300

For all the children

I GENESIS

Not even I had foreseen all that would befall us the day she arrived at Klieg's Karnival. When she at last had stopped running and built her home, she allowed herself to be brought to our world, bidden by her daughter and escorted by her husband, despite the foreboding that darkened her soul.

Her parents were siblings; her father was the sire of her first child. Her name was Nola, a name taken from one of the numerous television daytime dramas, which held her mother's attention throughout the day. Mollie Wayne preferred to remain indoors while her brother, Thad, tended the farm. What little education Nola was to have in her early life came from the small black and white RCA screen that crowded a corner of the kitchen counter ever since she could remember, behind and under which the Waynes had not cleaned since the day Old Mr. Wayne had set it into place.

It would be years before anyone thought to name Nola's son.

* * *

As I prepare to recount these events, I cannot help but marvel at how, unknowingly, we interweave the threads of our existence. It is easy to understand that one without benefit of my perspective might see these incidents as arbitrary, pointless, perhaps even cruel, as if the gods and The Fates grant one's wishes simply because they enjoy exacting the heaviest of tolls for the tiniest of blessings. I cannot, however, share this view. I am much more inclined to credit them with a profound and intensely ironic sense of humour than with evil intent. Though I, myself, at times, have viewed as a curse the *knowing*, which has ruled my existence from the day of my birth.

My poor mother must have felt cursed as well, as she was faced with the task of raising a daughter whose behaviour she could not understand. My unexplained fits of kicking and screaming upon being touched by anyone quickly consumed her patience, and, thereafter, her motherly instincts. Exhausted before I was two, she sent me to live with my maternal grandmother, who had no interest in touching any living thing aside from the six or seven stray cats she fed from the kitchen steps each morning.

Imagine for a moment what it would be like. Someone casually touches your hand, or a lock of your hair, and your mind is overcome with a wave of *knowing*. You feel in an instant a lifetime's fears, pains, and humiliations. You despair for every sin and transgression. You experience an ultimate fate. How could a child cope with such things? The mental images of horror and violence, of death and destruction? The sorrow of a broken heart, a soul dimmed, a light going out?

Classmates and neighbours soon came to know that I loathed physical contact in any fashion whatsoever, and the fact that I failed to grow more than four feet tall kept most of them disinclined to touch me. Surely no boys had any romantic interest in me. By the time I met my future husband, I had given up all hope that I could ever live anything remotely resembling a normal life. Within six months of our marriage, I could no longer conceive even wanting such a thing.

Normalcy is not what it seems. It is a façade, a face presented to hide the privation within. And for one such as I, a haven in which the outcasts are embraced is a welcome respite from the so-called sanity and compassion of common North American living.

*   *   *

Nola's curse was that she was born into poverty and ignorance, into a world with no regard for human life – nor life of any kind – beyond the pleasures it could provide. It was a world in which no limits of decency had been set, and Nola would endure what no child should.

The Wayne farm loomed on the outskirts of a small forgotten village in Alberta. The village itself was not unkempt. Each spring, the commercial buildings along King Street were repainted in bright hues as residents celebrated their survival of yet another harsh winter. Each autumn, gardens were ablaze with colour, fending off the greyness of days to come, lovingly tended by ladies who had never set foot outside the village and viewed with suspicion anyone who did. Self-contained and content within their world, the villagers retained their distance from the Waynes. A simple mention of the family set heads to shaking sadly, voices rising in disgust and anger, which masked a primitive fear. Old Mr. Wayne had inherited the acreage from his mother and, since that day, the family had shut itself away from its neighbours, only entering the village on unavoidable occasions. When Old Mr. Wayne died, leaving a son and daughter, the property began to grow over. Wild and poisonous things took root and, with time, choked the fields of any sustenance. Cattle and sheep wandered along the fence that bordered the road, straining their necks to reach the grass that thrived by the roadside.

It was more than a decade after Old Mr. Wayne's death, on a crisp and sunny spring morning, that Louise Markham drove past the Wayne farm on her way to the village, and saw a malnourished cow hanging dead on the fence. It was abruptly sickening and grotesque. The cow's emaciated neck had been sliced open by the rusted barbed wire, and jubilant, glutted flies buzzed about the wound. The eyes of the animal were filmy white and strangely hard in appearance, the tongue dangling oddly, black and infested with maggots.

Later that morning, Louise described the scene to her dearest friend, Aggie North, who shuddered at the account. Surely someone should point it out to the Waynes. The cow could be there for days before the family discovered it. But neither woman was eager to visit the farm, reminding each other that Thad Wayne had fired a shotgun at a taxman the year before. Over the next week, Louise sped past the property on her way to and from her gift shop with eyes averted.

At last, Louise telephoned Ned Thompson, a village deputy.

"You want me to do something about a cow?" Ned asked.

"A dead cow," Louise said. "A cow that's hanging rotting on a fence. A cow that's spreading God knows what-all diseases. Flies and maggots and kids walking by, poking it with sticks and – God, Ned, you have got to get out there and make those Waynes do something about it!"

"I could call the county health department."

"I've known you since you were a boy, Ned Thompson. You wanted to be a deputy – you wanted to protect the village because you think you're such a brave man. Now do something about that cow!"

So Ned went. At the foot of King Street, he left the patrol car to remind Mrs. Wilkins that her daughter had yet to pay her parking fines. He accepted a glass of lemonade and several homemade cookies, which he enjoyed lounging in the shade of the Wilkins' maples, before returning to the car. Just outside the proper limits of the village, he decided to check the catch of two young boys, who were fishing off a log that had fallen across the creek. Nearing the farm at last, he dallied along the road, looking at the cow and mentally counting the flies. Eventually he opened the gate, steered through and then dutifully closed it, before driving up the hill to the farmhouse.

Ned stopped the patrol car in front of the house. Thad was chopping wood in the yard, the axe whistling with each stroke. Mollie was seated on the porch steps, a naked child sleeping at her breast. Taking a deep breath, Ned stepped from the car.

Thad ceased his work and watched Ned approach.

"How do?" Ned asked. He tipped his hat and turned slightly to nod at Mollie.

"Do fine," Thad said. "What you want?"

Ned removed his hat and scratched at his head, trying to put a solicitous tone into his voice. "Well, Thad ... Seems you got a cow stuck on the fence down near the gate."

"So?" Thad said.

"You knew it was there?"

"Maybe. What's it to you?"

"Well, not me exactly. I've been getting some complaints in the village. Seems the cow's been dead awhile and people seem to think it shouldn't be there."

"What I care what they think? It's on my land, ain't it?"

"Well ..." Ned scratched his head again. "That doesn't seem to be the point, really. I'm getting complaints about it being a health hazard, so I thought I'd come up here and tell you about it. I figured you wouldn't want to leave it there so –"

"What makes you think you know what I wanna do?" Thad took a step forward. Sunlight glinted on the blade as he swung the axe to his shoulder.

Ned considered running. "I'm not saying I do. I just figured –"

"I figure you best get the hell off my farm. That cow's on my land and it stays if I want it to stay. But you –" Thad Wayne poked a sharp finger into Ned Thompson's chest. "You don't belong here and I'm getting rid of you."

"Now, Thad," Ned said. He took a step back. "No reason to get upset. Look ... It's not healthy having something rotting in the open. It's not healthy." He glanced at Mollie. "I see your sister's got a child." God knows where she got it, Ned thought. "You don't want that child catching some disease, now do you?"

"There you go!" Thad's voice thundered. "There you go thinking you know what I want and what I don't want! 'Sides, that ain't my sister's child."

"Well, there's a child here. And it's not healthy for a kid to be –"

The axe whistled as it sliced the air. Ned ducked and scrambled for his car as Mollie's laughter echoed across the yard. The axe shattered the windshield. It slammed into the side of the car as Ned wheeled the vehicle into a wide turn, splintered the taillight as Ned floored the gas pedal. At the base of the hill, Ned drove straight through the gate, wrenching it from its hinges. The fence collapsed and the cow hit the ground with a heavy thud, spewing aloft a swarm of flies.

Mollie brayed laughter, rocking back and forth on the porch steps. The child tumbled from her lap to lie silently on the ground, where the old dog nuzzled him gently and licked his face.

The child, of course, was Nola's. As the Waynes had always done, Mollie and Thad, though siblings, copulated outrageously. They thought nothing of bringing their infant daughter into their bed. As Nola grew into a compliant and attractive teenager, her father, more often than not, would approach her when Mollie was occupied elsewhere. He would bind her arms and legs and invade her with his tongue, his fingers, and his penis. Nola kept her soul and mind closed off as her parents ravaged her body for pleasure.

At thirteen, Nola was pregnant. She wandered the farm, lying in the fields of wild and poisonous things, the rotting hayloft, the unkempt garden. Her hands at rest on her ever-swelling womb, she was grateful Thad found her repellent in such condition. When the first waves of labour pains hit she was taken by surprise. She was in the hayloft. She managed to make it down the ladder without falling, reaching the house after what seemed an hour, stumbling up onto the porch and screaming for Mollie.

In response to their daughter's cries, Mollie and Thad appeared in the doorway. They were both naked, Thad's hands clutching Mollie's buttocks, her legs wrapped around his waist.

"What is it, Nola?" Mollie said.

Nola doubled over. "Hurts!"

"That's just your baby coming out." Mollie stepped to Nola's side, pushed her down on the porch, and spread the girl's legs. "See? It's just coming out is all." She took a rope from the porch floor and tied Nola's arms to the railing. "You just scream if you want to," Mollie said. She climbed back aboard her brother. "You let us know when it's out and we'll untie you."

Struggling against her bonds, Nola screamed repeatedly, a part of her thankful for the thought that this might kill her at last. Her head swam, her wrists burning from the rope. Her throat was parched and raw and, just as she was certain that she could endure no more, suddenly the pain was gone, and Nola fell back against the railing.

Mollie untied her, bit through the umbilical cord, and scooped up the baby to rinse him briefly under the spigot. Mollie ripped Nola's dress and pressed the baby to her nipple.

"What's it doing?" Nola cried.

"It's eatin', girl," Thad said. "That's how you gotta feed it."

Nola looked down at her child. She saw the mass of afterbirth, which Thad was poking with his fingers.

"You a mother now," Thad said. He lifted his head and smiled at her.

Nola wished she were dead.

They never named Nola's son, simply called him Baby. Nola, frightened of this thing that had come from her body, left him to Mollie and Thad. For that matter, she avoided her parents as well, and Thad resorted, when not with Mollie, to having sex with the various animals.

Frustrated after the visit from Deputy Ned Thompson, Thad mounted a newborn calf and was kicked, trampled, and ultimately killed by its mother. Baby stood silent – unblinking, uncomprehending – as Mollie and Nola dug a grave for Thad. Quite understandably, Nola felt nothing but relief, as she had never forgiven Thad for the times he had hurt her.

Mollie, however, was inconsolable. She lay about the house, drinking whisky and weeping, frequently screaming at terrors only she could see. Baby, completely on his own, slipped beneath the porch to sleep and eat with the dog.

Nola was sixteen and quite beautiful, her figure lithe, her features delicate. And she began to wonder what lay beyond the Wayne acreage. Unable to stand Mollie's noise, Nola wandered off the farm and into the village. She did not care what became of her child, who was, to her mind, but a crying, leaking, stinking reminder of their father's lust. The villagers saw her, darkly tan against the brightly painted storefronts, and tried to remember if they had ever seen her before. At the midpoint of King Street, she found the diner and went inside.

Harvey, who owned the place, always had an eye out for an attractive girl. "Can I get you something, pretty lady?"

"Water, please," Nola said. "I haven't got any money."

"How'd you get here? You ain't from around here."

"Boyfriend dumped me," Nola said. "Had a fight. We was just passing through." She had heard these lines spoken on Mollie's favourite daytime drama the day before.

Harvey was appropriately sympathetic. He gave her a cola and a bag of chips and turned to prepare a burger with onions. She had just finished her chips and was ready to start on the burger when Ralph Greeson, a truck driver who occasionally passed through, stepped up to the counter.

"Hello, Harvey," Ralph said.

Ralph was known for wearing long pants and long-sleeved shirts even in the hottest weather, and he wore a blue bandana to keep the sweat from dripping into his eyes. He was nearly six feet tall, and his muscles were strong. But he moved awkwardly, and possessed little self-confidence, especially when it came to women. Harvey knew that Nola would be perfectly safe with Ralph.

"Maybe Ralph can take you where you was headed," Harvey said to Nola.

Nola looked at Ralph. He was certainly not a handsome man – nothing like the men on daytime dramas – but he was much younger than Thad and he had a kind face. Nola had watched enough television to think she knew how to manipulate a man: she batted her lashes; she hung her head; she struggled to cry ...

"I'm headed to Winnipeg," Ralph said, appraising her. "What about you?"

"Me, too," Nola said.

In the transport truck, Ralph kept his eyes focused on the road ahead as Nola played with the radio dial, flipping from station to station. He and Nola exchanged hardly a word that afternoon. Most women terrified Ralph and, around those who did not, he felt shy and awkward. Nola was smaller than he, and he knew she could not physically overpower him. But she was the most beautiful girl he had ever seen, and she did not look at him with a lip pulled down or her eyes narrowed. He thought he would be relieved when they reached Winnipeg and she left his life.

For dinner, they stopped at a fast food restaurant next to the highway, which Nola chose because of its bright façade. She was awed as she watched children play in the colourful indoor playground. These children had parents who looked at them with expressions she had seen in the eyes of actors on television: tenderness, caring ... love?

After she and Ralph finished their ice cream, they returned to the transport truck. As Ralph drove until night, Nola grew increasingly sad. Nola had learned that love really does exist, for she saw it on the faces of the people. She knew what had been denied her, and she closed her eyes against tears.

"Are you sleepy?" Ralph asked. Reaching back, he pulled a curtain to reveal the built-in sleeper. "You just climb on up in there and go to sleep if you want."

"Thank you," Nola said.

Ralph drove for several hours, smoking a cigar as Nola slept safely behind the curtain. She was beautiful and sweet and shy and he wanted her, but he felt he could never share these thoughts, for he was ashamed of what she would see.

* * *

Ralph had lived a difficult childhood, being the son of two alcoholics. His parents had argued ceaselessly from the first day he could recall, and his father had left on more than one occasion, only returning when his funds had run out and he had sobered. Their anger and cruelty were usually reserved for each other, and what Ralph endured was his parents' neglect. The only adult who expressed the least interest in Ralph's life was his father's brother, Ron. One summer morning the year Ralph was twelve, his mother, while preparing breakfast, drunkenly, proudly, and cruelly informed her husband he was not, in fact, Ralph's true father. He left immediately, taking nothing more than his car keys and wallet. Ralph came running from the shower wearing only a towel as his mother began to rant.

She was holding the frying pan of spitting grease and bacon

when Ralph burst into the kitchen, terrified. Her face contorted and she hurled the pan. Ralph scrambled to flee, his damp feet slipping on the tile. Bacon sizzled against his skin, hot grease blistering his back, his buttocks, his arms and legs. Grabbing a wire whisk from the counter, his mother beat him savagely, even after his skin had split open and Ralph had passed out on the floor. She only stopped when her arms were so tired she simply could not continue.

Ralph remained unconscious for more than two days. When he awoke, he was in the hospital, and his Uncle Ron was seated beside him, waiting to take him home.

"Your mother hanged herself," Uncle Ron told him. "And rightly so, from the looks of you." That was all he ever said on the subject. Ron never mentioned, nor did Ralph ask, what had become of the man Ralph knew as his father.

When Ralph left the hospital, his back, arms, and legs healed to be covered with scars, which were hard and spidery white. As he looked at his body in the bathroom mirror, he felt only shame. He was determined no one would ever know. And his mind played endlessly the last words his mother ever said to him: "It's all your fault! Hear me, you little bastard? All your fault!"

Ron made a home for Ralph. He did the best that he could, being an unmarried man. Ralph attended a local school, and for the first week thought it would be all right until one of the children saw his back while he was pulling off his sweater. She screamed, and then she started laughing, as the other children did when she told them. They took to calling Ralph terrible names, making sure he heard them when he hurried by. Ron was a trucker and, shortly after the incident at school, Ralph asked to assist him on his runs. Ron agreed on the condition that Ralph continue his schooling, and he tutored Ralph in the truck. At seventeen, Ralph graduated with honours, and he could drive the truck as well as Ron, easily hitching and unhitching the trailers.

Ron died peacefully in his sleep when Ralph was nineteen. He never told Ralph their true relationship, but he left Ralph the transport truck. Ralph had assisted Ron for years, everyone knew and liked him, and Ron's former clients renewed their contracts with Ralph. For nearly two years before he met Nola, Ralph lived in the transport truck, reconciled to being alone.

*   *   *

When Nola awoke it was morning, and daylight streamed through the windshield of the truck. Ralph was asleep on his stomach on the seat, snoring softly. One of his legs rested on the floor and his arms were cocked above his head. His clothing was in disarray, and Nola could see the scars that covered his back. Unable to resist, she reached down to touch them and Ralph awoke with a start, crying out and sitting up.

"I'm sorry," Nola said.

"They're ugly," Ralph said. "I didn't want you to know."

"It doesn't make any difference," Nola said. "I don't care. Look." She held out her arms to show him the scars on her wrists, left by the baling wire Thad had used to bind her. "See?" she said.

Ralph looked at the scars and tears stung his eyes. For years he had felt ashamed, hiding himself from others, avoiding any contact with the rare woman who expressed desire for him. He had always dreamed of finding a girl who would not scar him further, nor be repulsed by those he already possessed.

"You hungry?" Ralph asked.

Over breakfast, Nola watched him quietly, listening to his soothing tones, noting the patience with which he spoke to the waitress. She wanted to ask him what had happened to his back, but she certainly did not want to know. He was kind and gentle, she was growing to like him, and she did not want to imagine the cruelty. She was glad that Ralph had not asked her about the scars on her wrists.

"We'll be in Winnipeg soon," Ralph said when they were back in the truck, driving east, and Nola wondered what she was going to do. Seeing the look on her face, Ralph asked her what was wrong and she burst into tears. He could not bear to see her cry, and he pulled the truck to the side of the highway. "Please don't cry," he said. "What's wrong?"

Nola told him the truth. She had never been to Winnipeg, knew no one in Winnipeg, she had, in fact, been running away.

"From your boyfriend?" he asked.

"Ain't no boyfriend," Nola said. "I made it up."

"Well, then ..." Ralph could not bear to see her cry. "There somewhere you'd like to go? I'll take you anywhere you want."

The thought of leaving him made her heart ache. "I just want to go wherever you're going," she said. After she had spoken, she could see that he did not want to lose her either. Shyly, she reached out. Her hand touched his and felt his fingers quiver. She studied his face, determined to find any trace of Thad within him. She found none. Moving closer, she eased her way into his arms, which wrapped instinctively and warmly around her.

"You're so pretty," Ralph said. "So sweet ..." Ralph leaned down and softly, tenderly, kissed her on the lips.

Nola marvelled at this wondrous new feeling.

When Ralph drew back, his eyes searched her face. "I don't suppose you could ever fall in love with me? I don't mean right now – not today, just ... ever?"

She wasn't certain how love felt, but if it was anything like she understood from television ... "I think so," she said. She accepted his kisses, and trembled with the gentle movements of his body. As she clung to him, her hands gliding over his skin, she knew that – having been so abused himself – he would never knowingly hurt her.

It took Mollie three days to realize Nola was gone. When the whisky still was empty, she stumbled out onto the porch, calling for her daughter and Baby. When Baby appeared from beneath the porch, she seized and shook him, demanding he tell her where Nola was. Unable to answer, frightened, and hungry because the old dog had managed to kill only a single goose, Baby began to wail. The old dog jumped to attention. She leapt expertly onto Mollie's back, sinking her teeth into Mollie's neck ...

In the field behind the barn, an old sow began rooting up

Thad's torso.

At the police station, Ned Thompson was debating retirement. He cringed as Louise Markham stormed to his desk.

"Over a week and that cow's still there," Louise told him. "Only now it's laying half on the roadway and someone's run over its head. All smashed flat with its tongue squeezed across the road like some kind of disgusting snake. Didn't you speak to them?"

Ned professed that he had done what he could, but there was no further action he could take. "That fool man came at me with an axe!"

Louise sniffed. "Ned Thompson, you're a coward. Get your shotgun, we're going up there this minute."

"But, Miss Mar– "

"This minute!"

With a heavy sigh, Ned lifted his shotgun from the gun rack and followed Louise to the patrol car. The windshield and taillight had been replaced, but a good-sized dent remained in the side, which Louise made a point to inspect. Once inside the car, she noted the slivers of glass, which still littered the floorboards.

"Can't you vacuum this out?"

"Yes, ma'am," Ned said without looking at her. He thought about what Thad Wayne would do next. Take a swing at Louise Markham? Sever her head and feed it to the pigs in the slop bucket?

At the entrance to the farm, Louise directed Ned to pull the car to the roadside. She pointed at the cow, half flattened and smeared across the road.

"See it?" she demanded. "How would you like to be driving past that twice a day?"

Ned swallowed hard, wishing that Thad would sever Louise's head, or at least her tongue. "Listen," he said. "I don't think this visit's going to do much good. Why don't I just head back to town and round up some of the boys and we'll haul this thing out of here?"

"Why don't you get some guts and drive up the goddamned road," Louise Markham said.

"You don't know what these people is like," Ned told her.

Louise frowned. She snatched Ned's shotgun and stepped from the car, striding up the dirt road toward the house.

Bitch, Ned thought, and called out, "Get back in the car, Miss Markham, I'm driving up there. No sense you walking."

As they crested the hill, Louise leaned out the car window. "What's that there in the yard? Ned, what's going on, is that a dog?"

"Looks like." Ned stopped the car in front of the house.

Within seconds, Louise Markham was doubled over, vomiting onto the ground. Once her stomach was empty she continued to heave, wishing for water to swallow so she would have something to expel.

In time, the sickness passed. Louise heard a growl and looked up, her vision cloudy. She wiped her eyes with her sleeve and set her mind to digest the scene before her. The dog, blood running from her mouth, crouched low, ready to spring. Behind the dog, sprawled lifeless on the ground, lay the mutilated body of Mollie Wayne. Tiny hands tearing at flesh and forcing pieces into his mouth, Baby was seated in the dirt beside Mollie. Seeing Louise, Baby smiled and pushed himself to his feet. He tottered across the yard, the dog close behind, and offered Mollie's arm to Louise.

"Hungry," Baby said. And again, "Hungry?" His eyes darkened with confusion, unable to understand why Louise did not wish to share.

"Ned," Louise said quietly. "Ned ... get the gun."

Ned sat, stunned and staring, leaning against the front tire of the car. He buried his face in his hands as he choked back further vomit.

Louise got the gun and shot the animal herself. It was a clean shot, right between the eyes, but it blew off most of the dog's head. Louise strode to Mollie Wayne's body, looking down on the torn flesh, the flies, and the blood surrounding her, seeping into the ground.

"Hungry?" Baby asked.

Louise turned. She marched to Baby's side, pulled Mollie's arm from his grasp, and heaved the limb across the yard.

Baby wailed.

Being childless, Louise Markham began to daydream about taking this one home with her. Holding him tightly against her, she rocked him, imagined raising him, caring for him, loving him ... How would she feel to have a child after all these years? Would it no longer seem that somehow her life to this point had been wasted? But then Louise realized that she would never be able to look at this child or, perhaps, any child, without recalling the moment Baby had offered the arm to her.

No. She could never ... ever.

When Baby stopped wailing, she carried him to the spigot beside the porch. She stripped him of his clothes and washed him gently beneath the spray of water, wiping away the blood and dirt. She instructed Ned to radio for assistance, but the man sat motionless, staring at the dead dog.

Louise finished washing the boy. He certainly was not clean, but she knew she had done the best she could without soap. She hoisted Baby onto her hip and carried him back to the car. She gave him crackers from her purse to munch while she fumbled with the police radio. At last she managed to radio the RCMP. Ned finally snapped out of his daze and radioed for an ambulance as well, and it wasn't long before the yard was full of sirens and flashing lights, not to mention the reporters – one from the village and, surprising to Louise, a van from the city, with television cameras and facilities for a live radio broadcast. Within hours, the story was picked up and aired on stations across the country. Incredibly, throughout the weeks that the story would air, Nola would only catch brief snatches of the reports, never enough to know that this was her Baby, her Mollie, who had all North America both fascinated and horrified.

Faced with the spectacle at the Wayne farm, the news people did not vomit and neither did the RCMP officers. At first, Louise did not want to mention Baby's cannibalism, but eventually she did so, pulling one officer aside. She was afraid that ingesting Mollie's flesh would somehow harm the boy. The officer shook his head sadly and glanced at Baby, who sat in the dirt, staring at the dog.

"Hungry," Baby said.

Louise, terrified that the child would repeat his earlier performance, snatched him up and held him squirming. "So what do we do with this boy?" she asked the officer.

"Any other family?" he asked.

"There's a brother. I mean – her brother," Louise said.

"He here?"

"I don't know," Louise snapped.

"Hey, Tony!" The officer called to his partner, who appeared from the crowd that had gathered around Mollie. "There's supposed to be a brother. Get some help and see if he's around somewhere."

Tony, in turn, called three of her colleagues. The four fanned out across the yard, one going into the house, the rest disappearing into and behind the barn and various outbuildings.

"No one in the house," one called back. "Man, it stinks in here!"

At last, Tony found Thad's torso, which the sow had rooted from the ground. Moments later, the officers were fighting the sow to pull what was left of Thad out of the field. The television crew duly documented the removal of the body.

"Holy shit," said the officer beside Louise. "What kind of fucking place is this?"

Louise was past vomiting, and studied what was left of Thad with Baby asleep in her arms. "So what do we do with this boy?"

"Hospital first. Then on to county, I guess."

"You guess?" Louise thought of just marching from the farm with Baby in her arms. But, as it was, it would be months before she could bring herself to eat meat, or dishes with tomato sauce, and the sight of a child eating anything in public whatsoever – popcorn, hot dog, what have you – would make her nauseous.

At the village diner, Aggie North was concerned that Louise had not returned from her errand. Sipping a coffee and stabbing her salad with a fork, she repeated to Harvey what Louise had told her. "Went up to make them do something about that cow," Aggie said. "Damn thing smeared all over the road."

"Surprised they wasn't gnawing on it," Harvey said, and they both laughed.

"Never know what those Waynes are going to do," Aggie said. "You know Ned was saying they've got a child? I'm not speculating how they got it, but sure as I have two eyes and a tongue, the Waynes have a child up there on that farm."

"Wait a minute," Harvey said. "You hear that?" He turned up the radio with a flick of his wrist.

"– the Wayne farm in Hasp County," the announcer said. "The farm is the sight of one of the most gruesome sets of killings in recent history. Deputy Ned Thompson and shopkeeper Louise Markham had come to the farm with a complaint about a dead cow. When they reached the yard, they discovered the body of farm owner Mollie Wayne, her throat apparently torn out by the family dog. In a routine search of the grounds, the body of her brother Thad was found half-buried behind the barn. Authorities do not wish to speculate as to the cause of Thad Wayne's death, though it appears that he was either bludgeoned or trampled to death. In addition to the bodies of the Wayne siblings, a young boy approximately three-to-four years old was found in the yard. At present, authorities have no clue as to the child's identity and, in fact, had no idea of the child's existence until several days ago. Authorities say he'll be taken to the county hospital for evaluation and treatment, and we will keep you informed of further developments. From the Wayne farm in Hasp County, I'm Sheila Beck."

Harvey turned down the radio and glanced at Aggie North. He was speechless. He was thinking about the cow, which the Waynes had left to rot.

"I can't believe it," Aggie said. She pushed away her salad.

Harvey produced a bottle of whisky from under the counter and took a long swallow.

Aggie accepted the bottle, the whisky burning her throat. She touched her lips with a napkin. "It's awful. It's ... satanic."

"Hellfire!" Harvey said. "There'll be no end of curiosity seekers pouring into town! I'd better call Melvin and order some supplies."

Aggie wanted to go directly to the Wayne farm to find Louise, but Harvey pointed out that in all probability Louise was no longer there. Since the radio had time to air the story, she was likely giving further statements to the police or at home, recovering from her trauma.

Aggie telephoned Louise at home. "Darling, are you all right? We heard on the radio. It must have been awful."

"Ghastly! Dead animals and dead people and cannibalism –" Though Louise had not intended to mention the latter.

"Cannibals!" Aggie shrieked. "Cannibals?"

"Good God, Aggie," Louise snapped. "I never said that."

"Of course you did. I heard you!"

"No. You must not have heard me correctly. I said – oh, never mind, Aggie, where are you?"

"At the diner. Do you need me, darling? Would you like me to come out?"

Louise made tea and served it in her spotless parlour. She set out a tray of cucumber sandwiches but could not touch them herself. Luckily, Aggie was not hungry either after the one tiny sandwich she tore in half and nibbled.

"Cannibals?" Aggie asked, more softly this time.

"I said animals, Aggie. The dog. And a pig. There was a pig eating Thad Wayne."

"Oh!" Aggie dropped the remainder of her sandwich. She gulped at her tea. "Oh, Louise, it must have been ... Was there a lot of blood?"

"Swimming in it," Louise said. Her nerves had been considerably calmed by several ounces of sherry. "Just swimming. And the child! Poor thing looked like he hadn't been bathed since birth."

"Satanic," Aggie said. "Do – do you think he's Mollie's?"

"Who else?"

Harvey had told Aggie about Nola and Ralph Greeson of course, long before they had heard about the commotion at the farm, but there was no reason for Aggie to make any connection. No one knew the Waynes had produced Nola, just as none knew Nola and Thad had produced the child.

"You don't think," Aggie said, "that Thad ...?"

Louise sniffed. "Nothing would surprise me when it comes to the Waynes ... More tea, dear?"

As it turned out, Harvey was right about the curiosity seekers. They swarmed on the village as flies had swarmed on the cow and, later, Mollie Wayne. A man from *Time* magazine took up residence in the diner and, once he learned where it was, on the bench in front of Louise's gift shop.

"I'm not talking to you," Louise told him. "I don't like your magazine, I don't like your moustache, and you smell like beer." This quote appeared in the *Time* story, along with a photograph of Louise entering the shop, a sensational caption printed beneath it: "Louise Markham: a nose for blood."

"What a terrible thing to say," Aggie consoled her.

"Animals. Animals and journalists and curiosity seekers ... What did they do with the boy?"

That was the question on many people's minds. They took him first to the county hospital, but by the time the reporters found his room he had been moved under secrecy. Sheila Beck managed to sneak into the record room, found a form stating he was transferred to Calgary, but by the time she arrived there he had been, once again, transferred. No amount of cajoling, no bribe, could get her the information. Police escorted her from the hospital.

The small village was soon once again forgotten. The curiosity seekers and reporters wandered off in search of more gruesome points of interest. The villagers – with few exceptions – both recovered and profited from that day at the Wayne farm. In the diner, Harvey cooked over a brand-new stainless steel stove, always with an eye out for an attractive girl. Deputy Ned Thompson retired and tossed in nightmares. For years to come, Louise Markham would feel nauseous at even the thought of children eating, and Aggie North would prod with "Cannibals, Louise?"

Though the Wayne acreage should have properly passed to Baby, it was sold to pay the years of back taxes. The taxman who had dodged Thad Wayne's shotgun blast took great pleasure in conducting the auction. The religious cult that acquired the property was considered quite an improvement over the Waynes. Some of the cult's more artistic wares could be purchased from a corner shelf in Louise Markham's gift shop.

As for Nola and Ralph, they delivered the consignment on time, and loaded another. They headed east, passing, as The Fates would have it, an unmarked car carrying Baby to the Children's Aid Society in Ontario.

At the county hospital, doctors found that the Wayne child had intestinal worms and was undernourished, but otherwise perfectly healthy. He had good tactile skills and swiftly put the square pieces into the square holes, round pieces into the round ones. He identified various animals in photographs, but was totally confused when it came to appliances and modern conveniences, other than things like pickup trucks and television sets. They assured each other that his vocabulary would improve over time.

Only one thing bothered the doctors and nurses. The child refused to sleep in a bed. Each night, the nurses would cover him lovingly with blankets and shut off the light ("Not afraid of the dark," one nurse noted on his chart). Minutes later, he would climb from the bed and slip beneath it, turning around and around like a dog before settling down to sleep. If they tried to pull him out from under the bed, he growled at them.

When reporters began to converge on the hospital, he was transferred to Calgary for psychological tests. Perfectly normal, the doctors concluded, aside from his preference for sleeping on a pile of blankets or clothing, the bed above shielding him from view. Sheila Beck traced him there, and though they managed to get her away from the hospital, the doctors felt it necessary to move the boy as quickly as possible. Since he had been de-wormed and inoculated, the boy was healthy, they said. He was intelligent with every chance of "growing up to be normal."

Baby was about to be taken by Children's Aid workers when it was deemed vital to fashion a birth certificate. Date of birth was chosen by the doctor's best estimate, and entered in the proper space on the certificate. As a worker's hand hesitated over the line

First Name, a young nurse spoke, without thought, the name she had always intended to give her own future son.

"Heath," the young nurse said.

She stifled a cry of protest as the name was briefly considered, then written clearly onto the line. For years it would sadden her to have so inadvertently given away something so precious. Decades later, having never become the mother she longed to be, it comforted her to know that a child carried the name that she had bestowed.

The newly-named Heath was transferred to Ontario. There, Heath spent the next few years in the care of the Children's Aid Society, until he was adopted at nine by Frank and Margaret Clifford.

With the Children's Aid Society, Heath did well in his studies with a pronounced love of reading. His vocabulary grew with each passing day. At five, he read as well as many children twice his age. But his identity was difficult to suppress, and stories of his life on the Wayne farm circulated among the staff at the home.

Margaret and Frank never heard the cannibalism aspects of the stories, though they were not spared details of what daily life on the Wayne farm must have been like. In late July, the year Heath turned nine, they were given copies of all the newspaper articles and the results of the tests done by the various hospitals.

"The poor thing," Margaret said when she looked through the articles.

"It's disgraceful," Frank said, shaking his head. "When can we adopt the boy?"

"Well," the Children's Aid worker said. He dabbed his ample cheeks with a handkerchief. "Our policy is to wait a few months before any permanent papers are signed. This way, we can be assured that as little as possible will go wrong and, if by some chance the child cannot adjust to the family – or vice versa – it is easier to bring him or her back to our care. I'm sure you understand."

Margaret shook her head. She and Frank and Heath had already spent several days together. Who would not want such a darling child? Heath had been wonderful, smiling into her eyes, holding their hands as they strolled to the park.

"It's best for the boy," the worker said. "We'll place him with you as a foster child until we see how he adjusts. I see you have another child?"

"A boy," Frank said. "He's eleven."

"And how does he feel about Heath coming to live with you?"

Frank grinned. "Well, that's one of the reasons we looked into this in the first place. We've been trying to have a second child for some time now."

"The boys get along famously," Margaret said. "To be honest with you, it was really Horace who suggested this to begin with. He overheard us talking one night and ... You see, the doctors couldn't ever figure out why I couldn't conceive after Horace."

"I see ... But keep in mind, there is no telling the possible difficulties. Give it a few months. If everything is fine then, we'll sign the papers. It's just a precaution."

"Look," Margaret asked, "is there something you're not telling us?"

The worker shook his head and smiled reassuringly. Then, "There is one thing."

"Yes?"

"The boy doesn't like to sleep in a bed."

"I beg your pardon?" She was confused. She had been prepared for much worse.

"He likes to sleep under the bed. He's done it for years."

Margaret laughed. "Well, for heavens sake! What possible difference could that make? We all have our idiosyncrasies."

The only thing about Heath that would ever cause Margaret discomfort was the odd way he had, at times, of looking at her: silent, unblinking. She had rarely seen such a look on the face of an adult, let alone a child. It was a look of utter absorption, as if he were a county inspector and she a midway ride. On those occasions, she would excuse herself from the table or room, anxious to place a closed door between herself and Heath.

They gave Heath his own room. It was next to Horace's room

on the second floor, with high windows that faced the woods bordering the backyard. As expected, Heath took the blanket and pushed it under the bed, turning around and around before settling to sleep. Having been forewarned, Margaret had spent the previous afternoon sweeping and scrubbing the floor.

Margaret was rarely disturbed by that which made one individual. She had grown up amidst the troupers of Klieg's Karnival.

A decade before Nola Wayne's birth, I became a resident of Klieg's Karnival. It was the week following my marriage to Hamilton Klieg, younger brother of the Karnival's founder, Arthur. The day I arrived I was still known by my given name, Alice Clemmons. I was twenty-two. I could not at that time have imagined all that would befall us, but had I known, my choices would have been no different. I accepted Hamilton's proposal because I loved him deeply, with passion inconceivable to those who have never known it; because he was of my stature; and, contrary to what I had come to believe was possible, he was the first person with whom I could have physical contact without the *knowing*.

I did not continue formal education following my graduation from high school. Though my grandmother owned her home, and our expenses were minimal, funds were not sufficient. My limited academic achievements did not attract scholarships or other financial assistance. I took a job in the city as a ticket seller for a movie theatre, working untouched behind a glass partition, seated on a high stool.

I knew that when she left me with my grandmother, my mother had been headed to the city. I wondered if I might sell her a ticket one day, if I would recognize her nearly two decades later as the smiling young woman in a faded photograph. To my knowledge, in the three years that I worked there, my mother never passed through the theatre doors, but Hamilton did.

It was late November. The sky and city were grey, but Hamilton was bright in a blue and yellow sweater. Business was slow and, after he purchased his ticket, Hamilton lingered making idle conversation. I thought him handsome. I found myself daydreaming about him once he entered the theatre. After the film, he boldly asked if he might buy me dinner after work.

I did not see myself as a candidate for romance. My loathing of touch aside, I was never what one might call a pretty woman, being perhaps just a bit too plump for my short frame, with eyes a bit too large in proportion to my button nose, and lips a bit too thin – lips that, to my mind, were never meant to be kissed. But I felt an immediate kinship with Hamilton, and there was an inviting openness in his manner. He told me about his life at Klieg's over spaghetti and a basket of bread. After touring the country for the previous eight months, the Karnival residents were enjoying hiatus, wintering on Vancouver Island. Hamilton, for the interim, was living in the city, working as one of Santa's elves in a Hudson's Bay Company store, and as emcee at a local burlesque house.

I was intrigued, for there was no trace of bitterness or self-pity in Hamilton. Prior to that day, I believed that all carnival dwarves were exploited, surely unhappy in the lives they led. But it was clear that Hamilton was content, and I doubted he wasted any time, as I did, wishing for a "normal" existence.

Hamilton made no attempt to take my arm as he walked me to the bus stop. He did not try to kiss me as I stepped onto the wheezing vehicle. I was relieved, for I could not imagine how I would explain that I should not be touched.

Over the next few months, we spent most of our free time together. We attended gallery openings, concerts, films, and theatre. We ate in fine restaurants, greasy diners, and once, when there was a break in the cold, from a picnic basket on the roof of the burlesque house. Still, he made no attempt to touch me, and I did not know he was falling in love. Hamilton was, truly, my first friend. I had quickly pushed aside any thoughts of romance.

One afternoon as we were leaving a restaurant, I tripped over the threshold. Hamilton stopped my fall, and it was a moment before I realized that the *knowing* had not come.

"Are you all right?"

I nodded, my body trembling, my voice incapable. I was thrilled and frightened, uncertain what this could mean, overwhelmed by unknown and unexpected possibilities.

Hamilton released me, and then took me into his arms and kissed me. I was shocked, yet I welcomed his touch. Until that embrace, I never knew the joy of holding another. Our fingers were entwined as we walked to the burlesque house, my skin alive with new sensations.

Little by little over the preceding months, we had discussed much about our lives, but I had not told him about the *knowing*. In his dressing room, the notes of the band in rehearsal resonating through the cracks in the floor, I explained as best as I could about my gift, and the price exacted by The Fates.

Hamilton smiled slyly. "But today nothing happened?"

"The *knowing* did not come," I said.

"It's a sign," Hamilton said. He dropped to one knee and held forth the ring he had carried in his pocket for the previous seven days.

I was happy to leave my old life behind. My name aside, I brought nothing from my earlier existence when I moved with Hamilton to Klieg's. I quickly felt at home at the Karnival, grateful for its atmosphere of playful indulgence.

As I was to learn, Hamilton had always kept dogs, and spent his time training them to enact elaborate tricks. In his youth, this had made him somewhat of a neighbourhood celebrity, and he supplemented his allowance with backyard performances. Neighbours were eager to pay a dime each to be delighted by his amazingly acrobatic dogs.

It was while watching one of these performances that Arthur conceived Klieg's Karnival. It appeared in his mind as a recollection of a fully-formed world. The front ticket booths were red and white, with blue and yellow awnings. Above them was the sign, neon lit in purple and gold, blinking out the name in letters six feet high: "Klieg's Karnival." Entering the lot, with wood chips crunching underfoot, the midway split, going left to the games of chance and skill, brightly painted and loud with agents, going right to the rides, looping and spinning with passengers screaming and a rainbow of lights ablaze. In the centre of the lot, encircled by the midway, stood the giant freak tent with painted banners depicting the wonders within. Inside the freak tent was the main stage, surrounded by the sideshow cubicles. Seated on bleachers in front of the stage, or standing against the sidewalls craning their necks to see, audiences were dazzled by the animals: a well-loved bear that specialized in waltzes and other intricate dances; a twenty-foot boa, which tied and untied itself into knots that you had to witness to believe; a monkey family of skilled musicians; and Hamilton's acrobatic dog act.

Within the sideshows were several "pickled punks" – deformed foetuses, both human and animal, preserved in formaldehyde and displayed in large glass jars; a two-headed lamb and a goat with four front legs, each stuffed and set upon a bale of hay; a collection of shrunken heads, swaying in a cubicle flooded with music from African drums; The Painted Woman, tattooed from head to foot, who performed a "posing show"; her husband, The Rock Headed Man, who burned himself, drove spikes through his nostrils and hooks through his cheeks, all without apparent injury; The Snake Lady, proud mother of the above mentioned boa, Tiny; Philippe, who danced in the spectacular ballroom act with Bilbo, the bear; Strongman Hank, always a crowd favourite, who lifted ever-increasing weights and, on occasion, full bench loads of onlookers; fortune-teller Madame Olga; Magician Balzod the Great; and "Siamese" twin boys, Chris and Toby. Arthur considered it quite a coup when the hermaphrodite Tim-Tina joined the troupe midway through Klieg's first season.

Just outside the freak tent, a trailer raised its awnings to reveal what was billed as a "Reptile Show." In compartments behind thick panes of glass were mambas and cobras and rattlers and diamondbacks; Gila monsters and iguanas and chameleons and frilled lizards; giant scorpions and albino tarantulas and hissing cockroaches and a baby alligator. "Have your picture taken with a giant snake!" a placard in front of the trailer dared. These photographs of patrons with snakes coiled around their arms, held far away in their hands, or draped about their shoulders, showed faces in various stages of pleasure and fear, and were posted at strategic points along the sides of the trailer.

In a small petting zoo, exotic fowl, lambs, goats, a pygmy zebra, and a pair of Shetland ponies saddled for rides, hissed and honked and bleated and neighed, gobbling feed pellets from the hands of squealing children.

On the midway, numerous food concessions (what troupers call "grab joints"), including popcorn wagons, hot dog carts, and cotton candy stands, wafted enticing aromas. The games of chance and skill offered prizes of every description, their bells and shrill whistles announcing each winner. The Haunted Mansion loomed dark and menacing over the merry-go-round. The Fun House beckoned with music and laughter. The cars of the double-looping roller coaster climbed and dipped and whipped through sharp turns, and would eventually operate in the shadow of Goliath. One of the largest roller coasters in carnival history – and certainly the largest on the day it was first constructed – Goliath would ulti-mately cost Arthur his life, but for years it would be a source of pride as it dominated the midway.

It was Klieg's third season when I arrived, newlywed to Hamilton. Our home was a spacious and rather well-appointed tent. This was dismantled at the end of our stands, and erected in the backyard of each new destination.

The backyard was off limits to the public and security guards manned its gates. Huge rolls of bamboo screening were unfurled and lashed along its tall fence to shield the area from view. Here, the trucks were parked in long parallel rows, awaiting tear-down and our departure. Several large trailers housed separate facilities for community bathrooms and showers. Meals were prepared in the cook tent, which was, in reality, a large canvas top attached to the trailer that housed the kitchen. Tables and chairs and benches were crowded together beneath the cook tent's canvas top and in the adjoining yard. These were popular gathering places not only for meals, but for smoking, drinking, card games, and reminis-cences. Open spaces served for rehearsals, and tents and trailers – homes for Karnival residents – were scattered throughout. Arthur resided in his office-trailer and the workmen in the sleeper trucks.

In addition to his duties regarding the dog act, Hamilton was busy each day supervising the design and construction of new rides: the single and double Ferris wheels; the scramblers; the giant swings; the spinning teacups and saucers; the bumper cars, and the mini-cars for little ones. As I had no stationary home to build and care for, no children or pets, and no career, I spent my time exploring and absorbing the Karnival. I avoided the midway during opening hours, but I enjoyed roaming in the early morning or late at night when the lot was closed to the public. I was awed at the efficiency as Klieg's was torn down and packed into trucks, to be reborn with great speed when the caravan pulled to a stop.

It was fascinating to watch as, over and over, a huge empty lot was transformed within hours. If we arrived in morning light or early afternoon, workmen immediately set about framing the Karnival. If it was later in the day or night, the initial order of business was to unload and start the generators. These powered giant floodlights, which were hoisted high on cranes to illuminate the ongoing work.

First, the freak tent was positioned in the centre of the lot. This tent had a most ingenious feature: in clement weather, a portion of the canvas above the main stage could be rolled back by use of a long cord attached to a pulley, allowing sunlight to bathe the performers.

While the freak tent took form, raising of the midway began. Some of the rides – such as the Fun House and the Haunted Mansion – were large semi-trailers with modified interiors. These were parked broadside along the outer perimeter of the midway. Huge façades were put together and secured to the sides of the trailers, transforming a plain box into an Old West saloon, a haven for ghosts and witches, or the op-art Fun House, which was cranked upwards to allow a second floor of play. Flat contraptions of metal telescoped into staircases at the trailer doors.

The bigger rides, such as the roller coaster and Ferris wheels, were assembled from large segments, like a giant's toy set. Once these were built, workmen walked and examined every inch of track and girder, double- and triple-checking every rivet, nut and bolt, and electrical connection. County officials inspected each ride, the bravest accompanying workmen as they scaled the intricate creations.

Many of the grab joints and games of chance and skill were housed in smaller trailers that were dropped, without wheels, into place on the midway. These would lift metal awnings to reveal the enticing foods, the games and colourful prizes. The smallest trailers, scattered throughout the lot, housed the public washrooms, First Aid stations, and the various Karnival gift shops. Concessions not housed in trailers were fashioned from large wooden flats marked "a," "b," and so on. These went together with incredible ease and were brightly painted and festooned with lights.

Streetlights were set at points along the midway, and tables and benches into open areas. All necessary power was supplied by the generators. The generators chugged endlessly all through the day and into the night, and miles of electrical cords ran rampant like snakes behind the scenes.

Much later, I would readily note the differences in the framing of each stand. But throughout my first season with the Karnival, each time it was reborn, to my eyes Klieg's looked virtually exactly as it had the time before. So perfectly had Arthur conceived the Karnival, as new rides and concessions arrived on the midway, they seemed to have been there always.

Tear-down always occurred at night. Early in the evening on the final day of each stand, the giant floodlights were hoisted high on the cranes. When Klieg's had closed, the floodlights were switched on. Security swept the last of the public from the lot and tear-down commenced. This was accomplished with even greater speed and in opposite order, leaving the lot once again empty, looking as if it had never known our world.

I was not one to enjoy the rides, neither did I care to try my hand at games of chance or skill. But I was intrigued by the freak tent, and most particularly by its colourful banners. The images they depicted were at once completely real and wholly fantastic. I studied them for hours, fascinated in a way I do not know how to explain. In so doing, I soon made acquaintance with Madame Olga, who read Tarot and crystal ball from her own curtained cubicle in the sideshow.

Madame Olga was a middle-aged woman of some bulk, her movements extended and graceful. She wore long flowing gowns that whispered at her ankles, and necklaces too numerous to count, made of gold and silver and polished stones. Her head was wrapped with a turban of silk, crimson and yellow and beaded with white. Bangles clanged together on her wrists, and rings on every finger sparkled as they caught the light. Her cubicle was hung with heavy dark draperies, and thousands of fluorescent stars glittered on the fabric.

After much persuasion, I allowed her to read my fortune.

"You have an astonishing gift," Madame Olga said with longing and regret. "And yet this tortures you, because you have not embraced it."

I wanted to slap the woman's face. She must have seen something in my eyes, for she laughed and collected the cards into a neat pile.

"You are young," Madame Olga said. "In time you will learn —" She looked straight into my eyes. "Or your gift shall destroy you."

At that time, I had no interest in exploring my gift. I expanded my circle of acquaintances to include other members of the sideshow troupe. I was pleased to be invited, on occasion, to join Tim-Tina, Balzod, and the "Siamese" twin boys, Chris and Toby for a late night or early morning game of croquet.

Tim-Tina performed in the cubicle furthest from the freak tent entrance. (I shall refer to her in the female, as that was her preference.) She exaggerated her duality by dressing as if a man and a woman both had been split right down the middle, and then half of each neatly joined together. If one looked quickly — and most especially, if she was in the midst of a crowd — it was easy to mistake her for two separate people. The hair on the left side of her head fell long and lustrous to her shoulders. On the right it was clipped short and slicked back. Her left eye was decorated with mascara and bright powder, the cheek below rosy with blush. The right side of her face was heavily browed and devoid of makeup, sporting a dark swab of stubble, which she encouraged with secret lotions and oils. Her costume was fashioned from a wedding gown and a tuxedo, the white lace and white satin of the gown ending in a clean vertical line, mirrored by the black silk of the tuxedo. The neckline of the gown met perfectly the collar of the jacket. The bodice swelled over her single breast, as the jacket lay flat on the right side of her chest. The hem swept up to her waist in front, bared a flash of supple left leg, and swept down to touch the ground behind her, ruffled where it met the seat of the pants.

With precise timing and supremely executed lighting cues, she presented herself to the audience first as Tim, standing with only the right side of her body visible. After "he" had recited beautifully written and romantic vows, the lights would dim briefly and she would turn, to be discovered by a pink spotlight as Tina. Tina would recite "her" equally beautiful vows. The lights would switch off, then quickly back on, and Tim-Tina would stand facing the crowd to reveal that the two were, indeed, but one.

By her own choice, Tim-Tina ended each performance by pulling open the front of her costume, exposing her single breast, her muscular chest, her flat stomach, her vagina and penis. Turning and posing on her platform, Tim-Tina appeared to take no notice as her audience whistled and whooped and stared, the men jostling each other and making rude comments. Women rarely entered Tim-Tina's cubicle, anyone not of legal age was barred admission, and, in several jurisdictions, Arthur paid protection to county bag men to avoid obscenity charges.

There were no such concerns with Balzod's act, and he performed in the cubicle closest to the entrance. Balzod the Great was very tall and very slim and looked very old, with unruly tufts of silver hair sprouting above his ears. He was an expert magician, a trouper of some sixty-odd years, having joined his first show at the age of eight. A member of the monkey family served with admirable skill as magician's assistant. "And now!" Balzod would proclaim, his black cape rustling, displaying a liner of red as he spread his arms. "I would like to introduce my lovely assistant. Ladies and gentlemen, the enticing – the entrancing – the ravishing and beautiful – Mademoiselle Zelda!" The curtain would sweep aside, and the monkey would scamper to Balzod's platform. Dressed in a silk gown and draped with paste diamonds, a blonde bouffant wig perched atop her head, she elicited peals of laughter from the audience.

I was particularly taken with Chris and Toby, who were handsome and charming and sang incredible operatic harmonies. I was deeply saddened when, only midway through that third season, the twins were crushed to death by Tiny during their twentieth birthday party. They had been celebrating alone with The Snake Lady in her tent. The Snake Lady left the Karnival not long after, Tiny coiled into her suitcase.

"You really shouldn't go," Tim-Tina said. "No one blames you for what happened."

"But I blame myself," The Snake Lady said. "We were having such fun, I never dreamed she'd think the boys were ... but Tiny ... she thought ..."

Tim-Tina shuddered, envisioning the tangle of bodies, the sudden attack of the boa squeezing life from those beautiful boys. Tim-Tina knew she would not mind losing Tiny's acquaintance. "Have a good, long life," Tim-Tina said, and she kissed The Snake Lady goodbye.

According to Madame Olga, The Snake Lady would have a wonderful life: "I see a cottage, surrounded by woods. I see a man, handsome and strong. I see a union, a birth, an Eden."

I was with Madame Olga when she uttered these words. At the mention of Eden I thought of its serpent, the boa, the death of the boys, and the dream that had invaded my sleep for the preceding five nights, from which Hamilton would awaken me, my body slick and trembling.

Once The Snake Lady had left, Madame Olga followed me to the tent I shared with Hamilton. As I turned to enter, she touched my arm. I recoiled, seeing at once her painful death. I stepped back.

Her eyes clouded with confusion. "What is it?" she asked.

Before I could speak, she supplied an answer. "You knew this would happen."

Of course, she was right. For nights in a row I had dreamed of a boy trapped within a mirror encased in a gilded frame. The boy screamed as a giant serpent twined itself around the frame, scales pulsing against the glass. At last the mirror shattered, and the boy hurtled into my face as deadly shards of bone.

"I see," Madame Olga said. "And so you blame yourself for what has happened to the boys."

"Not exactly," I said. "But I cannot help thinking, had I tried to discover what it meant ..."

"Perhaps you were not meant to know."

"Then why? Why present these things to me if I am not meant to understand them?"

Madame Olga closed her eyes, breathed deeply, and then opened her eyes as she exhaled. I saw how she would look in her casket, her face in repose belying the unbearable pain of her passing. "That is a question I don't know how to answer," she finally said. "All I know is that a talent, unexpressed, will grow in upon itself. Perverted and twisted and never escaped."

Perhaps it was the guilt I felt for the twins' deaths, or a longing to gain some sense of control over my destiny, that made me consent to Madame Olga's tutelage. Soon after this conversation, I began my training in the Tarot. I believed I could learn to master the *knowing* by giving it an outlet other than touch.

About this time, Arthur was approached by a young woman wearing a veil. She asked if Klieg's were still hiring freaks. When Arthur nodded, she lowered the veil to reveal a full beard.

"Is it real?" Arthur asked.

She took his hand, guiding it to her face. As he gazed into her eyes, his soul immediately recognized hers, though his mind knew only that he felt he had known her forever. It would not be long before he began to court her affections.

Her name was Anna, and the beard was natural. As Arthur lingered by her table at meals, or "accidentally" encountered her in the yard, he often asked how she had groomed her beard into such a stunning display. But this was a secret she would not share. "If I told you, sweet Arthur, you would perhaps lose your fascination for Anna, no?"

Nothing could dispel what Arthur felt for this lovely woman. As the freak tent filled with spectators, Arthur would slip inside and gaze at Anna, wishing he had not put her on exhibit, but knowing it was all that kept her near him. One night, hearing two teenage girls giggle and sneer at Anna, he resolved to marry her and retire her from the sideshow.

"If I marry you, Arthur," she said, "I cannot – I will not – give up my work."

"Surely there is something else you can do."

Anna shook her head. "There is nothing."

"But of course there is!" He could not bear to see her ridiculed again.

"But you do not understand," Anna said. "In their world I am a freak. I am less than a person. But here, in the dark of the tent, with the spotlight on my face and, beyond that light, a wall of eyes gazing with awe ... Here I am exotic. Each person who looks at me wishes, if only for a moment, that he or she were here in my place. That life were different and exciting and not an endless treadmill. Here I am more than a person." She touched his hand. "Do you not see? Do you not see, my sweet love?"

Yes, he saw. And he loved her all the more.

It was beautiful to see them together, walking through the lot arm in arm, feeding each other in lantern light, alone in a corner of the cook tent. None of us was surprised when they announced that autumn that they were soon to marry.

The wedding was held in the sunshine of the yard. Hamilton served as best man, and Tim-Tina as maid-of-honour. The monkey family played a symphony and threw rice as Philippe and Bilbo led the dancing. Balzod produced Anna's bouquet and disintegrated it into thin air when she tossed it back over her shoulder. A discreet distance away, reporters and cameramen documented the event.

In the hush that followed the newlyweds' kiss, I squeezed my husband's hand and whispered softly. "A daughter. From the daughter a son, and another."

But in my mind were other words, which I was too frightened to voice: "Salem. A witch."

Arthur and Anna's devotion to each other continued to deepen throughout the years. Their wedding was featured in *Life*, *Macleans*, and the amusement trade's *Billboard*, in addition to several newspapers. As further articles about them appeared over time, it was apparent that the public enjoyed a sincere and affectionate fascination with the couple.

With the words I whispered to Hamilton, I accurately foretold Margaret's arrival. Anna gave birth to her child in the spring of our fifth season. Arthur and Anna kept Margaret always within sight, checking her covers as she slept, rushing to her side whenever she cried or awakened. They held and kissed and tickled her. They played games and performed stories: creating outrageous voices for the characters, they exaggerated the action, waving their arms or standing on their heads as plots required. Margaret was generally delighted by these antics. She was a bright and curious child, if somewhat timid and overly sensitive. She enchanted all of us, though I was loath to touch her. I did not want to know how such a vulnerable soul would suffer.

Only weeks into the Karnival's tenth season, Madame Olga was crossing the yard when a heart attack felled her. The pain showed on her face even after her body had ceased to function. We all mourned her passing, but Arthur had an additional concern: Klieg's was without a fortune-teller for the sideshow.

"I need your help," Arthur told me the next morning. "People expect to see a fortune-teller. We don't have a full sideshow without one. I need you to take Olga's place."

It was daybreak, and we were alone in the cook tent. My hands rested on the table and my eyes focused on my wedding band. To read as a course of study, or for various troupers as practice, was something that I had come to enjoy. But to read for someone who expected to believe, who perhaps may make decisions based on what I foretold ... Could I truly see what the cards sought to reveal? I did not know if I was ready to see clearly in such manner, but touching a customer was beyond question. I did not want to submit to such intensity of *knowing* under these circumstances.

"We'll call you Madame Isis," Arthur said without waiting for my answer.

That afternoon, though I felt a new camaraderie between me and the other sideshow performers, I was uneasy as I entered the freak tent. Reaching what had been Madame Olga's cubicle, I could see that the entrance was veiled by linen draperies, which were printed with a garish Egyptian motif. Her banner on the sidewall had been covered with a placard announcing, "Madame Isis reveals YOUR Past! Present! Future!"

I said the name aloud for the very first time. I thought it fitting, for I knew that the Ancients – not only in Egypt, but also in Central America – held a particular reverence for dwarves, believing that we were directly connected to the gods. I decided nearly at once I liked the name, though, truth told, there is not a drop of Egyptian blood in my lineage this lifetime.

I stepped into the cubicle and paused for a moment. All physical traces of Madame Olga were gone. The walls were hung with the same garish linen as the entrance, blue and gold and green. Peacock feathers were bunched in large urns, which balanced on pink and white marble pedestals. The table was round, approximately three feet in diameter, and covered with a bright purple cloth fringed with yellow. Centred above the table, suspended from a bronze chain, a bowl-like oil lantern cast dancing shadows of feathers and furniture onto the linens and floor. Close together in front of the table, two low camel seats awaited those who were to be my customers. Behind the table, facing the entrance, my chair was high-backed and gilded and carved with lotuses, set upon a short platform. On the table, near the right arm of my chair, was a small wooden box, into which I would put the silver that crossed my palm. Near the left arm of my chair was the oversized deck of Tarot cards, brilliant with colour and design.

"Madame Isis," I said again. I stood between the camel seats, looking across the table as my customers would. I tried to imagine how I might appear through their eyes. Silently, I prayed that I would be able to assist those who came to me for answers.

Skirting the camel seats and table, I stepped onto the platform and eased into the chair. I leaned against its high, carved back, and grasped its lotus arms with my hands.

"Madame Isis," I said, and reached to spread the Tarot into a rainbow of fates before me.

My fear of incompetence proved to be groundless. Reading the cards came easily. My customers were pleased and, appropriately awed, did not seek to touch me. I soon came to enjoy the parade of new faces that greeted me from across my table, anxious for answers, for hope, for meaning. I gave each customer what I could, warning of an accident that might be avoided or minimized, but otherwise giving only positive predictions, for all the people I met were in need of something affirming in which to believe.

As she grew, Margaret asked me repeatedly to read her fortune. At last I consented on her eleventh birthday.

"A son," I told Margaret. The Knight of Wands, the Wheel of Fortune, the Knight and Queen of Cups were in the spread on the table, and the young girl watched me with wide eyes. "A son calls forth a brother. A sister to the second bears three."

Margaret later told me that, for years, she carried this reading as a shield, protecting her belief in the importance of her life. Though she did not understand it all, she knew she had a purpose which could only show itself in time. (Ironically, nearly two decades later, when her son, Horace, sent her and Frank to the Children's Aid Society, my reading did not come to her conscious mind.)

These years of Margaret's childhood were kind to the Karnival and its residents. Due to the favourable press coverage, an impressive roster of performers, and rides and games of chance and skill that were newly-built or refashioned each season, our bookings increased. We cut our winter hiatus from four months to three. For several weeks during our twelfth season, the Karnival buzzed with expectations of a three-week stand in Mexico, but the deal eventually fell through.

Hamilton and I were deeply in love. Though we learned during this time that we could not have children, our marriage was fulfilling. I was thankful that we were never apart for more than a few consecutive hours. I ached to touch him. It was as tortuous to be in his company and not have physical contact as it was to be without him. I longed for his embrace, to feel his heartbeat against my own. I held his hand at every opportunity and slept wrapped in his arms at night. I often told him that he was my compensation from the gods for the burden placed upon me this lifetime, and for this reason alone I always knew that he would outlive me.

At last I stopped viewing my gift as a curse. This gave my life a balance I had never before experienced. As I had hoped, by channeling my energies through the Tarot, it was rare that I endured an unwanted *knowing*.

Yet, as the seasons passed, The Fates continued to conspire.

In our nineteenth season, Klieg's spent thirteen days in early June at Toronto's Exhibition grounds. Arthur and Anna had then been married nearly sixteen years. Margaret was fourteen. Lovely and sensitive, Margaret worked the ticket booths, and was always popular with local boys, who loitered and purchased unneeded tickets just to be near her. Margaret worshipped and was adored by her mother. She spent hours grooming Anna's beard and hair in preparation for her appearance in the freak tent. Arthur was Margaret's anchor, and whatever fears would manifest, his inherent strength provided all she needed to once again feel safe.

The eleventh day of our Toronto stand saw Arthur reluctant to leave for New York, to finalize arrangements for an autumn tour of Europe. That morning, all of us gathered at Arthur's limousine, and he and Anna clung to each other as if they were to be separated forever. They had never before been apart. From the first day he had hired her, whenever Anna performed Arthur was always nearby. On his previous trip to meet with the promoter, both Anna and Margaret had accompanied him to New York.

"I will miss you, my sweet love," Anna said.

Arthur hugged her more tightly, whispering words that were meant for her ears alone.

"Don't you come back without that contract, now," Balzod said, for he was still disappointed about the cancelled trip to

Mexico so many years before. Balzod was about to turn ninety. He was certain he would die before Klieg's had ever played outside North America.

"Just come home to me, my darling," Anna said.

"No funny business now," Arthur said.

"Stay out of trouble, Daddy," Margaret said. She kissed him and placed a protective arm around Anna's shoulders.

I turned away, thinking of how it would feel to be parted from Hamilton, unable to bear the look of sadness in Arthur's eyes.

Black thunder clouds rolled in over Lake Ontario early that afternoon, but, without a single drop of rain, darkness settled on the teeming Exhibition grounds.

Hamilton filled in as talker for the sideshows. He delivered his spiel from Bilbo's shoulders as the bear twirled in skilled pirouettes.

The moon began to rise. It shimmered in the sky reflected in the surface of the lake. The sell-out crowd surged forward, and two young boys – drunk with curiosity – were drawn into our midst.

The boys had ridden a streetcar to the Exhibition grounds. It was a ride during which the two had delighted and disgusted their fellow passengers with tales of the freak tent.

"They got a lady that's half a man, y'know?" Joey had said. "Like, she's got a man's privates."

"You seen her?" Mark asked.

"Naw, the strongman keeps you out less you're old enough. Cause she shows her parts."

A young married couple turned in their seats. The husband looked at the boys and then back at his wife and then back at the boys again. "You two want to keep it down over there?" he said.

"I don't believe a lady with man's parts," Mark said. "Ain't in the possibles."

"Is," Joey insisted. "They got a lady with a beard. A real beard."

"Ladies don't have beards, butt-brain."

"Does, piss-breath. Why you think they call them freaks? Cause they're freaky!"

This sent the boys into peals of laughter. Several fellow passengers, despite all efforts, smiled and looked shyly away. The husband smiled. His wife jabbed him in the ribs and he let out a groan and then faced the boys as if to speak once again.

"You two are disgusting," a teenage girl said.

The boys stopped laughing. They glanced at the girl and tried to turn their backs in the crush of passengers.

"I won't believe it till I see her," Mark insisted; thus, upon arrival at the lot, they began to run when they spotted the tent.

I did not see the boys enter, though, as I was to learn in subsequent visions, they came in very near my table, slipping under the canvas through a gap where a sidewall's peg had come unearthed. I was reading Tarot for the driver of the streetcar that had brought the boys to the Exhibition grounds. But as their eyes grew accustomed to the dim light of the freak tent, the driver and I held no interest for the boys.

Remaining in the shadows out of sight, Joey and Mark moved quickly and reached Balzod's cubicle, where the man was gesturing on his dimly lit platform. Joey paused to watch, but Mark goaded him – "This guy's no good, come on!" – and Joey followed, glancing back as Balzod sawed Mademoiselle Zelda in half. They reached Anna's cubicle, the crowd growing restless, the lights not yet lit, and the boys hurried on, impatient with their progress.

And then, catching them unaware, they were jolted and thrown back by the cord that roped off Tim-Tina's area. It was strung across the aisle between two metal stands. Recovering, they speculated as to where Strongman Hank could be, and began to look for a vantage point from which to view Tim-Tina's act without their being seen.

There was a clang as Mark kicked one of the metal stands. "Damn freaks."

"What?"

"Look!" Mark pointed to the sign that was swaying back and forth attached to the cord. " 'Next performance ...' That's twenty damn minutes from now!" He lit a cigarette, which had come from a forgotten pack carelessly left beneath the front seat of Joey's father's car.

"Listen, Mark, I got an idea."

Mark sighed with exaggeration. "What?"

"She's got a dressing room behind her place – all of them do. If we could get a look in there we'd –"

"See her naked!" Mark took a long drag on the cigarette. "Maybe she's walking around in there with nothing on ... Man oh man, the guys are never gonna believe this."

"Maybe," Joey said, his voice thick and hungry. "Maybe she'll let us – you know."

"You think she would?"

"Sure," Joey said. "She's a freak, ain't she? Them freaks is always horny."

"Yeah?"

"Yeah. Cause no one wants to do it with them. I'll bet no one even kisses them."

At that moment, in another part of the tent, Anna was preparing to go on. For the first time in years, her heart fluttered with excitement.

Over sixteen seasons at Klieg's, Anna had grown bored with her act. Day after day, draped in silk veils, she lay on a divan, Arabian music flooding her cubicle, palm fronds and paste pearls decorating the walls. As the lights came up, Anna slid gracefully from the divan and began her dance, peeling away the veils one by one. Then, with a climax of music, she whipped away the final veil and faced her audience, whose mouths dropped open at the sight of her beard. Several seconds later, she was swallowed by blackness when the lights switched off.

But this night, with Arthur away, she risked the innovation she had been considering for years, despite the fact that Arthur had forbidden it the one time she discussed it with him. Anna had her cubicle carpeted with straw, over a foot thick. In the centre stood a huge wooden stake with heavy iron chains to be fitted around her wrists and ankles. Dressed in flowing silk beneath a wool wrap and a cloak, she watched the gathering crowd through a slit in the canvas. When the lights came up, she was led into the cubicle by "The Slave Master" – Strongman Hank, who had left his post near Tim-

Tina. A broad man, dressed ominously in black with a monkey perched on one shoulder, Hank fastened Anna to the stake with the chains. Turning to the audience, he bowed solemnly, lifted the monkey from his shoulder and placed him atop the stake, before striding from the cubicle.

The monkey danced about in the straw, pulling away the cloak, then the wool wrap, the silk scarves, one by one until Anna was left only in shift and veil. Anna's heart beat faster. The tension in the audience mounted and she writhed, shutting her eyes as the waves of awe washed over her ...

By this time, the transit driver had left the tent knowing his intended bride would say yes, and I was reading for a middle-aged rural woman. Her prize hog had given birth to five-legged piglets and, having experienced unexplained mishaps around the home, she was convinced that someone was out to do her harm via witch-craft.

Hamilton later told me (for I have no conscious recollection of the event) I interrupted her reading. My head snapped upright, and my voice took on a monotone, though resonant, timbre. "Salem."

"Pardon?" The woman bent forward, awaiting this new revelation.

"Salem. A witch. A witch ... Salem ..."

"A witch has put a curse on me!" The woman jumped to her feet. "Oh, that explains it! That explains it all!"

My consciousness returned. My eyes focused. I looked at her and strove to collect myself.

"Who is she?" the woman demanded. "Tara at Pork and Save? Dolly at Curl and Comb? Damn it, you tell me who she is!" The woman reached across the table to grab my hand, and we heard the alarm.

Meanwhile, Joey and Mark had found Tim-Tina's dressing room. She was naked, watching herself in the mirror, her breast gleaming in the lantern light, her penis at rest.

"Hers is bigger than yours," Joey said.

"You complaining?" Mark laughed as he passed the cigarette and Joey took a drag.

"What're you kids doing in here?" Strongman Hank grasped Joey's ankle and pulled him across the floor.

Mark cried out, scrambling to his feet. He scurried along the back of the tent, out of Hank's reach, and turned to see Joey was running toward him.

"Let's get outta here! Hurry!"

Racing from the tent, the boys struggled against the maddening crowds when Joey pushed through a fortuitous gap, quickly out of sight. Mark called his name, feeling lost, shoving people aside until he collided with Joey.

Joey stood transfixed, staring in the direction from which they had come.

"What is it?" Mark asked.

Joey pointed and Mark turned. Smoke was rising from the folds of the freak tent. Flames, like giant tongues, were licking at the canvas.

"Damn," Joey said. "We got outta there just in time."

"Where's that cigarette?" Mark asked.

"I dropped it when that –" Realization hit like a punch in the stomach. A wail escaped Joey's throat as he whirled and fled through the crowd.

From the ticket booth in which she was working, Margaret heard the alarms of "Fire!" Slamming shut the cash drawer, she turned the key, allowing the booth door to bang closed behind her. Her teenage admirers stared curiously after her as she ran.

By the time Margaret reached the freak tent, most of us had escaped: Hamilton; Tim-Tina; Balzod; The Painted Woman and The Rock Headed Man; Philippe and Bilbo. The monkey family was crazed with excitement, anxious for news of their youngest, still inside. The dogs barked furiously. The rural woman and other patrons were awed and frightened and safe.

I was desperate. There was no sign of Anna.

"Mama!" Margaret's eyes searched the crowd. She rushed to my side. "Where is my mother?!"

A woman screamed and we turned to see Strongman Hank, framed by the roaring fire. He was holding Anna. She was wrapped in a blanket, cradled against his chest.

Margaret saw them, clearly – all of us did. As the canvas crashed down upon them, she would have run into the flames herself had Hamilton not seized her around the waist. She slipped to the ground, weeping, as I wished that I could console her, take her into my arms and assure her that her heart would heal and life would go on ...

Margaret would forever believe that her father was spared the flaming tent. What she was completely unaware of, however, was that from the moment the fire touched the straw of her cubicle, Anna knew she was destined to die. With all her soul Anna called for Arthur and, from his hotel room in New York, he found himself transported to her side.

The straw burned quickly, the flames sweeping across the ground and catching Anna's garments in seconds, but Arthur was helpless. His hands passed through the chains, unable to touch the emergency release on the locks. When Anna saw him, she felt a sense of peace, and she told him that she knew she would die, but their love would bind them forever.

Arthur knelt at her feet. Words of love poured from his lips, barely audible above the fire and the panic of the youngest monkey. Suddenly Hank was there, oblivious to the flames, fighting his way through the inferno with a blanket over his head, refusing to believe it was too late.

Hank pressed forward, kicking aside the straw, ignoring the heat that licked at his ankles. The chains were red hot but he unlocked them, his fingers blistering. He caught Anna's body as it fell from the stake and wrapped her in the blanket to put out the flames. He lifted her, ducking away from the rain of debris, a beam smashing beside him.

The monkey, seeing that Anna was free, escaped through the top of the tent.

Arthur stood in the centre of the cubicle, knowing that Hank had already failed, but proud and grateful for the attempt. The wood chips were turning to coals, the straw, the canvas, the beams burning, the roar like the roar of a crowd. He could see the people gathered a distance from the tent. They were wide-eyed, crying out in one anguished voice as the canvas gave way, smothering Hank and Anna within.

Arthur shut his eyes, and reopened them lying on his back on the floor of his hotel room in New York. And there he lay, weeping.

Hamilton dispatched two of the workmen later that night to retrieve him.

There was no funeral. Anna and Hank were taken to the crematorium (the irony of which was not lost on us), and a memorial was held in the Exhibition's chapel. Tim-Tina, heavy bags beneath her eyes, sat beside Margaret, clutching the girl's hand.

In the tent that night, Tim-Tina had heard Anna's screams, but she was searching for her robe so she would not have to run naked into the crowd. By the time she found her robe the screaming had stopped. Tim-Tina fled the tent, passing Anna's cubicle unaware that Anna stood chained to the stake.

Arthur was at the podium, sobbing through a eulogy for his beautiful Anna and the brave Strongman Hank. Tim-Tina slipped her hand free of Margaret's and left her seat, pushing her way out into the sunlight. On the lot, the remains of the freak tent smouldered in the heat of the afternoon. Tim-Tina looked away. For the first time, she wished that she had never come to Klieg's.

It was a moment before she saw the boy curled beside the chapel wall. His hands were clasped between his legs as his body trembled. She touched his shoulder gently, and he opened his eyes.

"Are you all right?" Tim-Tina asked.

He shook his head.

She knelt on the ground, reached out and held him. His face pressed into her breast, his tears wetting her black silk blouse. She let him weep, her mind blank, until he lifted his head to look at her.

"You're the man lady," he said.

She nodded.

"I did it," he said.

I did it. The words echoed about her brain, slamming into the sides of her skull. "I don't understand," she said.

"I did it," he choked. "I dropped the cigarette ..."

She held him more tightly, her heart aching. He couldn't be more than twelve, his body caved in upon itself, his face wrenched. "No," she said softly. "No. You did not do this."

"But I did!" he cried. "We wanted to see you! We wanted to see – !"

"Don't," she said.

"He grabbed me ... he grabbed me because we weren't supposed to be there. But we wanted to see you."

I did it, she thought, and was chilled.

"I dropped the cigarette and I ran and ran and suddenly it was on fire and – and – !" His fists beat at her arms and she bore the blows. "I did it I did it I killed them! I killed them!"

"No," Tim-Tina said. "No." She pulled him into her breast and rocked him. As if from miles away, as if someone else had taken over her body (Tim without Tina? Tina without Tim?), there was her voice. "I heard you yelling ... it must have been you ... And Hank. I was frightened ... I jumped out of my chair to look for my robe, and the lantern ..." The thoughts she had managed to fend off until that moment rushed into her, filling her. "It shattered on the floor. The canvas ... and the wood chips ... All of a sudden everything was ... as if it had been doused with gasoline." The boy studied her, but she did not see him. "I did it. I spilled the lantern. I did it." She looked at him then, tried to smile into his eyes. "It wasn't your cigarette ..."

"You're just saying that," he said. His eyes searched her face. "You're just –"

"I wish I were," Tim-Tina said.

The breeze swept down to caress them.

"Maybe," Joey said. "Maybe it was both of us."

To my enduring shame, I was unable to carry the burden placed upon me at this time. Once again I cursed my gift. Why only helpless brief glimpses of what would profoundly affect the people I loved? It seemed that The Fates were taunting me to subject myself to the *knowing*. Yet, were I to *know*, what toll would The Fates exact if I should attempt to change what must be? I felt betrayed, as betrayed as Margaret must have felt as she faced me after the memorial service.

"Why didn't you save her?" the girl demanded.

"I did not know, child," I said. My heart swelled with remorse. "I did not know."

"Bullshit," Margaret said.

The mourners gasped.

From the podium, Arthur stared at his daughter, powerless in the depths of his grief.

"Margaret, please," Hamilton said.

"I'm sorry, Uncle Ham, but I mean it." She bent down, her face close to mine. "Bullshit! You're the fucking fortune-teller! And people are saying you knew!"

"By all that is holy on this earth, I swear to you, Margaret, I did not know."

"I don't believe you!" The girl lost all control. "Salem! Salem! A witch! Salem!"

I drew back my arm to slap her.

Hamilton grasped my wrist. He glanced at Arthur, who wept as he watched the disintegration of his family. "Now, Margaret, you stop this!" Hamilton said. "You can't blame your aunt!"

"She knew! And if she didn't she should have, but we all know – she did!" Margaret's eyes were dark with fear and anger, shadowed by hatred. She turned once again to me. "We both know, don't we?"

"Child, please –"

"I will never forgive you. Ever," Margaret said.

As she stormed away, my self-confidence dissipated.

That afternoon, Hamilton oversaw tear-down. I was in our tent packing our belongings when Balzod stopped by to offer his sympathies. I never sipped more than a shot glass or two of wine with dinner, but Balzod poured me a drink from his ever-present flask of vodka. When he left some time later to prepare for departure, the flask remained behind. There began a downward spiral I made no effort to arrest.

We left Toronto, heading west, crossed the border in Niagara Falls, and entered the United States. Klieg's began a series of five-nighters, zigzagging west and south. Much of this is a blur to me, recalled only in brief snippets. What I cannot forget is the overwhelming feeling of being alone, despair which only deepened with each drink I took.

Arthur refused to leave his office-trailer and it fell upon Hamilton to keep the Karnival operating. Hamilton's duties took up to eighteen hours a day and I was often fast asleep when he returned to our tent at night. We saw little of each other at this time, and as all the Karnival staff was in a state of shock and mourning, it was easy for me to hide, for some weeks, what I had so quickly and thoroughly become.

That July we moved on to Nevada. We set up in a seemingly-endless expanse of flatness, which no one had claimed. The dry heat of the desert permeated our bodies. At night, we sank into breathless cold. As the Karnival was shutting down one evening, I sat ashamed in the makeshift tent we had converted for the sideshow. I struggled to focus on the Tarot cards as an irate woman glared from across my table.

"This is crap," she hissed. "I want my fucking money back."

I was too drunk to stop her as she reached into the small wooden box at my side. She extracted the three silver dollars with which she had crossed my palm.

"Fucking waste of my time, you fucking midget," she said, and then I was alone with the cards, wishing I had never learned to see them.

I do not understand what possessed me to do what I did that night. In my drunken state, I believed as Margaret did, that Anna's death was my fault. I had perversely convinced myself that restricting my gift to the Tarot had destroyed all hope of mastering the *knowing*. As Madame Olga had warned me, I refused to embrace fully what the gods had granted and, seeing no redemption, I only wanted an end.

Much later, once I had returned from the hospital and sobered, never to drink alcohol again, Hamilton explained with careful words what had transpired. He had awakened to my anguished voice, crying out incoherently from the Karnival lot. He found me standing barefoot upon a pyre of tumbleweeds, scissors held in one hand, a lantern in the other. Hamilton tried to approach me, but I brandished the scissors. Calling for help, he was soon joined by the rest of the troupe – even Margaret, though she hung back. They watched as I raised the scissors. I thrust the blades into my left eye, blood spurting as I drew the tiny ball from its socket.

Hamilton ran forward and wrenched the scissors from my hand. I began to swing the lantern, intent on burning myself alive. Suddenly Margaret tackled us and we landed softly in the sand, the lantern breaking nearby.

"Stop it stop it stop it stop it!" Margaret held me down, and this is what I remember: I could see, all at once, all that would befall her and all that ever had. I knew how she would die, far from that moment, painlessly in her bed with her loving husband beside her. But there was no overwhelming intensity to make me ill.

"I'm sorry," Margaret said. "It wasn't your fault ..."

Just before I passed out in Hamilton's arms, I realized what I had done.

Months later, Margaret and I would speak of that night. "When you read for me on my eleventh birthday," Margaret said, "I thought that you were – magical, I guess. And you are but, somehow, I thought that made you stronger than the rest of us ... But you're just a person, aren't you? Some things you know, some things you don't."

"I swear to you, child –"

"It's okay, I believe you."

"All I had were words – meaningless in themselves. Your mother told no one but Hank. Do you think Hamilton and I would have allowed her to – ?"

"I know," Margaret said. "I just wanted to say I'm sorry I accused you. I'm sorry for all the horrible things I said."

"I cannot blame you for anything you have said or done."

"You should," Margaret said with a shy smile. "But since I know you won't ... then just don't blame yourself. Please. Mama would be horrified if she knew we were fighting."

My actions that night had provided a release, and the Karnival moved on. Though our trip to Europe was postponed until the following year, we played out our dates for the rest of the season and accepted several late bookings.

Anna's death quickly dimmed Arthur's light. He had once spent his days wandering the lot, noting needed improvements and talking for the sideshows. He now remained in his office-trailer for days at a time, counting the gate and keeping the books. Hamilton took it upon himself to act for his grieving brother regarding neglected affairs. He started drawing up plans for a new, larger freak tent, and placed ads in the dailies of the towns we would play as we began our stands through the American South.

The Snake Lady returned to us in Georgia, Tiny dead, two new baby snakes coiled around her body. She was sorry to hear that Madame Olga had passed on, particularly because she wanted to complain about the quality of her prediction. "Oh, yes," she told Tim-Tina. "He was handsome and strong and we did have a beautiful cottage in the woods. But the birth she envisioned, while his, was not mine."

Balzod, at the age of ninety, collapsed in the heat one afternoon and died not long after, Klieg's not yet having played outside North America. We agreed, out of respect, to continue for some time without another magician. We decorated what had been his cubicle as a small museum of magic, which proved to be quite popular and would eventually inspire the world-renowned Karnival Museum.

A Sword-and-Fire Swallower named Fritz joined the troupe in Atlanta. Polly and Peg, a set of conjoined twins ("Siamese" to the customers) attached at the hip and buttocks, signed on in New Orleans. The Amazing Armless Artist wandered onto the lot and was doing portraits with his feet for a week before Hamilton realized he was there and asked Arthur to put the man on salary.

As for myself, I replaced my left eye with one of glass. When I cleaned it each day, it served to remind me that none of us is meant to see all things.

During our tour of the American South I began my rise to fame. In Fort Lauderdale, Florida, I read for an actress whose locally-based television series was facing cancellation. I predicted an Emmy and renewal for her. She refused to believe me, and later she thanked me from the podium, and recounted the full story of her visit to Klieg's in every television and radio interview.

Attendance tripled during our twentieth year. We at last toured Europe, extending the season well into December.

Upon our return to Canada, we were all exhausted from the excitement of the tour, looking forward to our winter hiatus. All, I should say, but Tim-Tina, who was, without question, the most profoundly sad soul I ever encountered.

*   *   *

Tim-Tina had never formed a strong sense of identity, and joined Klieg's because, as she would often say, "This is the only decent place I'm worth something the way I am."

She had been born in a tiny seaside village, which existed because of the continued abundance of local whitefish. Rebecca Hardwick gave birth to her child alone, in the bedroom she shared with her husband, Ed, when he was not at sea. She was forever grateful that she had done so. While her child was not exactly the daughter for whom she had hoped and planned, neither could it rightly be called a boy.

To Rebecca, the child she named Tina was a girl, despite the fact that, as well as a vagina, Tina possessed a penis the size of Ed's thumb. Rebecca made certain that her child's secret was covered in Ed's presence, always bathing, dressing, and changing the child herself. She was glad that his work kept Ed often away at sea.

Tim-Tina's first memory (and in fact, she would awaken years later from nightmares, the words still ringing in her ears) was that of her mother's insistent voice: "Keep your skirt down. Always. Never let anyone see – never. Do you understand, little girl?" Tim-

Tina knew only that she was different, bearing a shame that would have to be hidden, even from her own beloved father.

When Tim-Tina was five, Rebecca abruptly took ill. She passed away from an infection that could not be diagnosed even after death. Ed dyed Tim-Tina's best sundress black, and as he was helping her prepare for the funeral, he discovered his child's secret.

Dressed as a boy with hair hacked short, Ed's child wept at Rebecca's funeral. Whereas Rebecca had been blind to Tim-Tina's penis, Ed was blind to Tim-Tina's vagina. He retired from the fishing boats and took up doing odd jobs for villagers. He renamed her Tim and, as she grew, he browbeat and bullied her to "toughen" her. She was ridiculed by classmates, whose parents never forgot nor neglected to mention that for five years she had been a girl. She was a boy, Ed reminded her at every opportunity, and she was more confused than ever. She was incapable of understanding what her life was meant to be, and hours of her childhood were spent weeping in her room.

After more than a decade of living as Ed's son, she awoke one morning to find her sheets sticky and crimson red. She was bleeding. Panicked when the flow increased, but afraid to approach her father, she stuffed her vagina with cotton socks, wore extra underwear and a pair of short pants beneath her jeans, and took the bus to the city.

She was certain she was dying. Panic abated with the growing belief that her torment would soon be over.

But she wasn't dying, the doctor explained. She had entered puberty and begun to menstruate, though this did not mean she could ever have children. He told her what she was and, without her consent, exhibited her to his colleagues, his nurses, and an endless parade of medical students and personnel from nearby hospitals. They photographed and treated her like a specimen. They explored her in an operating theatre, her legs in stirrups, lights glinting on frightening implements.

Three days later she sneaked out of the hospital, knowing where she was headed. A nurse had joked about carnival sideshows, and Klieg's, struggling through its first season, was on the outskirts of the city.

Arthur felt a great sympathy for her, but he was anxious to know why she would put herself on display.

"What else can I do?" she asked. "I have no family. As the doctors explained, I can never have children. What man or woman would want me? What kind of life can I have for myself anywhere else? At least here, nature's cruelty can feed and clothe me. What do I care how many more eyes see? All I want is to be what I am and not be asked to be anything else."

Over the years, Tim-Tina had fallen in love with Strongman Hank, who often protected her from attack. When Hank died in the fire set by her lantern, she lost all hope of ever being loved and all desire to ever love again.

Shortly after our return from Europe, Tim-Tina discovered a lump in her breast. She consented, despite her fears, to visit a doctor because she hoped to learn she was soon to die.

"That's a horrible thing to say," Margaret told her. "Don't you know how I would feel if something happened to you?"

During the period in which Margaret and I were estranged, Tim-Tina had taken it upon herself to become a companion to Margaret. It was more than the guilt she felt for spilling the lantern. She did not want Margaret to suffer as she had, since Arthur's depression had left the girl virtually parentless. But Tim-Tina had underestimated Margaret's feelings for her, because they were as unexpected as they were alien.

Though Tim-Tina prayed for a negative prognosis, once her breast was removed she returned from the hospital sentenced to live. But she again was uncertain how she could go on.

Margaret cared for her as we wintered on Vancouver Island. Tim-Tina spoke little about the future, but as the Karnival prepared for its twenty-first season, she confessed to Margaret that she did not believe she belonged with Klieg's any longer.

"I'm nothing," Tim-Tina said. "I'm just a body with a penis growing out of a vagina."

"You can do something," Margaret said.

"What?" Tim-Tina asked. "Get married? Have babies? I don't

even know what I am anymore ... A man? A woman? Just a body with double sex parts!"

"You're a person," Margaret said. "A beautiful, beautiful person."

"Sure," Tim-Tina said. "A beautiful person ... But nobody loves a hermaphrodite. Nobody but a pervert."

"That can't be true," Margaret said.

But it was true for Tim-Tina. In some of the towns and cities that Klieg's had visited, she had tried to find companionship. Regardless of how she presented herself, in heterosexual environments she was beaten up by men, laughed at by women. She had turned to homosexual environments where only the wolves with twisted smiles and evil eyes wanted her, never the handsome men with love in their hearts, never the lesbians who wanted more than dominance and power.

"How can I expect you to understand?" she asked Margaret. "You're young. You're normal. You have people who love you ... I've seen how that Clifford boy looks at you."

Margaret was silent. Frank Clifford had signed on as a workman when Goliath was first constructed. He spent his days building and inspecting the rides, tearing them down when it was time to move on. And yes, she had felt that stirring, her pulse quickening, whenever she was close to him. But at this moment, she only knew what she felt for Tim-Tina. "I love you," Margaret said softly. She pulled the man-woman into her arms, stroking her hair. When Tim-Tina lifted her head, Margaret kissed her. She hugged Tim-Tina more tightly, her mouth opening, welcoming Tim-Tina's tongue, which sent desire shivering rampant throughout her body.

But then Tim-Tina scrambled to her feet. "No! No, Margaret, it's wrong!" Tim-Tina's eyes were wide and red. "No. No ..."

"But I love you," Margaret said.

"It's not the same thing. It's not that kind of love."

"Oh, but it is," Margaret said. She often lay awake listening to Tim-Tina's troubled sleep, wanting to climb into bed with the beautiful man-woman, hold her, and kiss her. "I want to make love to you," Margaret said.

"No!" Tim-Tina began to pace and Margaret felt she could see the fight – man versus woman – going on within the single body.

"You don't know what you're saying," Tim-Tina said. "You don't know!"

Margaret was calm, watching her. "I love you." She smiled, taking a step forward.

"Like a friend," Tim-Tina pleaded. "Not like a lover. Not me, Margaret ... I'm not a man ... I'm not a woman. I'm a freak. A thing! Nobody loves a thing, not like that, not the way you're saying!"

Margaret reached out for her.

Tim-Tina pulled away as if Margaret's touch were fire. "It's wrong!"

"Was my mother a thing?" Margaret asked. "Was my father's love for her wrong, was he loving a thing?"

"But it's not the same!" Tim-Tina cried, her shoulders sagging. "It's not the same ... Someone else loves you, Frank Clifford loves you."

"And?"

"And you should be with him! You should be saying these things to that boy, not to me! Look at me ... I'm old, Margaret ... I'm a freak! I've made a living showing my body to sick people –"

"Curious people," Margaret said. "Different isn't –"

"Different is! I was never a person to those people. I was a thing, with one breast, a cunt, and a cock. A freak of nature! A non-person, a thing! A thing!"

Margaret slapped Tim-Tina's face. Tim-Tina crumpled, and Margaret knelt beside her. "I love you," Margaret said. "My mother loved you ... The Snake Lady and Uncle Ham and Madame and my father – we all love you."

"But it's not the same! It's not the love of a man for his wife, a woman for her husband ... It's not the love of two young people just starting out, two old people who have shared their lives, given children to the world. I have nothing to give ... Nothing but a freak body."

"Love," Margaret said. "You have love." Margaret kissed her, pulling her into her arms. She peeled away Tim-Tina's robe, her hand caressing between Tim-Tina's legs, moving aside the ever-flaccid penis to stroke her vagina. "I love you ... I love you ..."

They clung to each other, kissing deeply, Margaret gasping with the consummation of their love. Afterward, Margaret lay with her head on Tim-Tina's chest, one finger gently tracing the mastectomy scar.

"I do love you," Tim-Tina said. "But we can't ... never ... We can never do this again. He can give you a life, Margaret. All I can give you ..." But Tim-Tina turned toward the canvas of the floor, the words unsaid.

Margaret would always wonder how she went from loving Tim-Tina to loving Frank. Perhaps Tim-Tina was right, she would think. Perhaps she did not love Tim-Tina the way she would grow to love Frank. Yet she would always remember that night with Tim-Tina, envision their union, in her dreams, even her waking hours, until she felt she would die if she could not relive it. But Tim-Tina spurned her advances, touching Margaret's cheek and shaking her head.

Soon Tim-Tina began dancing with Bilbo, the bear. Philippe had fallen for a local woman and was preparing to leave the Karnival. It was Arthur's suggestion that Tim-Tina take his place in the ballroom act.

Tim-Tina looked at her hands in her lap. At that moment, facing Arthur in his office-trailer for the first time since the night he hired her, she was ashamed of her lovemaking with Margaret. She was ashamed of the fire, ashamed that Arthur was broken.

"Please release me from my contract," she said.

"Nonsense," Arthur said. "I won't hear of it."

Tim-Tina was torn. She did not want to leave the Karnival, but neither did she think she could stay after losing her self-control with Margaret. But, as these were feelings she could not voice to Arthur, she said, "I know nothing about the bear."

"Philippe will teach you – he's agreed to stay on for another two weeks. It's not as if you have to teach the bear. It's simply a matter of your learning the steps."

With nowhere to go – and no one else who wanted her – Tim-Tina yielded. As she rehearsed with Bilbo in the heat of the yard, she watched Frank and Margaret walk together through the Karnival lot. Tim-Tina could not help envying Frank those glorious moments, basking in Margaret's adoring gaze.

Tim-Tina's heart was broken. She did not want to endure further loss, nor another unrequited love. Her cancer began to spread.

Frank proposed to Margaret on the second anniversary of their first date. Margaret hugged him, kissed him, and told him they would have to wait.

"But why?" he asked.

"We're so young, Frank. And I don't know what I want to do with my life yet. Sometimes I think I want to stay with the Karnival, but then my father wants me to go to university as soon as I get my diploma."

"When is that?"

"I mailed in my finals last week. If I get good marks – and I'm certain I will – then it's only a matter of stopping in some city to take the provincial exam and that's it ... But – marriage, Frank, I don't –"

"All right," he said. He kissed her. "I can wait. If you love me today – you do love me?" When she nodded, he laughed and said, "Then you'll love me a year from now. You'll love me whenever you know what it is you want to do."

She accepted the ring he slipped on her finger, the tiny diamond sparkling in the sun. "I love you, Frank Clifford," she said.

She received perfect marks on her finals and arranged to take the provincial test on our next swing through Alberta. She passed but, with Frank waiting to marry her, she wondered if she should bother with university or simply begin their life together.

"Is there any reason you can't do both?" Tim-Tina asked from her bed. Blankets were tucked tightly around her, and a glass of water stood next to the pill bottle on the table nearby. "Marry him, Margaret. Find a nice town to settle in and go to university."

"But the Karnival –"

"The Karnival is no kind of life for you two. The Karnival is for freaks, for gypsies, for people without love, without families to raise and roots to put down. You need roots, Margaret. Roots from which a family will grow ... A family that will love you and care for you, and you them."

Margaret could not tell Tim-Tina the true reason she did not want to leave. When she slept with Frank she could not help thinking of the beautiful man-woman, so alone in her tent, failing with age, cancer eroding her body. If Margaret were to leave, who would care for Tim-Tina? Who would hold her hand and comfort her the way she had comforted Margaret?

From her last hospital bed, breathing her final breaths, tubes running in and out of her body and doctors and nurses hovering, Tim-Tina squeezed Margaret's fingers and forced a smile. "I'll be gone soon," she said. "I'll be gone ... Now there's nothing to hold you, nothing to keep you there. Marry him, Margaret ... Marry him and raise a family. And be happy. He loves you."

Standing by the graveside as they lowered the casket, Margaret could not help but think that Tim-Tina had died to free her so she could marry Frank and bear Horace.

III FISSURES

Margaret left the Karnival with Frank and Horace soon after she had given birth. Though she never intended to remain so distant for so long, it would be more than a decade before they returned to Klieg's. Arthur convinced himself that Margaret's leaving was best for her and her family. He missed her terribly, but busied himself with improvements to Klieg's as the monkey family rehearsed their symphonies and the acrobatic dogs perfected new tricks. The bear was retired to a home on Algonquin Island because he would dance no longer after Tim-Tina's passing.

Margaret and Frank settled in a lovely suburb of Niagara Falls, Ontario. Frank found employment with the parks department. He worked during the day while Margaret cared for Horace, and cared for Horace at night while Margaret attended university. Margaret majored in literature. She approached her courses with enthusiasm, but the books they studied were dark, heavy with philosophy and death, and midway through her first year she dropped out.

Seeking to change her perspective, Margaret decided to write children's books. She illustrated them herself, clumsily at first. Horace was her critic. If he sat still and listened, she knew she had done well. If he did not, she set the book aside possibly to rewrite later. With the money left from her schooling, she and Frank converted the garage. She installed a printing press, set and inked type, and cut plates for her illustrations. She took the finished pages to a binder, from whence they emerged, as if by magic, as real books with lives of their own.

Once she had completed several books, she selected the best six, left Horace with a trusted neighbour, and sped off in the car to visit local bookstores. She was greeted with little enthusiasm, though managers were polite in their refusals. Striding to the parking lot, it struck her that bookstores were not her only option. She stopped in the middle of the sidewalk and turned to survey the stores across the street.

Toward the end of the block she saw a children's clothing shop. In the front window, among the displays of clothing, were teddy bears and dolls, a child's tea set, building blocks, and toy cars. She hurried to the corner, her foot tapping as she waited for the light to change. She pushed ahead of the other pedestrians and, once inside the shop, looked around for a salesperson.

"May I help you, Miss?"

The woman who spoke was the proprietor and, after she said, "How perfectly lovely!" several times, she ordered five copies of each book. Thereafter, Margaret paid sales calls on all the specialty stores for children and expectant mothers. Within a few years, Clifford Press was a viable business. Margaret's books were well-loved in homes throughout the country.

Margaret wrote twenty-eight books by the time Horace turned six. That was the year she signed what would prove to be her most lucrative contract. A major restaurant and motel chain, which catered to the family travellers, began to carry the series in more than three hundred locations. As The Fates would have it, Nola and Ralph soon discovered the books.

They had been together for nearly a year, but Ralph had not yet learned that Nola could not read. In restaurants and truck stops, Nola chose her meals by looking at the pictures in menus or the plates of food on other tables. Most restroom doors had pictographs of either a male or female form, but it was easy to watch who went in and out, or to time her visits with Ralph's, going through the door that he did not. There were no occasions that demanded Nola read or write, and so Ralph remained unaware for some time that she was illiterate.

One afternoon, as Ralph was paying for lunch, Nola saw on the wall behind the cashier the display of Clifford Press books. She was intrigued by the lively, colourful covers. Seeing her wonder, Ralph purchased what was then the entire collection.

Back in the truck, Nola looked through the books. She was delighted by the illustrations and Ralph was happy to see her smiling.

"Read me one," Ralph said.

Delight evaporated. Nola stared at the pages of the book in her hands, and the markings she knew must be the words of the story, lost. Her heart pounded.

"Well?" Ralph said. "Can't decide?"

"I can't," Nola said. "I don't know how." Her eyes clouded. The illustrations became as fogged as the letters she could not decipher. Then she was angry and wished she had never wanted these books.

Ralph reached for her hand. "It's okay," he said. "I'll show you." That moment he began, ever patiently, to teach Nola how to read.

Over the next few years, Nola progressed slowly, and she was eventually able to read to Ralph with little assistance. When Nola told him that she was pregnant, they were both pleased that she would be able to read to her child.

Ralph felt it was time that they see about getting married. But the young lovers were unable to obtain a licence. Nola had no identification, and the clerks could not proceed without proof of her birth. Back in the cab of the truck, after a day and a half of arguing with bureaucrats, Nola snuggled into Ralph's arms.

"We don't need them to get married," she said. "We'll do it ourselves." She picked up one of the cigars on the dashboard and removed its paper band. "With this ring I wed ye," she said. She slipped the paper band onto the proper finger of Ralph's left hand. It stopped after the first knuckle, but at least it fit.

Ralph hugged her close. "I do," he said. He kissed her deeply.

"I do, too," Nola said.

It was mid-December when Nola and Ralph awoke snowed in on a lonely side road. Nola was in labour, and though Ralph was frightened, she assured him she was not. As the pains intensified, coming more often, he read to her from Margaret's books and chipped an icicle from the side mirror for her to suckle.

Nola had done all that she could to forget her early life, including the birth of her son. But as she lay in the built-in sleeper, Ralph holding her hand as her second child entered the world, she could not help thinking of Baby. She found herself saying a silent prayer, that he was either happy or blessedly dead.

"Honey," Ralph said.

Her eyes were closed, her mind finishing the prayer, and as her breathing slowed she raised her arms to take the gurgling baby from Ralph.

"It's a girl, honey," Ralph said, but his voice was tight. "A very pretty, special little girl."

Nola struggled to sit up. "What's wrong?"

"Nothing, honey, she's –"

"What is it?"

With a sigh, Ralph lifted the baby, letting the blanket fall away.

Nola studied her daughter. "My God, Ralph," Nola said, "she's ..."

"Special," Ralph said.

The baby was pink and plump and healthy. In addition to all the standard parts, the baby had a third arm. The arm extended from the right side of her chest, just below the nipple, the fingers curled as if forever caught in the act of grasping the air.

"What does it mean?" Nola asked.

"I don't know." Ralph wrapped the baby in the blanket and placed her into Nola's arms.

"She's very pretty," Nola said. "Do you think she's okay?"

"I don't know," Ralph said. "Maybe we should ask someone."

Once the sun had risen and melted enough of the ice and snow, they took the baby to the nearest hospital. As nurses and interns gossiped and stared, a doctor explained.

"She seems perfectly healthy," the doctor said.

Nola and Ralph breathed a sign of relief. "What about – ?"

"No need to be concerned. Birth anomalies are much more common than people realize. It will be a simple procedure to have the offending limb removed."

"The what?" Nola said.

"The offending limb," the doctor said.

"Offending who?" Nola's eyes narrowed. "I just wanted to know if she's okay."

"She will be perfectly normal," the doctor said. "After the operation, of course."

"Now, wait a minute," Nola said.

"Are you saying," Ralph asked, "that you want to operate to take her arm away?"

"Of course. Isn't that why you're here?"

"I've told you a hundred times now," Nola said. "We just wanted to know if she's okay."

"She's healthy, if that's the question. But, really, Mrs. Greeson ... Don't you want a normal child?"

"Who are you?" Nola demanded. "How do you know what's normal?"

"You need only look around you." The doctor smiled, thinking that he had, indeed, said something meaningful and intelligent.

"What kind of answer is that?" Nola said.

"We're just regular people," Ralph said. "We don't know much about medical things."

"As I mentioned earlier, birth anomalies are not uncommon. Quite frequently, we are called upon by parents to ensure that their children are able to live normal lives."

"What?" Nola said. "You mean you go around cutting up babies all the time? Just to make sure they look like what you think they're supposed to?"

"That's a little dramatic," the doctor said.

"That's sick is what it is," Nola said, and Ralph said, "Honey, now let's be calm here."

"When a child is that different from what is normal, life can be quite difficult."

"Maybe if you didn't cut babies apart there'd be no normal. And then my baby would be fine just the way she is."

The doctor stared at her, looked at Ralph who was nodding slowly, and pushed back his chair. He silently escorted them to the door.

Back in the truck, Ralph turned to look at Nola, who was cuddling her daughter and kissing her face.

"You okay?"

"I don't know," Nola said. "Do you think he's right?"

Ralph studied her. "I think you did the right thing," he said. "After all, it's the kind of thing that you can't undo. I just wouldn't feel right if ... Anyway, she can decide for herself later on if she wants to."

"I just couldn't stand the thought of some man taking a knife ..." Nola pulled her daughter close. "Besides. Things like this don't happen for no reason, right?"

"Well ... Sounds right."

"So there must be a reason for it. Right, Ralph?" To Nola's mind, bad things happened because of bad people, and that train of thought led to Mollie and Thad. "Right, Ralph?"

Ralph saw in her beautiful eyes the desperate plea for agreement. "God must have very special plans for her," he said.

"I think so, too," Nola said. She snuggled her daughter, humming softly.

Ralph's thoughts floated on the notes of the song. "As long as we love her," he said, "and we teach her how to love herself, then everything is going to be all right."

They named her Chloe and Nola read to her every night, cuddled against her in the built-in sleeper. Over time, as Clifford Press released new books, Nola and Ralph purchased these as well. Ralph constructed an ingenious storage space in the built-in sleeper to house the series.

Margaret had published fifty-seven books, and her son, Horace, was eleven, when she and Frank brought Baby – then nine and properly named Heath – into their home.

That September, in the lovely suburb of Niagara Falls, Margaret watched as Horace took Heath off to his first day of school. At the corner, Heath turned to wave to her, and she wished for the same sense of loss she had felt when Horace first left for school so many years before.

After school, Heath brought home a starving dog he had found scrounging in a ditch. Margaret's first impulse was revulsion. The animal brought to her mind Hamilton's dog act, her mother, and Tim-Tina ...

"Oh, honey, we can't keep him," Margaret said. She stood blocking the doorway.

"But we have to!" Heath insisted. "Nobody else wants him!"

She did not have the heart to refuse him. "Well ... We'll have to take him to a vet first. Where's Horace?"

"He stayed after school to play baseball," Heath said.

"Well, come on then. We'll pick him up on our way."

The veterinarian gave the animal a thorough examination, administered shots, ear drops, and pills for de-worming. She treated him for fleas and ticks, prescribed a special diet, and assured them the dog would be healthy "in no time."

That night, beneath his bed, Heath and the dog – which Heath named "Dog" – slept peacefully, leaving it to Margaret to explain to Frank, who did not arrive home until late.

"I thought we told Horace he couldn't have a dog," Frank said.

"I know, I know ... But Heath found it and the poor thing was dying from starvation and Heath seemed so attached, so determined to save it ... I don't think he had a good day at school, he didn't seem to like it, I don't think he made any friends. But when I asked him about it he said he guessed it really wasn't any different from his other school and ... I just couldn't tell him no. After everything the child has gone through and now coming to live with us and everything so different for him ... I think it might help him adjust."

Frank sat back in his chair and lit his pipe, which was a habit he had acquired after leaving the Karnival. "Well, I understand that, but what is Horace supposed to think? You tell Horace no, you tell Heath yes. Are you forgetting that Horace has some adjusting to do?"

"Of course not," she said, thinking perhaps she was.

"I think it's only fair you explain to Horace your reasoning," Frank said.

She did, the next morning in the upstairs hallway after Heath had gone down to breakfast.

Horace simply rolled his eyes and sighed. "Aw, Mom, do you think I'm thick or what? Course I know why you told Heath he could keep Dog, I'm not stupid. Besides, he's a good kid but he never talks to anyone around the neighbourhood, yesterday in school, nowhere. He just watches people. And sometimes if they start teasing him, he growls ... Growls, Mom. It'll probably be good for him to have someone to pal around with."

"Why doesn't he pal around with you?"

"Because he doesn't want to. I ask him, lots of times. He just shakes his head because he doesn't like the other kids and I'm usually playing baseball or something."

"Why doesn't he like the other kids?"

Horace shrugged. "Why doesn't he like sleeping in a bed? Don't get all freaked out about Heath, Mom. He's fine. We talk sometimes when we're supposed to be asleep ... I mean – he likes it here and everything, he likes you and Dad. He just doesn't seem to like people in general. He just likes to sit and read."

Pulling Horace close, Margaret kissed his cheek and thanked him for being so understanding. He smiled at her, returned her kiss, and clomped off down the stairs and into the kitchen. She could hear him talking with Heath – "Morning, Heath. How's Dog today?" – and her heart swelled with pride. She marvelled at how she and Frank had managed to raise a child so wise, so caring and sure. She had seen many children over the years, and most of their mothers seemed torn between love and disgust. But she was grateful because she had Horace.

That night, Margaret gathered up copies of all fifty-seven of her books and brought them upstairs in a box to Heath. He likes to sit and read, Horace had said. Though some of the books might be more suited to younger readers, she thought she would try.

Heath looked through the box. He lifted books in turn, opening them, wondering at the pages, fingers caressing the illustrations. "You made these?"

"Yes," she said. Her writer's ego anticipated rejection.

"Wow," he said.

She dropped to her knees beside him on the floor. "They're for you. I know you like to read."

His eyes were wide. "For me?"

She nodded.

He reached out to hug her. She was certain she could feel tears on his cheeks but, when he pulled back, his eyes were dry and he was smiling. "I love to read," he said. "And since you wrote them I think I'll love them even more."

Her heart swelled as it so often did with Horace. She thought that she would feel sad when Heath next left for school. She searched through the box and pulled out a book. "It's about a dog," she said. "I thought you might like to read this one first."

He took the book from her, touching it with gentle fingers, and opened it with care. He studied the picture of the dog on the title page before reading aloud: "*A Dog's Tale.*" He smiled at her and reached for her hand. He held it as he read to her, and she thought that she had never heard the words aloud, other than the times she had read to Horace. But that had been her voice and somehow different from this.

Margaret closed her eyes as the words washed over her....

* * * * *

Dog lived on a farm in the country. The farm was large and gave him many chances to run and play, to roll in the grass and gaze at the sky. He slept in the shade of the giant oak tree and talked with the squirrel who lived in its branches. He slunk through the tall grass in the meadow, enjoying the feel of it touching his fur, softly, like the hand of his master who lovingly stroked him when they sat together on the porch. Dog talked with the cattle who grazed in the pastures and spoke with the crow in the cornfield.

Dog knew that once a week — on Wednesdays — Master climbed into the red pickup truck and rode away, going through the gate at the bottom of hill and down the road. Dog would follow the truck to the gate and wait there until Master came back. Leaving with corn, sometimes with other vegetables or a calf, Master returned with things that Dog did not know and had not seen before. These strange things went into the house and Dog would soon forget what they looked like, because he was not allowed inside past the mudroom. Nevertheless, he remembered that Master brought home wonderful strange things, which lived in the house with him. Dog could not help but wonder from where those things had come.

One day when Master went out, instead of waiting at the bottom of the hill, Dog went back up to the house and nuzzled the door. Dog wanted to see those wonderful things again and get to know them. Master had not latched the door, and after working for some time with his paw, Dog managed to pull the door open just enough to slip inside. He stood for a moment in the mudroom, his heart beating rapidly. He was frightened and excited about what he might find.

From the mudroom, a door opened into a large room. The room smelled of meat and vegetables and apples. Dog knew this was what Master called the kitchen. Along the walls were shelves holding objects that looked like the dishes Master used to bring Dog food and water. Dog figured that these were the dishes from which humans ate. There was a large table (Dog knew what that was: there was one on the porch) and chairs. Dog imagined Master sitting in one of the chairs, eating food from the dishes which would rest on the table.

There were other rooms in the house. In one there was a rug on the floor, but this rug was much nicer than the one on the porch. All around the room were things that looked like chairs, only bigger. When Dog climbed up onto one, it was soft and warm and very roomy, not hard and confining like the chair on the porch. There were small tables with shiny objects and a dish with Master's pipe. There was something that looked similar to the lantern Master carried out to the barn when it was dark and there was no moon. Dog stood in awe, looking around at all the colours and the patterns and remembering the softness. He thought about how beautiful it all was. Dog thought that perhaps he might like to live in a house like this.

Suddenly Dog heard Master's truck chugging up the hill. He turned and ran hurriedly from the house. Dog ran through the kitchen and mudroom and out onto the porch and across the yard, barking to welcome his master. He hoped Master would not find out he had been in the house.

"There you are," Master said, smiling. "I was wondering where you were when I didn't see you by the gate." He patted Dog's head, and Dog yipped and wagged his tail. "You're a good boy, Dog," Master said, and patted him again. "Now, if you'll excuse me, I've got to get these things into the house."

Dog sat down and watched as Master carried a box into the house. Then Dog jumped up, putting his paws on the tailgate of the truck to look in. Master had brought home another beautiful colourful thing to put inside his house, but Dog could not imagine its purpose. It was large and flat, rectangular in shape, and it had what looked like trees and grass on one side, but it could not be real trees and grass, being flat. Then Master returned and picked up the beautiful colourful thing and took it into the house.

The back of the truck was empty now, and Dog walked across the yard. He would lie in the cornfield and think about all the wonderful things he had seen today.

He was lying in the cornfield almost asleep when Crow called and Dog jumped alert. Dog looked around and saw the large black bird sitting on the scarecrow.

"What are you thinking so hard about?" Crow asked Dog.

Dog settled down again in the corn. "I was inside my Master's house today and I saw all these beautiful colourful things. They were soft and warm and I would like to have things like that."

"What for?" asked Crow. "We have beautiful soft colourful things here in the fields and woods and pastures."

"It's not the same," Dog said, and sighed. "I wish I knew where those things came from."

"They come from the city," Crow said. "Everybody knows that."

"What's the city?" Dog asked, his mind spinning with the thought of a magical place filled with soft warm colourful things.

"Have your master take you," Crow said, flying away. "But it's not like the farm."

And so Dog decided that was exactly what he was going to do — go to the city with Master. Dog waited and waited, counting the days until Wednesday. At night in his dreams he wandered soft roads and gazed at a world alive with beautiful colourful sparkling things, like those things he had seen in the house.

Finally Wednesday arrived. When Master started out, Dog jumped into the back of the truck and crouched down, hiding behind the spare tire. Dog was afraid Master would see him when Master got out to open the gate, but Master did not see him. Once they were on the road, Dog lifted his head and looked around, excited that finally, finally, he would get to see the city, which produced the beautiful things.

Dog watched as the trees and pastures began to change into tall brick towers spitting out smoke. The air did not smell very good and Dog wondered what this place could be. It was not beautiful and colourful, so it could not be the city of his dreams.

The smoking towers disappeared. Now they were on a wide road with cars and trucks everywhere. There were loud sharp noises, which seemed to come from the cars and trucks. Dog noticed that when Master pressed on the centre of the steering wheel their truck made this same loud noise. Dog put his head down and covered his ears, because the noise hurt him.

After some time, the truck stopped and Master got out. Dog lifted his head and saw tall buildings and many people walking around on what looked like hard white ground. Was this the city? Dog sniffed the air and jumped out of the truck. The ground was hard — very hard — and hot. People walked by him so quickly, pushing him along, that soon Dog had lost his way. He could no longer see Master and Dog slunk over to the side of a building and sat down.

Was this the city? he wondered. Where were all the beautiful things he had expected? Where was the colour, the softness? Dog began walking along beside the wall when he saw a window and jumped up, placing his front paws on the windowsill to look inside. There they were! There were the things he had come to see! People were inside touching them, picking them up, putting them down. Other people were putting things into boxes and carrying them outside, going along the hard white ground only to take the boxes once again indoors, where the beautiful things would be safely unwrapped and admired. So yes, this was the city, and there were the beautiful colourful things, inside behind glass and bricks and stone.

Dog turned around and looked up and down the street. Nothing but people and hard white ground and cars and more buildings. Why were there no beautiful things outside? Where were the trees, the grass, the animals? Why did the air sting his nose and the noise hurt his ears?

If all the beautiful things were inside maybe they would not stay beautiful outside. Maybe they would turn hard and white and dull, like the ground. Dog watched the people carrying their beautiful colourful things into the buildings and closing the doors. Maybe these people had these things because outside was not beautiful, and Dog wondered if these people stayed inside all the time with their things, only coming outside to buy more soft colourful things. Dog thought he would not like to live in the city, would not like to have all those beautiful colourful things if he would have to stay inside all the time or walk on hard hot white ground because there was no grass, no cornfield, no crows or cattle with whom to talk. These people must like their city and their buildings with their things inside, but Dog knew he would not. Dog knew that he would be happier on the farm, outside, and he wondered why Master came here to buy these things when they had the grass and the cornfields, the pastures and woods of the farm.

"Dog! Dog, what are you doing here?"

Dog looked up and saw Master. Dog had never been so happy. He was not lost, he would not be trapped here! Master would take him back to the farm. Dog jumped up and down and barked with joy and Master patted his head.

"Come on, boy," Master said. "It's time to go home."

Dog walked proudly beside Master to the truck and jumped into the cab with him. He lay down on the seat, his head resting beside Master's leg. He sighed.

"So what do you think of the city?" Master asked.

Dog barked, saying he did not like the city, he would rather be on the farm.

"I know what you mean," Master said. "The city's no place for a farm dog. You need the fresh air and the grass and the fields."

Dog snuggled down on the seat, happy and content, glad that he was a farm dog with a kind, loving master.

* * * * *

Heath finished reading and the room was silent. After awhile, Margaret opened her eyes. Heath was still, seeming to be staring at the book in his lap. But his eyes had a distant look about them, and his lips quivered. She sat up quickly and squeezed his hand.

"I was born on a farm," he whispered.

Margaret watched him, not knowing what to say.

"I had a dog there, too ... she took care of me and we ..." Then he glanced at her and smiled. "Thank you, Margaret."

"I'm glad you like it," she said.

"Did you grow up on a farm?"

Margaret shook her head. "My father owned a carnival. Still does, actually."

"A carnival?"

"You know, there's rides and games and −" She stopped herself just in time. "It's like a circus, but without as many animals."

Heath thought about this and Margaret wondered if it could be true that the boy had never seen a carnival or circus. "I saw a circus on television once," Heath said as if reading her mind. "Do you have circuses near here?"

Margaret considered the tourist traps in Niagara Falls. "Not a real circus," she said. "Not like the old days."

"What about a carnival?"

"Klieg's? They're still travelling − all over the world. All across North America, Europe, maybe even Mexico by now."

"Wow," Heath said. "I'd like to see it."

"Would you? Well, we'll have to take you then. I'll find out what their route is, where they're going to be. And when it's close we'll take a day and go."

"Has Horace seen the carnival?"

"He was born there."

"Really?" Fascination brightened his face.

Margaret laughed. "Yes. But I doubt he remembers it."

"You think he'd want to go?"

"That doesn't matter," she said. "If he doesn't want to go that's no reason why we can't. Okay?"

"Okay," Heath said.

"Now I think you'd better climb into –" Don't be neglectful, she thought. "I think it's your bedtime. You'd better take Dog for a short walk before you two go to sleep."

He gathered his books with care and put them on top of the bureau. Then he kissed her, thanked her again for the books, and woke Dog. Dog squinted at him and climbed to his feet, following Heath out of the room and down the stairs.

Carrying the empty box, Margaret passed Horace's room, saw him lying on the bed, and went in. She sat beside him and kissed his forehead. "Homework?"

"I was listening to your story, Mom. I haven't heard that one in a long time."

"You stopped letting me read to you years ago," she said.

"I know," Horace said. "But, listening to Heath ... it was pretty and kinda sad. Like Heath was the dog and ..." He trailed off, uncertain of the words. "I don't think I mean that," he said. "Like Heath wanted to be the dog."

She thought she knew what he meant. "I don't think he's been very happy," she said. "When he was on that farm ... Well – I think dogs are the only friends he's ever had."

"You know what I think?" Horace said. "I think – sometimes – Heath could go off with only Dog for company and never miss anyone."

"Oh, I don't know," Margaret said. She hoped it would never be true. She hoped that Heath would miss them. She hoped that Heath would never just run off.

As Margaret tucked the covers tightly around Horace, Heath stood in the front yard with Dog. He was thinking about

Margaret's story when a high, thin, angry voice shattered the night:

"Nola? Nola! Where the hell is you, girl? Nola!"

Heath turned, expecting to face the owner of the voice. But his gaze fell on the empty yard, the tall evergreens, the flowerbeds.

"Nooolaaa!"

He covered his ears with his hands, shutting his eyes.

"Baby? Where are you, Baby? Baby!"

Terror spurred him across the yard to reach Dog. He threw trembling arms around the animal's neck, burying his face in the softness, the fur tickling his nose, his eyes. Dog whimpered and nuzzled him, tongue licking his face.

"Heath?"

Don't look don't look! Heath thought. But Dog was wresting away, fighting against Heath's grip.

"Heath?"

He could feel the body coming closer. Dog pulled free, barking and running across the lawn. Now is when it happens, Heath thought. Now is when she –

A hand touched his shoulder. He whirled to see Margaret.

"Are you all right, sweetheart?"

Terror subsided. He nodded, unwilling to trust his voice. Heath pushed himself to his feet and forced a smile, unable to hold Margaret's gaze.

"You're certain?"

"Yeah."

She slipped an arm around his shoulder and pulled him close. "Then let's go in. You'll catch a chill out here on that wet grass."

In his room, Heath lay awake. He turned over and over on the floor beneath the bed. Dog whined in sleep and stretched, his paws resting on Heath's stomach. Terror returned, and Heath hugged himself, knowing that, above him, walking about and calling his name was –

NO!

Heath buried his face in the blanket. The room plunged into darkness. Maybe she wouldn't see him, wouldn't find him here. But she was calling, just as she'd done before ...

Michael Mortensen

Heath's eyes flew open. Bolting upright, he struck his head on the bottom of the mattress. He pulled the blanket out from under Dog and crawled through the shadows to the doorway.

"Baby!"

Across the hall, he could see Frank and Margaret's door, left ajar so they could hear should the children call. He pushed himself to his feet and surveyed the hallway (Was she out there, just waiting for him to step out so she could grab him and – and –) and then he dashed across the hall to Frank and Margaret's bedroom. He eased the door open and looked into the room. Margaret and Frank were asleep. Dragging the blanket behind him, he crawled underneath their bed, then froze for an instant as one of them shifted on the mattress above him. He laid out the blanket, working it with his hands, turning around twice before falling into fitful sleep.

On subsequent nights, when the voice was overpowering, he would return to their room, to the haven beneath their bed. They would never know of his presence, but on those nights Dog would find him there and curl up warmly beside him.

Margaret remained unaware of how her book affected Heath. When she awoke with Frank in the morning and found Heath and Dog were not in Heath's room, she assumed they had left for Dog's morning walk. She set about preparing breakfast, too busy scrambling eggs and toasting muffins to wonder why she did not hear the front door before Heath entered the kitchen.

Once Frank left for work and the children for school, Margaret sat at her desk and hunted out the letter. One arrived dutifully each year and included a copy of the Karnival's route. To her surprise, Klieg's had been in Toronto only weeks before and was making its way west, across Ontario, into Manitoba, Saskatchewan, Alberta ... not scheduled in the East again until the following summer.

She sat staring at the route, asking herself why she had not thought of this before the children started school ... She had seen the route. She must have noticed how close the Karnival would be. Why had she not thought to introduce Heath to Arthur?

She hated to admit it, but she did not want to see her father, could not bear to see him, the man who had virtually vanished with the smoke from her mother's body ... She loved him, yes, but she did not miss him in her life. The fire, my self-mutilation, and Tim-Tina's passing had become her memories of the Karnival. But she chided herself for her selfishness, thinking inanely, Sorry, Daddy, can't visit or write. Makes me think of death ...

She was seized with an urge to see him.

With shaking hands, she pulled out a notepad and dashed off a message. Consulting the route, she sent the telegram to Kenora, asking him to telephone. Margaret, she thought, don't be surprised if he doesn't.

Arthur telephoned the next morning. "Margaret, dear, is something wrong?"

"Daddy! It's so good to hear your voice! Nothing's wrong. How are you? Are things going well?"

"Very well, thank you. Got all kinds of excitement coming up. We've got a rock band planning on shooting videos and there'll be a reporter from *Rolling Stone*. Going to do a special issue on the band and the Karnival. Not bad, eh, Margaret?"

"That's fabulous, Daddy."

"Everyone's excited. I've been reading your books."

"Really?"

"I'm so proud of you, they're wonderful! You aren't writing one about a carnival, I suppose?"

"Not yet, Daddy. I will, though, I promise."

"That'd be nice. Can you believe what some people are doing these days? Setting up rides in supermarket parking lots and calling it carnival – ha! The world needs to see it, needs to know what it's really like before –" But he stopped and she tried to envision. A tear? A lump in his throat? Was he thinking of Anna? His youth?

"Daddy, I want to see you."

"Margaret! Oh, Margaret ... It's been too long. Too too long."

"I know, Daddy. I'm sorry."

"No sense in being sorry, Margaret. Sorry is a word we can forget. When are you coming?"

"I was thinking Christmas week. You'll be wintering and –"

"We'll still be working, Margaret. Just outside Vancouver. Got that special stand for six whole weeks! The lot will be closed to the general public, but it'll still be carnival time, crazy time, pretty much like you remember it. Please come."

She fought her disappointment. She had been planning a quiet time with her father, the chance to reabsorb the atmosphere of her past without the crowds, the rides turning endlessly, the call of the agents and talkers, and lure of the sideshows. "All right, Daddy, I –" She rushed into the story of finding Heath. Children's Aid had assured her the adoption would be finalized before Christmas. "He wants to see the Karnival, Daddy, and – and I want you to meet him."

"That's fine, Margaret. That's fine. You telegram and let me know when we can expect you."

"Thank you, Daddy, I –" But, inexplicably, she could not say it. "Thank you. Good luck with your magazine story."

That afternoon, she began work on a book about a carnival. But, after writing only five paragraphs, she set it aside and closed it up in a drawer of her desk.

That night, she began to have nightmares.

She told the family about the proposed trip during dinner the following evening. Heath almost spilled his milk, and Dog, beneath the table, thumped his tail rapidly.

"Well," Frank said, "this is quite the surprise."

"Oh, I know, Frank," Margaret said. "But – well, Heath and I were talking about Klieg's the other night and I haven't seen Daddy for so long, none of us has. Horace hasn't seen the place since he was a baby and I think Heath should meet his new grandfather and –"

Frank cut her short, waving his fork. "You don't have to sell me," he said. "I think it's a great idea. I'd love to see the old Karnival again."

"Have you seen it?" Heath asked.

"Of course. I used to work there. That's where your mother and I met."

"Boy! What was it like?"

Frank laughed. "It was incredible! The best part was meeting your mother, of course, but – there's an excitement about it, an electricity you never feel anywhere else. You can touch it, it seems, and when the crowds start rolling in ..." Frank sighed. "There's nothing like it."

"I can't wait to see it," Heath said. "I can't wait."

"Well, you'll have to wait," Frank said. "Christmas is almost four months away."

That's forever, Heath thought.

"You'll love it," Horace said. "They've got a dog act you wouldn't believe. They were even on television once!"

"I'd forgotten that," Margaret said.

"A dog act?" Heath asked.

"Oh yes," Margaret said. "Run by your Great Uncle Ham. There are six dogs – I think it's six – and they do tricks."

"I liked the pyramid," Horace said.

"The totem pole," Frank said.

"What's the totem pole?" Heath asked.

"They all get on top of each other, see?" Horace said. "The biggest up to the littlest. And then the one on the bottom starts walking around and the one on top stands on his hind legs and boy! They don't fall or anything!"

"Boy," Heath said, "I'll bet Dog would like to see that, wouldn't you, Dog?"

Dog thumped his tail.

"Dog and I are gonna love it," Heath said. "When we were talking the other night we thought maybe you'd just forget about it and we'd never see a carnival or circus or anything."

"Gosh," Horace said as Margaret tucked him into bed that night. "Never even seen a clown, I'll bet. No magic ... nothing. Nothing but –" He stopped himself and shook his head. "It must've been awful."

For Heath the weeks went slowly. In early October, he was walking home from school when he came across a girl weeping on her front lawn. Her name was Shay Garrett, but the neighbourhood children called her "Gargantuan Garrett" because she was twenty pounds over her "ideal weight." Her new kitten had been startled by a car, and retreated to the heights of the tree in her yard. Shay had tried to climb the tree, but her weight had caused the branch beneath her to collapse. She was as terrified that her parents would be angry about the tree as she was that her kitten would be hurt.

Heath rescued the kitten, took blame for the branch – which Shay's parents quickly forgave given what they understood to be the circumstances – and the two children soon became friends.

Shay, a year older, was a year ahead of Heath in school. But she took to having lunch with him because his stoicism frightened the other children. No one ever made fun of her in Heath's presence.

"You're the only one who's ever liked me," she said to him one afternoon. And, on another occasion, "Some day, I'm going to go a long long way away from here. Someplace where people don't care what I look like or how much I weigh."

"You can live at my grandpa's Karnival," Heath said. Margaret had explained, in careful words, about the residents of the freak tent. "Nobody there would care how fat you were. You could be fatter than anything and no one would care."

Shay aside, the children at school held no interest for Heath. He daydreamed about Klieg's, so distant, until he felt he would never see it. Waiting another day seemed to prove that Klieg's was just a word. It took forever just for Halloween to arrive. Summer weather stretched unseasonably long that year. For Heath, Halloween day seemed just as far from Christmas as the day so long before when Margaret first told them about the impending trip.

Halloween morning, Heath stood at the window in his room. He looked out over the yard and the woods beyond. Horace was at the picnic table, carving the top off a pumpkin. His hands were orange with slime as he scooped out the pulp and seeds. Beside Horace at the table sat a second pumpkin, that one reserved for Heath. Margaret had planned on their doing the pumpkins together, but Heath had told Horace he would do his own later.

"Jack-o-lantern," Heath said. That's what Horace had called it:

a jack-o-lantern.

There were no jack-o-lanterns at the Children's Aid Society home. There were paper cutouts of black cats and witches on broomsticks and skeletons. There was a party in the dining room, with a barrel of water into which you had to stick your face until you caught an apple in your teeth. There was candy for the children, and punch for everyone. The groundskeeper told ghost stories in front of the fireplace until the matrons sent the children off to bed. Alone with strange noises they were not certain they had heard before, the children dreamed of witches and severed hands and spirits come back from the dead. Heath would not sleep on those nights. He would remain in a bundle beneath his bed, the blanket pulled up to cover all but his eyes. He had to stay awake watching for Her.

"Baby? Where are you, Baby?"

But his new family made Halloween sound like fun. Margaret told him about trick-or-treating, dressing up and going from house to house, getting candy and apples and cookies. "But you don't eat anything – anything – until you get home and your dad and I check it, okay?" Frank told him about soaping windows and scaring other kids, "Not that I'm encouraging this type of behaviour, you understand." One of the high school football players came around to sell something called Spook Insurance. This meant, Margaret explained as she opened her purse, that the team would stop by to scrape the soap off the windows, pull the toilet paper from the trees, hose the eggs off the car and driveway, should there be any "tricking." Horace said he would be happy to have Heath go trick-or-treating with him if Heath wanted.

"Okay," Heath said, but a part of him remained apprehensive. What if there really were witches? He knew there were fortune-tellers – Margaret had said so. What if there really were were-wolves and vampires and ghosts, and Halloween was their night to be out and around? What if they thought he would make a delicious meal? A thirsty vampire? A successful sacrifice?

A chill passed through him and he turned away from the window. You're not a baby, he told himself. Those things aren't real.

"Heath! Hey, Heath!"

Heath turned back to the window, leaning out. Horace stood at the table, holding up his jack-o-lantern to show off the face he had carved: huge round eyes and an apple for a nose and a wide grinning mouth with two marshmallow teeth.

"Hey," Heath said.

"What do you think?"

"Looks creepy," Heath said.

"Yeah," Horace said. "Come on down here, will ya?"

The thought of putting his hand into the pumpkin churned Heath's stomach. But he thrust his fingers into the yielding orange flesh. It was cold and stuck to his skin – like brains, something inside him said – but it also felt strangely pleasurable. He squished the pulp in his hands, watching it squeeze through his fingers.

"Save the seeds," Horace said. "Mom puts them in the oven and roasts them and we eat them."

"Eat them?" Heath asked.

"Sure."

"What do they taste like?"

"I don't know, just seeds, I guess. They don't really taste like pumpkin or anything, just ... seeds."

Heath finished scooping out the seeds and pulp, putting it all dutifully into the bowl on the table. He wiped his hands and looked at the hollowed out pumpkin.

"What are you going to make?" Horace asked.

"I don't know," Heath said. "Any kind of face I want?"

"Sure. Any kind of eyes, any kind of nose, any kind of mouth."

"I gotta think about it." Heath studied the pumpkin for some time, chin on his arms, as Horace watched him. At last Heath lifted his head, picked up the knife, and began to carve.

When he had finished, the eyes were thin slits, curving up and down as if they were worms crawling across the orange face. The nose was a single tiny hole. There were larger holes on either side, just below the eyes ("Those are her cheeks," Heath explained). A thin, barely perceptible line ran between and connected them.

"Where's her mouth?" Horace asked.

"Right there." Heath traced the line with the knife.

"Not much of a mouth."

Heath smiled. "Not much of a talker."

When Margaret saw Heath's jack-o-lantern, she did not like it, but she did not know why. Nothing wrong with it, she tried to tell herself. Nothing at all. It's a child's pumpkin for heaven's sake, just a child's pumpkin ... But she was glad she did not have to keep looking at it. She set the pumpkin down on the right side of the front door. Horace's jack-o-lantern was on the left, and the two stared down the driveway toward the road, one on each corner of the small porch floor. She inserted the candles and lighted them with a long match, glancing up to see the boys, who lay on the front lawn with Dog. Their legs were stretched out behind them, chins resting on their hands as they surveyed their work.

"Looks creepy," Horace said. "Creepy, kid."

Heath was solemn. "At midnight, they'll roll off the porch, roll down the driveway and into the road, searching, calling for their bodies, calling for —"

Margaret hurried inside and shut the door.

She thought of the Karnival, the visit to her father, wondering why she felt so unnerved. Anxious, she thought. Just anxious to see Daddy after all these years. Quite often she woke in the middle of the night, knowing she had dreamed about him, yet unable to touch the vapours of her subconscious. I'll be glad when this is over, she thought. Halloween has always given me the willies. But she was fully aware that it was a lie.

Her uneasiness flourished. Frank was not home by the time the boys left the house with Dog. When the doorbell rang, it was a moment before she convinced herself it was safe to open the door.

The porch appeared deserted. Margaret stepped beyond the threshold. Two teenage boys leapt from the shadows, one on either side of her. They babbled sounds, the jack-o-lanterns held in front of their faces like gross orange heads. Margaret screamed. Laughing, the boys ran off, dropping the pumpkins, Horace's rolling down the driveway and into the gutter.

She was huddled on the couch when Frank came home. She

held him and kissed him and begged him not to answer the door.

"Why don't you go up and lie down," Frank said. "You look exhausted."

"I am," she said. She had not slept the night before and, once she dragged herself from bed, realized she had not finished making Heath's costume. Heath hadn't been satisfied with just a head and paws, he had to have a tail also and –

"Hush now," Frank said. He pulled her into his arms. Her behaviour frightened him, but he told himself it was only the stress: wanting to have the adoption finalized after all these weeks; anxious to see her father and the Karnival, but afraid, too, because of the memories. He had heard her in her sleep, calling for Tim-Tina.

Frank kissed Margaret and walked her up the stairs, ignoring the doorbell, which rang several times. He tucked her into bed and brought her a glass of white wine to calm her nerves. He left the bathroom light on, the door open, and went down the stairs to swing the front door wide to a witch and an alien.

"Trick-or-treat!"

After the children left with their lollipops and bubblegum, Frank spotted Horace's jack-o-lantern in the gutter and went to retrieve it. He picked it up, cradling it in the crook of his arm as he peered up and down the street. There was no sign of the boys or Dog ... Turning back to the house, Frank noticed that his hands were sticky and damp. He looked to see that the pumpkin was split completely along one side. His finger traced the gash in the bright orange skin, as he thought how disappointed the boys would be. Then it occurred to him that he could repair it, using toothpicks as dowels to pull the two sides together.

Frank carried the pumpkin head into the house as two dogs and a pirate (Dog, Heath, and Horace respectively) made their way through the labyrinth of neighbourhood streets, the boys' treat bags growing heavier with each stop.

At Shay's house, they asked her to come trick-or-treating with them, but her parents said no because she was not allowed to have sweets.

"I can't," Shay said.

"Not even just to walk around with us?" Heath asked. "They let your brother go."

"They don't trust me," Shay said. "Like I couldn't eat just any old thing just any old time I wanted to."

"Shut that goddamned door!" Shay's father shouted.

Shay bit her lip, hung her head, and swiftly shut the door.

"That wasn't very nice," Horace said as they walked down to the street.

"Yeah," Heath said. "They're not very nice to her, that's for sure. Her dad and brother even call her names and stuff."

"That's horrible," Horace said. "What's her mom like?"

"Well," Heath said, "I guess she's not quite so bad. But she cooks all day – and I really do mean it, all day long – cookies and pies and all kinds of stuff, and she never lets Shay have a single bite of anything."

Horace stopped. He looked at Heath, thinking, and then looked back at Shay's house. "They don't hit her, do they?"

Heath shook his head, his eyes wide.

"I mean it, Heath. Mom says if we ever know about anybody who's getting hit, we're supposed to –"

"Naw, they don't hit her," Heath said. "Really, Horace, they don't, I know, but ... It's not right," Heath said, "but they sure don't seem to like her very much."

Heath's fears of witches and goblins quickly faded. Once Shay receded to the back of his mind, he found himself enjoying the new ritual. He liked the feel of the costume Margaret had made for him: the cowl with the droopy dog ears, the paws that flopped over his hands and shoes, the tail that swished the ground behind him. He wished he could wear it all the time, especially to school, but he doubted Margaret would let him do that. And Frank, concerned about Heath's lack of more than a single friend, had given him a talk a few days earlier about being strong and being an individual and not being afraid to let people see what makes you You. Frank did not know he was wrong in assuming that Heath was afraid of the children at school.

"Hey, wait a minute," Horace said. He put a hand on Heath's

arm. "You don't want to go there." He indicated a house sitting far back from the street, shrouded by trees, dark but for a single light burning in a front window.

"Why not?" Heath asked, several steps up the walk.

"That's Old Man Martin's house," Horace said. "He doesn't like kids. A couple years ago he grabbed Jenny Mayfield and tried to touch her."

Heath looked back up the walk toward the house. A chill passed through him. Dog retreated to the far side of the street and growled deep in his throat.

"Come on," Horace said. He tugged Heath's arm. "Let's go."

As they watched, Old Man Martin came out onto his porch. He peered down the walkway, and Heath felt as if the man were looking right at him. Heath felt paralyzed.

Old Man Martin took a step onto his walk and Horace took off, running down the street. "Come on!"

Heath was unable to follow. He could hear Dog whining softly, but he stood watching as the old man approached and came to a halt only steps away.

"Who are you?" Old Man Martin demanded. He was only a foot taller than Heath, his shoulders stooped, wire rimmed glasses pinching a large hooked nose, a wrinkled face working thin lips. "I said who are you, boy?"

Heath gulped. "H-H-Heath, sir."

"Well, H-H-Heath, mind if I ask what you're doing staring up at my house? You planning a robbery? You in one of those gangs, just a little thing like you?"

Heath wished he could run. "We were trick-or-treating."

"I see. Then you're in a costume? You're not a real dog, then?"

"N-no, sir. I'm a boy."

"A boy. How old are you?"

"Nine."

"Nine."

"Almost ten."

"Almost ten." Old Man Martin ran a quick mental calculation. "I've got sixty years on you, kid."

"Y-yes, sir."

"You're scared to death, aren't you?" The old man chuckled. "Scared to death. Stop shaking, H-H-Heath. I'm not going to do anything to you. I'm just an old man, is all. It's those young men you ought to worry about."

"Y-yes, sir." Heath was thinking about Jenny Mayfield.

"So. If you're out trick-or-treating – if you're not casing the joint for a robbery – why didn't you come up to my house for a treat?"

Heath could not answer. He looked around quickly for Dog.

Old Man Martin stepped back. "What are you looking for?"

"M-my dog."

"A real dog?"

Heath nodded.

"Not another young hooligan in a dog costume?"

"No, sir."

"Not a cat in a dog costume?"

"N-no, sir."

"Stop shaking, boy, please! You got any idea what it's like having people scared of you all the time? No one comes up my walk for a treat. No one brings me a Christmas card. I'm an ogre, I am."

Heath thought the old man's words sounded sincere. The old man sounded hurt. Heath took a step forward. "I was going to come up."

"You were, eh? So why didn't you?"

"Horace said ... Horace said not to."

"And who's Horace?"

"My brother."

"Your brother." Old Man Martin thought a moment. "You don't mean Horace Clifford."

"Yes, sir."

"I didn't think the Cliffords had another boy. When they get you?"

"Last summer. I'm a – I'm adopted."

"Oh, I see. I was adopted, you know."

"Really?"

"That's right. My pappy was loony – loony, I tell you. Picked up a shotgun and blew my mum's head clean off her shoulders, then did the same to himself. I was in her belly, so I don't remember it. But that's what they told me. He was loony, they told me, so –" He shrugged. "I don't suppose you have a history as colourful as that?"

Heath shook his head solemnly. "I don't know. I was born on a farm, but ..." His voice trailed off, and he imitated the old man's shrug.

"Sure, I know. They haven't told you the whole story yet, have they? Maybe they're thinking they never will, but, believe me, boy, you got a right to know. You got a right to know what loins sprung you."

"Yes, sir."

"Else wise – else wise you go living your life with little pieces of hell floating around in your head. Little pieces, like jigsaw puzzles, little pieces that don't quite fit together. But you know. You know there's something horrible, something dark, a blot on your soul. And if you never know what put it there, you spend your whole life asking, Was it something I did?"

"Y-yes, sir."

"You have to know the answer to that question, boy. No two ways about it."

"Yes, sir."

"So. You want your treat or not?"

Heath hesitated. It seemed that the old man was trying to be nice – even though he was a bit scary. But he was only scary because he was different. That was being an individual, wasn't it? He was an individual and his feelings were hurt and ... Heath wondered where Horace had gone, thought it might be all right if Dog were with him.

"Problem, H-H-Heath?"

"I don't know," Heath said. "Horace said ..."

"Horace said what?"

"Jenny Mayfield," Heath started.

Old Man Martin burst into laughter. "Not that old story

again!" He threw back his head. "Thought I'd heard the last of that one!" When his laughter diminished to a smile, he met Heath's gaze. "Jenny Mayfield showed up here, couple years ago I guess it was, with a handful of rotten eggs and a huge bar of soap. She got to going on my windows with that soap and tossed those eggs at my door and I'll tell you ... I did grab that girl. I was plenty angry and I would have beat the living sh– I would have given her a spanking, I would, only I'm not as spry as I used to be. And off she went, screaming at the top of her lungs that I tried to do things to her." Old Man Martin's glasses bounced on his nose. "Bah! Never arrested me, I promise you that."

"I ... They didn't?"

"No, they didn't. And you know the Mounties – they always get their man ... Still scared?" Old Man Martin chuckled. "Well, okay. You stay here and I'll go on up to the house for your treat." With a patient smile, he turned and made his way up the walk.

Heath began to feel foolish standing on the sidewalk waiting. He glanced up and down the street. There was no sign of Horace, and even Dog had deserted him. Heath shrugged and started up the walk. Reaching the porch, he met the old man on his way out the door.

"Well," Old Man Martin said, "decided to come up after all, did you?"

"Yes, sir."

Old Man Martin smiled. "Open your bag, Heath."

Heath held the bag open.

"Wider, boy." Then, "Is that your dog over there?"

Heath whirled and the old man made a quick movement. Heath stared at the handcuffs cold on his wrists, stared up at the old man wide-eyed.

Laughing, Old Man Martin pulled him toward the door ...

Margaret, tossing restlessly, awoke. She had been dreaming of her father, seated on his lap as he told her a story, in the middle of which he fell silent. When she looked at him, his head flushed orange, swelling to three times its normal size. She began to scream, and the head dropped from his shoulders and into her lap. She scrambled to push it away from her, unable to escape its ugliness as it rolled across the bedroom floor. It grinned at her, eyes sparkling, and came to rest against a chair leg.

With the dream faded, she thought of the boys. She swung her feet out of bed and left the room. From the hallway she could smell Frank's pipe, and this reassured her. She called to him down the staircase and waited until he appeared below her.

"Yes, love?"

"Are the boys home yet?"

Frank hesitated.

"It's awfully late, don't you think?"

"Now, Margaret, it's not a school night ... They're together and they've got Dog. No sense you worrying yourself."

"But I told them to be home before nine-thirty and –" She stopped. There was barking outside.

"There, see?" Frank said. "There they are now." But when he opened the front door the boys were nowhere in sight. Dog was jumping up and down in the yard, wagging his tail.

"Frank?"

"Now, Dog," Frank said, "where are the boys?"

Dog ceased jumping and stood in the yard, just barking.

Margaret rushed down the stairs to grip Frank's arm. "You don't think something's happened to them?"

"I don't know, love," Frank said. He was a quiet and simple man, and he had lived a quiet and simple life. Though he knew that horrible things routinely happened to other people, nothing terrible had ever befallen him. He had not been a victim of abuse or neglect, no bones had been broken, no scars inflicted. He could not conceive that something untoward had happened to his sons, but his mind raced, searching for a way to calm Margaret. "We'll just wait a bit, see if they come in. They can't be far behind. Dog was with them, wasn't he?"

Margaret nodded.

"Okay, then. Give them ten minutes and then I'll go out looking for them."

"Couldn't you go now?"

Frank studied her. "All right." He rummaged in the hall closet for the flashlight. "You stay here in case they come home. I'll be back every few minutes or so. Just to check. Don't want to be wandering around with them snug in their beds." He smiled but Margaret was too frightened. "You guard the house now, Dog," Frank said.

"Be careful!" Margaret called after him, certain that whatever had befallen her children was lying in wait for her husband as well.

Once spooked, Horace ran blindly. Each step brought a rise in panic until, out of breath, he simply had to stop. He tumbled onto a lawn, his sides aching, his eyes closed against the cool grass, his treat bag on the ground nearby. "Heath?" He fought to control his breathing. "Man, Heath, I thought I was gonna have a heart attack." He lay, still panting, until he realized he was alone.

Horace sat up and looked around. "Heath?" He peered down the street. "Heath? Dog? Heath!"

No answer.

Horace felt panic return. He wasn't sure that Heath could find his way home by himself. Heath didn't know the neighbourhood as well as Horace did, with all its twists and turns and shortcuts. They had already been quite far from home at Old Man Martin's.

As he thought of Old Man Martin, his heart began to pound. Remembering Jenny Mayfield, Horace snatched up his treat bag and ran back through the streets, passing groups of children, losing his sword but not stopping to retrieve it, out of breath again when he reached Old Man Martin's. But there was no sign of Heath or Dog. Horace stood on the sidewalk wondering what to do.

"Please, God," Horace prayed. "Let him be okay."

Horace wandered up and down streets, through twists and turns and shortcuts, calling Heath, calling Dog, returning every few minutes to stand in front of Old Man Martin's house. "Damn it, Heath," Horace muttered. "You weren't stupid enough to go in there, were you?"

A burst of laughter caught his attention. But it was only a group of teenagers weaving down the street. Probably drunk, Horace thought. Damn it, Heath, where are you?

Horace crept up to the Martin house. Peeping in the window, he saw the old man seated in a rocking chair, chuckling to himself and thumbing through a picture magazine. There was no sign of Heath, and Horace made his way out of the bushes and down to the street. He realized the best thing he could do was tell his parents. Looking around one last time, he started toward home.

Frank met Horace coming up the street. "Where's your brother?"

Horace shrugged. His eyes brimmed with tears. "Last time I saw him we were in front of Old Man Martin's house. The old guy came out and I took off. I thought Heath was behind me but – I don't know where he is, I looked everywhere!"

Frank hugged him, stroking his head. "It's all right. Don't worry, we'll find him."

"But, Dad, I shouldn't have let him out of my sight! If something's happened to him, I'll –" He buried his face in his father's chest.

Frank held him and ruffled his hair. "Come on. We'll get you home and I'll go out again looking for Heath."

*   *   *

Meanwhile, a thousand miles away, having done all she could to forget her firstborn, Nola was watching her daughter, Chloe. Chloe was topless, seated at Nola's feet colouring paper and floor with crayons. She was nearly three, and Nola adored her. Chloe was still plump and healthy, with big round cheeks and big round eyes. She seemed to understand every word that people spoke. Rarely fussy, she loved to listen to stories and play with her parents. She was equally content to amuse herself, finding fascination in spoons, bits of fabric, candles, and other household objects.

Chloe's third arm needed no particular attention, though it did make it challenging to dress the girl. For some time, Nola had tried to convince Chloe to let her chest-arm lay flat across her stomach, covered by a shirt or, weather permitting, a bulky sweater. But, despite the fact that the arm never moved, to have it at all restricted caused Chloe a great deal of discomfort. Taking up needle and thread and scissors – with nothing more than her own imagination and sewing programmes on television to guide her – Nola refashioned all the girl's blouses and sweaters and tee shirts to create a third sleeve or armhole as required, though Chloe generally went topless when inside the house.

They were then living on the outskirts of a small border city, their fifth rental house since Chloe's birth, in the fifth neighbourhood that at first appeared to be kinder than most. Shortly after Chloe was born, Ralph insisted that he did not want her confined to life in the transport truck. To be healthy, he said, a child needed a yard to play in, with sunshine to warm the face and nature to entice the mind. Neither did he want her to reach his age and be as he was, hiding from the eyes of others, no shell built against their cruelty.

Nola did her best to make a comfortable home for her family, and for this occasion she had decorated with orange and black crepe paper, a jack-o-lantern on the dining room table, a paper skeleton on the front door. The skeleton was on the inside, because she was determined not to answer the door, refusing to give out candy to those who called Chloe names and laughed.

"They're just kids," Ralph had told her. "They don't know any better."

But Nola wished – kids or not – that she could cut out their tongues, gouge out their eyes, sever their limbs. She hated this neighbourhood, hated this house, just as she had hated all the others. Taunting and judgment brayed ceaselessly around them.

Nola was seated at the living room window, pulling back the curtains just a bit to peek out. In her lap rested a gun. The gun rightly belonged in the transport truck, but Ralph had given it to her that morning when he left for a quick twenty-four hour run. It was meant to ensure their safety from Halloween trickery gone out of hand, but Nola had formed a different plan. The first child who set foot on her porch would be shot. Cleanly, she thought. Right between the eyes. Right in the mouth, the throat. Right between the legs, where their young sex parts lay dormant. That'll teach them, Nola thought. She turned her attention back to Chloe.

Chloe was eating her crayons again. Nola snatched the crayons away and picked her up, placing the girl in her lap.

"Sit still now, Chloe," Nola said. "I hear someone coming." She peeled back the curtain, her eyes scanning the darkness. Her fingers tightened on the gun as a smile widened her lips. At last, one had found the courage to approach the front door, shameless in asking for a treat from a home she consistently attacked.

"For God's sake, now, Chloe, hold still, hold still!" Nola took careful aim, but Chloe's right arm swung out at the gun, knocking it to the floor. "Damn it!" Nola was ready to strike the girl, but Chloe's innocent eyes immediately melted her. "All right," she said. "All right ... Get a book and I'll read you a story."

Chloe gurgled and scrambled down. She returned moments later with what had recently become her favourite. Handing Nola the book, Chloe climbed back into her mother's lap, snuggling into her body, content.

"Dog lived on a farm in the country," Nola read once Chloe had settled. "The farm was large and gave him many chances to run and play, to roll in the grass and gaze at the sky."

Chloe sighed, the knock at the door unanswered, the neighbourhood children safe from ambush, Nola's breast a pillow for her head. And a thousand miles away, the woman who would soon adopt her brother was showing the first outward signs of strain.

"You what!" Margaret stared at Horace. She wanted to slap him. "You left him at that crazy man's house? How could you!" Aware of how hard she was shaking him, she released him and stepped back.

"I thought he was with me, Mom, honest! Honest! I looked everywhere!"

Margaret's fury frightened her. She turned away, trembling. She went to the bar, poured a generous splash of whisky, and downed it. When she heard the front door open and close, the glass slipped from her hand and shattered on the floor.

Heath clomped through the entrance hall, his treat bag dragging on the tile. "Hi! Boy, Horace, where'd you go?"

"Huh?" Horace said.

"Heath!" Margaret gasped. "Where were you? Horace said you were at the Martin house."

"I was. He gave me these." Heath held up one hand.

Margaret stared at the handcuffs dangling from his wrist. "What is that?"

"Handcuffs," Heath said. "Mr. Martin gave them to me. They were his when he was a boy." Heath set his treat bag on the coffee table, toying with the handcuffs. "I've got a key and everything." He caught sight of Dog and shook his head. "Some watchdog you are, running off. Afraid of some harmless old man."

"You scared your mother to death," Frank said.

"I'm sorry. We were talking and then I went looking for Horace." Heath turned to study Margaret.

He's safe, Margaret thought, but for how long? Her heart pounded.

"Heath," Horace said, "where's your tail?"

"I gave it to Mr. Martin," Heath said, but his eyes were focused on Margaret. "He had a costume like mine once, but some kids pulled his tail off and –"

Margaret fell to the couch and burst into uncontrolled laughter.

IV IMMOLATION

That year, Hamilton and I took our first vacation – ostensibly to celebrate my fifty-fifth birthday – and we left Klieg's in early November.

Though the Karnival was normally on hiatus from December through February, Arthur was approached in late summer by Flye, leader of the internationally-famous rock band, The Maggots. Their latest album was inspired by Klieg's, Flye told Arthur. On a visit to the Karnival earlier in the season, the band had strolled the midway incognito. In response to the cacophony, Flye began to whistle a tune. That night, The Maggots returned to the recording studio, and left a week later having laid down the tracks for an entire album. Given this, they wanted to shoot several music videos at the Karnival. They would pay for us to open for their exclusive use through a six-week period in December and January. *Rolling Stone* wanted to chronicle the event. Arthur signed the contract without hesitation.

Hamilton and I travelled ahead to Vancouver, where we planned to join the Karnival when it hit town in mid-December. This meant that, for the first time in Klieg's history, the Karnival played without a live fortune-teller. Arthur arranged for a mechanical arcade gypsy, which customers could access with quarters. The conjoined twins, Polly and Peg, took over Hamilton's dog act for the interim.

Feeling restless, I spent little energy wondering why Arthur insisted we take the time away. I was merely pleased that he did. What I did not know until much later was that Hamilton requested of Arthur our vacation. Once again, I was interrupting customer readings with words not meant for their ears. Hamilton did not know what to make of it when, in a thin, high, and angry voice, my mouth began calling for Nola, for Baby ...

"I'm not sure it'll work," Hamilton told Arthur, "but I've got to get her away from here. Maybe a change of scenery is all she needs. I get scared when she's without control ... I'm really worried."

Hamilton and I boarded a flight from Edmonton to Vancouver, signing autographs as we went. Within hours, we were checked into a honeymoon suite with a spectacular view of the Pacific Ocean.

That afternoon, I received a call from Dolph Quentin, executive producer of the hit television series, *Scarlet Beach*. He had learned of our arrival through one of his location scouts who had seen us at the airport. Dolph offered me a guest part at an excellent salary. My scenes began shooting the following morning. The episode was scheduled to air in the spring.

Over the next five days, I was dressed as an Anglican nun, a newcomer to the "Our Lady of Sorrows" Convent in Scarlet Beach. My character was "helping" the stars of the series investigate the stalking and murders of "Miss Scarlet Beach" contestants. I was thrilled when I finished reading the script. In act four, I was to be revealed as a homicidal maniac whose first victim had been the nun she was impersonating. I thoroughly enjoyed the work and, delighted by the attention of the press, I appeared on local talk shows. It was not until our tenth day in Vancouver that I found myself with no bookings to distract me from the anticipation, which swept over me in waves.

Arthur telephoned that morning. "I've been leafing through the papers, Madame, and what do you know? There you are making some big splash in a television series. I hope you won't be leaving us for another career."

I laughed. Nothing could take me away from the Karnival. Klieg's was my home. "After thirty-three years, Arthur, how could you even think such a thing?"

"Just checking," he said. "I've been going over things with a lawyer and – well, never mind about all that. We'll be arriving on the fifteenth. I hope you two will be plenty rested. Got a lot to do before Christmas."

Perhaps it was my mood, or the fact that I was seeing him away from his milieu, but when Hamilton awoke later that morning, I suddenly realized how old he had become. Though I knew he would not die and leave me alone, I was sad to see the toll the years had taken on his body. On the day we married he had been so full of vitality. Over time, his movements had slowed and, though he did his best to hide it, I knew his hearing was beginning to fail.

"Good morning, Madame," he said, and kissed me. He slipped an arm around my waist, leading me back to the terrace railing. We looked up and down through the rails to the beach, which was nearly deserted at this hour. "Up for a walk before the jocks take over?"

I leaned my head on his shoulder, inhaling the rich scent of him. "North," I said.

"Treasure, Madame?"

"I don't know," I said. I simply knew a direction insistent in my mind.

"There a time limit?"

When I shook my head, he turned me to face him and kissed me deeply. My arms tightened around him. Drawing me away from the railing, he led me back to the coolness inside. With sure hands, he undressed me, kissing every inch of my body, and we made love in each room of the suite.

Later, we walked hand in hand, strolling up the beach unhurriedly northward, welcoming the breeze and the lap of the water at our feet. Soon Hamilton was collecting seashells, setting them carefully into a tote bag. I scanned the sand before us, my hands at rest in the pockets of my dress. Abruptly swooping in, seagulls and terns circled above and around us, calling out with shrill voices. Watching the birds, I did not see the head. It rested far to our right on the crest of a sand dune.

"Excuse me! Hello!"

Hamilton, bent to retrieve a shell, turned to look at me.

"Excuse me! Over here!"

I spotted the head in the sand. I peered forward. "Yes?"

"Do you think you could help me?"

I reached for Hamilton, clasped his hand in mine, and we stepped to the bottom of the sand dune. We had been summoned by a young woman – not yet twenty, as we were to learn.

"I am sorry to disturb your walk. But you see, I – I don't seem to be able to move."

"Can't you roll?" Hamilton asked.

"What?" The girl's eyes shifted back and forth between us.

"Roll," Hamilton said. "Can't you roll?"

"What are you doing there, my dear?" I asked.

She turned her eyes with a look of relief, for she did not share Hamilton's dry sense of humour. "Oh. Well ... You see, there was a party here last night and some of the kids got carried away and decided to bury me. Then the cops showed up because of the beer and pot and noise – and then ... Well, everyone got rounded up except for me because I was over here."

"Is that all?" Hamilton said.

"So I figured I'd been lucky that far and if I just waited until this morning ... I don't suppose you'd be willing to dig me up? It's impossible to move in here and I've got to go something awful. I'd have huge sand flea bites all over me if I'd been able to scratch." She smiled winningly. "Please ... it's terribly uncomfortable."

"All right," I said.

"There was a shovel over there." She indicated a point to her left with her eyes. "I'm not sure if it's still around."

Hamilton released my hand and clambered over the dune. He returned moments later with the shovel.

"I don't suppose you saw my clothes," the girl said.

Hamilton's eyebrows shot up and he shook his head.

"Just my luck." The girl appeared to shrug. "Oh well, we'll deal with that somehow. Thanks so much for helping me."

"You're welcome." Hamilton began to work carefully with the shovel. After several minutes he had dug enough to reveal the neck and shoulders, and the rise of the girl's breasts. She was no longer simply a head.

"What is your name, my dear?" I asked.

"Annette." Her lip curled. "I've never really liked it," she said. "It's a lovely name."

"If you say so." Annette chuckled and winked at Hamilton, who had exposed her breasts. He was trying to avert his eyes and dig without hitting her with the shovel. "What's your name?" she teased him.

He cleared his throat. "Hamilton, but people just call me Ham."

"That's a wonderful name for a man," Annette said. "Hamilton ... It sounds so – so strong."

"Thank you," Hamilton said.

"And you're Madame Isis," she said, turning to me.

I nodded. "I am pleased to meet you, Annette."

"Pleasure's mine. You know, I've got a box full of newspaper and magazine clippings about you. You and that actress? She made you sound like Joan of Arc and Mrs. Stanwick all rolled into one."

"Mrs. – ?"

"High school drama teacher. Brilliant woman." Annette worked her arms back and forth in the sand. "Just a bit more," she said to Hamilton, "and maybe I can push myself out of here. Anyway, Madame Isis, I've been wanting to meet you for years. Of course my family thinks I'm nuts, but then they're no pillars of sanity, so – You're really for real, aren't you?"

The girl had such a way of speaking that it was difficult to keep up with her. I was just staring, but Hamilton ceased his digging to stretch his back and wipe his brow. "The finest seer in the country," he said.

"Are you just born with it or can you develop it? The sight, I mean."

"A little of both, perhaps," I told her.

"I think I've got a bit, you know," Annette said. "Just a bit, mind you. Like ... dreams and stuff. I wake up sometimes just knowing things. One time my brother – his name is Danny – anyway, I woke up thinking, 'Danny had an accident.' In his car, you know, and sure enough, later on that afternoon I found out he had an accident. In Madrid of all places, thousands and thousands of miles from here! He wasn't hurt or anything, and I guess I knew that too." Annette freed her arms, placed them on either side of the hole, and tried pushing herself from the sand. "Maybe a bit more," she said to Hamilton. She turned her attention back to me. "Do you think I could buy you breakfast?"

Our eyes met and held. "You haven't any money," I said.

"I know, but I can just make a call. Daddy has more money than most countries."

"First," I said, "I think we should get you something to wear."

I gave Annette my dress. The girl wore it open at the back so it would fit across her breasts. It barely covered her pubis, but Annette appeared undisturbed. "I'll phone the house and have someone send over something," she said.

We created quite a stir as I, in my slip, and Hamilton, shovel at rest on his shoulder, escorted the oddly dressed girl through the lobby to the elevator. Once in our suite, Annette went to make her telephone call. Afterward, she wandered out to the terrace and asked to use the shower. When Hamilton and I were alone on the terrace, looking out through the rails to the ocean, he reached for my hand and frowned with mock disapproval.

"At the very least," he said, "you could have carried down a blanket for her."

A large leather shoulder bag had arrived by the time Annette emerged from the shower. Not modest about her repeated nakedness, Annette unwrapped the towel she wore and slipped into jeans and a tee shirt. She fitted sandals onto her feet and stood, turning around for our inspection. "Better?"

We nodded.

"And look at this." Annette reached into the bag and pulled out a bottle of champagne. "The best," she said. "For you. For saving me. Don't worry, it's non-alcoholic. And, if you don't mind, this is for me." She lifted a plastic sandwich bag. Inside were several joints of marijuana. She waited.

"Go ahead, my dear," I told her. I spoke instinctively – marijuana was standard with many of the Karnival residents – for my mind was focused on the echo of her words: "Don't worry. It's non-alcoholic." The girl possessed a *knowing*.

"You're sweet," Annette said. She selected a joint from the sandwich bag and wet it with her lips. "Daddy'll buy it and send it to me anywhere I want but he won't let me smoke in the house. Isn't that hypocritical?"

"What does he do, my dear?"

Annette laughed. "Well, he's supposed to be some top drawer executive, you know? But really I think he's just a big importer." She surveyed the joint. "You know, I really don't know why I continue to smoke this stuff. It's like ... like it doesn't really get me high anymore and it's only an exercise. Hmmm ..." But she lit the tiny cigarette, pulling the smoke deep into her lungs. "You know, Madame, I think there's a lot of things that happen –" She stopped, considering, exhaled and then took another drag. "Wait a minute. You know, sometimes things happen and you don't know why they're happening and you think, 'Boy, this is a big pain in the ass' and then something else happens, which wouldn't have happened otherwise, and – and you think, 'Oh, so that's why.'" She stopped again and broke into laughter. "Now that made a lot of sense."

"You're talking about last night," I said.

She nodded, releasing a puff of smoke. "I mean, I don't even like those kids. They're ... nincompoops." At this she broke into another fit of laughter. "Boy, this stuff is deadly. Daddy's going to make a killing on it. Hmmm ... Yeah, last night. I mean, here I was with a bunch of kids I didn't even like – don't even like – and they're burying me in the sand and ... But if that hadn't happened I wouldn't have met you two and ... And I'm glad I did. Really glad I did ... Thank you so much."

"Our pleasure," Hamilton said.

"Breakfast," Annette said, jumping to her feet. "I promised to buy you breakfast. Man, I'm starving! Daddy's going to make a killing, all right."

In the dining room, coffee waiting in porcelain cups, plates of food steaming in front of us, Hamilton made polite conversation while I studied the girl.

"Did you grow up here?" Hamilton asked.

"Pretty much, I guess," Annette said, stabbing her eggs. "Yeah, for the most part. We lived in the islands for awhile. I think that's where Daddy got all his connections. You know, it isn't such a hot ball of wax having a dope importer for a father."

Hamilton coughed lightly. He sipped at his coffee. "Are you certain that's what he does?"

"Oh, come on," Annette said. "No one has that much money without being a star, politician, or crook of some sort – not that they're mutually exclusive. Anyway, it's just my luck. I mean, someone's got to do it, right?"

"Not necessarily," Hamilton said.

"Sure, sure, I know. Morality. Laws. Do you think half the people making those laws actually follow them? Some of Daddy's biggest clients are politicians and corporate executives and people like that." Annette set her fork down. "Anyway, my luck isn't all bad. I escaped a night in jail, right? And you found me, right? I guess you didn't know I would be there or you would have brought me some clothes."

"My thoughts exactly," Hamilton said.

I laughed. "I did not know we would find you. I knew we would find something, but –"

"Treasure." Annette picked up her fork and attacked her potatoes.

Hamilton glanced at me with wide eyes.

"Something like that," I said.

"Like auto-pilot, right? 'Treasure, Madam?' 'North.'" Annette wiped at the plate with her toast and popped the bread into her mouth. "Know what? I'd love to see the Karnival." She sipped her orange juice.

"By all means," Hamilton said. "As our guest."

"Guest nothing," Annette said. "I've got plenty of money – more than I could ever spend. It may be drug money but it's just as colourful as any other. You found me. The least I can do is –"

"We'll see," I broke in, hoping the quake in my voice was not audible.

Annette looked up to study me. "Oh, I'm sorry. I didn't mean to impose, I –"

"Don't be silly, child." I forced a smile. "Sometimes it is better not to rush things."

Annette pushed away her plate. "All right." She finished her coffee and slid back her chair. She took money from her bag and put it on the table. "I hate to rush off but I do have an appointment. Can I buy you dinner?"

"Italian," Hamilton said. "It's her favourite."

"All right, then." Annette leaned across the table and kissed Hamilton on the cheek. "Thank you so much for digging me up. I'll call you later, all right?"

She had made no attempt to touch me. We watched her go, her bag slung over her shoulder, her hair swinging from side to side as she wove her way through the dining room.

Hamilton, not taking his eyes from the girl, reached over and squeezed my hand. "Is there something you need to tell me?"

I had no answer for Hamilton then, other than I believed that The Fates had led us to the girl. I could not express it, but I knew a first step had been taken, and the path must be followed to its end.

It was later that same day I discovered a new and intriguing facet of my *knowing*. As I was cleaning my glass eye, oddly, it appeared to take on an inner glow. It became transparent, like a flawless crystal ball. The mist that formed within soon faded, and I was looking into a bedroom of a stone mansion. The walls were blue, decorated with skilled murals of white clouds. A large bay window along one wall provided a view of the ocean. Off to one side was a big white bed, overflowing with a rainbow of elaborate pillows and plush animals.

I was powerless to look away. As I watched, a young woman entered the room. After a moment I recognized Annette. She crossed to the walk-in closet, and emerged an instant later with an ornate hatbox. She set the hatbox on the bed, bright red against the white of the comforter. She walked back and forth just looking at the hatbox, as if prolonging the pleasure of opening it until the last unbearable second.

Abruptly Annette sat down on the bed. She lifted the lid from the hatbox and spilled its contents onto the comforter. I soon realized that these were the press clippings of which she had spoken at breakfast.

She lit a joint from the sandwich bag and, smoking it slowly, one by one she lifted the clippings, savouring each as if for the first time. She must have been halfway through the pile when there was a knock and a whisper at the door.

"Annette?"

"Yes?"

"Are you all right, dear?"

"I'm fine, Mother."

"Your father just told me you were home. I've been so worried, you not coming back last night and – please, dear, could you open the door?"

Annette took a final drag on the joint and stabbed it into an ashtray. She scooped up the clippings, dropped them into the hatbox, and replaced the lid. Then she crossed the room and threw open the door. "Hello, Mother."

"Hello, dear." Her mother took a step forward, peering into Annette's eyes. She reached out with fingers that barely touched Annette's cheek, her arms. "You're all right. I was so worried."

"I don't know why," Annette said. "I'm perfectly fine. I was the only one who didn't get arrested and Daddy sent spectacular grass."

"Annette." The reproach was gentle, hardly a reproach at all. "Dear, I wish you wouldn't say such naughty things."

"The ostrich, Mother, is a large running bird of Africa with a long neck and tiny head, which it buries in the sand when –"

"Annette." Mother smiled. "Really, dear, you're teasing me."

"Of course, Mother. They don't really bury their heads, you know." Annette threw herself on the bed, rolling over onto her back.

Her mother eased onto the mattress beside her.

Annette took her mother's hand. "Is Danny home?"

"No, dear, he cabled last night. He's decided to stay on at the chalet. He wanted me to be sure and tell you he would like you to come."

"I hate it there," Annette said. "But I'll call him. Is he coming home for Christmas?"

"I don't think so, dear." Mother shifted on the bed, her hand slipping almost casually from Annette's. "And your father ..."

"What."

"Well, dear, he has business in South America. One of those god-awful little countries down there somewhere. We'll be flying out day after tomorrow."

"I see." Annette shut her eyes.

"I do wish you'd join your brother in Switzerland, dear. We're going on to Sydney and Paris and – we won't be back until February. There's no sense both of you being alone over the holidays."

"Maybe Danny will come home when he knows you're gone," Annette whispered.

"I'm sorry, dear, what did you say?"

"I said I think I'll stay here."

"Well, Malcolm will be available should you need anything. Perhaps invite him for a drink."

"Malcolm?!" Her laugh was bitter.

"Annette." Mother reached for her hand, settled on stroking her arm. "Are you unhappy, dear?"

There was no answer.

"Annette?"

"Of course not, Mother. I have everything money can buy. Why would I be unhappy?" She cringed as Mother kissed her forehead.

"That's a good girl," Mother said, standing. "Will you be down for dinner?"

"I have a date, thank you."

"Oh. Anyone we know?"

"I don't think so."

"What does he do?"

"Relax, Mother, it's not that kind of date."

"Oh. Well. I see. Very well, dear. Do you need a driver?"

"No, thank you, Mother, I'll take the red Jaguar." Annette turned away and her mother went out, easing the door closed. As the girl began weeping into the rainbow of elaborate pillows and plush animals, the room faded. I once again found myself looking at my opaque glass eye.

I was shocked about this new facet of *knowing*, but this feeling was pushed aside by my concern for Annette. I could not get the girl out of my mind, and I was glad we had plans to see her that night.

After dinner, Annette, Hamilton, and I walked the beach in silence. We heard the occasional burst of laughter, the clink of glassware. In time, as if by prearrangement, we slowed and seated ourselves facing the water. We watched as the blackness erupted into white foam, crashing into itself, sweeping along the sand only to retreat before reaching us.

"I've always loved the ocean," Annette said. "So peaceful, yet relentless ... deadly." She lit a joint and lay back, looking up at the stars through the smoke.

Hamilton took my hand.

"Danny – my brother – is staying in Switzerland," Annette continued after awhile. "Daddy and Mother are going to South America – buying drugs, I suppose, or something. Then on to Sydney and Paris. Merry fucking Christmas, Annette." She rolled over, pressing her face into the sand. "What a ridiculous life," she said.

The waves beat on the shore.

"You don't have children, do you?" Annette asked.

"The gods have not blessed us as yet," I said.

"I don't suppose you'd like a daughter."

"Very much," Hamilton said.

Annette sat up, her gaze steady. "I'm not kidding."

I felt the girl's intent was justified, but I could not encourage further estrangement from her parents. "You are welcome at the Karnival," I told her. "But life decisions such as these should not be made so quickly."

"I decided this years ago," Annette said, laughing at my serious demeanour. "I've just been waiting for you to show up."

The following day was my fifty-fifth birthday, and Hamilton arranged an evening on a chartered yacht. He and I enjoyed a sumptuous dinner, with dancing to a string quartet before and after, as we cruised the ocean. We returned to the harbour kissing each other under the stars. Back at the hotel, we spent the night making love, finally falling asleep as the sun began to rise.

We woke just after noon. As we were leaving our suite for lunch, we opened the door to find Annette weeping on the hallway floor.

We soon learned that it was no longer necessary to consider the feelings of Annette and Danny's parents. Two hours off the coast that morning, their private jet had exploded in mid-air. Annette did not need the telephone call from Transport Canada to know. She was about to bite into a cheese croissant when she saw, reflected in the plate, her mother's puzzled and anxious face, and felt the blast of heat from the bomb.

Annette did not want to return home by herself. She kept insisting that we were to be her new parents, that we were the parents to whom she wished she had been born. We were hesitant, but after a brief meeting with the family lawyer, Malcolm Lewis, we agreed to accompany her back to the mansion, where we would remain until the Karnival's arrival.

Annette's bedroom was just as I had seen it that day, gazing into my glass eye. The walls were blue, with skilled murals of white clouds, and a large bay window overlooked the ocean. The press clippings she collected were in the red hatbox and, seated in the bay window that night, I read them as she had done on countless occasions, while Annette tossed in the big white bed.

Annette notified Danny in Switzerland. She requested he fly home immediately, but he did not come directly to the house from the Vancouver airport. When he learned that Hamilton and I were temporarily living at the mansion, he arranged to meet Malcolm Lewis for lunch before facing Annette.

"Who're the pygmies?" Danny asked the moment Malcolm sat down at the table.

"Certainly you've heard of them. Hamilton Klieg and Madame Isis, the stars of Klieg's Karnival."

"Who hasn't? But what the hell are they doing in the house?"

"According to your sister, they have every right to be there –" Malcolm paused, as he often did, for dramatic effect. "As her new parents."

"What?!"

Malcolm shrugged. "That's what she told me. Her new parents."

"Fortune hunters," Danny said.

"Apparently not. I've checked them out and they've got quite enough of their own money – investments and what have you. He is part owner of the Karnival. These are celebrities, you know – you couldn't turn on the television last week without seeing Madame Isis."

"That's comforting."

"Personally," Malcolm continued, "I think Annette's dipped a bit too deep into your father's cache of drugs, but – I'm an employee. She inherits the majority of the estate, so, from where I'm sitting, she can do as she likes."

"I'll throw them out."

Malcolm shook his head. "I wouldn't try it."

Danny frowned. He finished his drink and ordered another. "Whatever you say, Malcolm. You just keep an eye on them. I don't want her giving the estate away to a couple of Munchkin rejects."

"Careful, boy. She's quite serious about all this."

"But ... pygmies?"

"Dwarves – I think. Call them vertically challenged, just to be safe. Anyway, Annette appears to genuinely care about these people."

"Come on, Malcolm, you don't mean to tell me –"

"What I'm telling you is, your sister loves that couple. Who can say why and who cares? And I'll tell you something else – they came to me when she asked them to move in. They didn't seem all that sure about it and wanted to know what I thought. I'll admit, at first I thought it was all an act. You know, play the family lawyer for sympathy, that kind of thing."

"So how do you know it wasn't?"

"I don't. That's why I looked into them. But I'm forced to give them the benefit of the doubt. Look, Danny, you know as well as I do how miserable Annette was with your parents. Now, I'm not too keen on this situation. I hate to think these people will be staying on after their Karnival arrives. What if Annette decides she wants the whole thing legal? It's quite possible, you know."

"You mean – have them adopt her?"

"That's what I mean."

Danny took a long swallow of whisky. "You can't be serious."

"Danny." Malcolm placed a hand on the young man's arm. "I don't know what's in Annette's mind, and I don't want to speculate. But I will tell you one thing. If you try in any way to drive this couple out you're liable to drive Annette away with them."

Danny's tone softened. He looked into Malcolm's eyes. "She's in shock. Mourning. This has got to be some kind of crazy thing she'll snap out of."

"And what if it isn't?"

Danny shuddered. "I'll have a ham and Isis on rye," he said to the waiter.

"Pardon, sir?"

Danny raised his glass in mock toast. "To the pygmies. And to Annette's pygmy mind."

I must state in Danny's defense that Arthur did not approve of our move into the mansion, either. "Where the hell are you?" he demanded when I telephoned. "The hotel said you checked out without leaving a forwarding address. I didn't know what to think!"

I explained as briefly as I could.

"Found her like some flotsam on a beach, you say?"

"Arthur. She is very sweet and has just lost her parents. We're stand-ins until she gets back on her feet."

"That could take months. And how the hell did some wild-eyed fan become your problem? We're due there in less than –"

"Arthur, please. I cannot – I will not – turn my back on this girl."

Arthur sighed. "Whatever you do, you just be there on the fifteenth. And you tell my brother, the next time he pulls a disappearing act like this, we're setting loose those dogs of his to hunt him down!"

Despite all his bluster at lunch with Malcolm, to his credit, Danny made the effort to simulate respect for his sister's decision. Though he did not go out of his way to seek our company, neither did he make us feel out of place. He chatted with us politely over meals, took us on a tour of the spacious grounds, saddled the pony and offered me a riding lesson. He had found his father's cache of cocaine and thus drifted above us all, as if we were merely audience participation theatre.

I soon learned that Annette had given up marijuana. With her parents gone, she no longer felt such a need to escape. "The fact that your parents don't love you," she said to me one afternoon in the garden, "is infinitely easier to handle when they're dead and unable to – as opposed to just unwilling." But on another occasion I was saddened to hear her say – quite wrongly – that the only people who ever cared for her, aside from ourselves and Danny, had done so because she stood poised to inherit not only the magnificent estate, but hundreds of millions of dollars.

Since our arrival at the mansion, Hamilton and I had not mentioned our impending departure. But with less than a week before the Karnival hit Vancouver – and Arthur's angry words still stinging – I felt it was time. After dinner one night, I asked Annette to accompany us on a moonlit walk through the grounds.

We came upon the maze and made our way through to the centre – she, Hamilton, and I. We sat on the marble bench, and I broached the subject to Annette. "You know we must be leaving soon."

Annette did not speak, but her words were visible in her eyes.

"As much as we enjoy being here, we do have the Karnival."

"I know," Annette said. "I've been thinking about that. I still want to go with you. Stay with you. Learn from you."

I was silent then. I glanced at Hamilton. I had wanted to hear these words, but the girl must be certain. "The Karnival is an entirely different world. It is nothing like this." I waved my hand to indicate the maze, the sculpted gardens, the palatial mansion.

"I know," Annette said. "But I want to leave all this. There's nothing here for me. Money – things. I've had things all my life – everything I ever wanted – and it means nothing."

"Annette –"

"If you don't want me," the girl broke in, "I'll understand. Just – just say the word and I'll –"

"Of course we want you. But you must be certain of what you want. What is right for you."

"I know. And I am. Like I told you before, I decided this a long time ago. I've dreamed about this all my life, ever since I first learned of you. I don't know why – I have no explanation for it – but I've always wanted to be with you. Needed to be with you. Please – please say you'll have me."

Undeterred by Arthur's raised eyebrows upon meeting her, Annette felt immediately comfortable at Klieg's. She took up working one of the games of skill, and spent her days handing out softballs and stacking milk bottles. She was, as it turned out, a fan of The Maggots. She lured them to the concession with good-natured taunts, commenting on their throws while loudspeakers blared playback, and video cameras captured the action.

With Frank, Margaret, and the boys scheduled to join us on the nineteenth, Arthur drove the workmen hard. He insisted on the freak tent's banners being repainted and the ticket booths being appointed with fresh awnings. On the morning the Cliffords were to arrive, he supervised the installation of a new sign for Goliath, the giant roller coaster.

"I don't want to see the damn thing swaying," Arthur told Hamilton. The sign straddled the track at the highest point, suspended by two metal supporting arms, which seemed unwilling to remain tightly bolted. It had nearly fallen twice, and the bravest of the workmen were busy fitting new bolts and replacing the light bulbs that had shattered. "We've got less than two hours," Arthur said. "I want everything – and I mean everything – absolutely perfect."

As for myself, I kept thinking of the prediction I had given to Margaret, the words I had spoken on her eleventh birthday: "A son calls forth a brother. A sister to the second bears three." I feigned ignorance when Arthur told us that morning – wondering why it had slipped his mind until then – that Frank and Margaret had adopted a boy at Horace's urging.

I was anxious to meet the child, but circumstances were such that Horace and Frank came to the lot in a taxi cab without Margaret, Heath, and Dog. Once Frank had been led away to their tent for a nap, Horace explained that his father was terrified of flying. Frank had guzzled four drinks within the first half hour of the flight, and soon passed out, drooling onto his seat. Suffering a nightmare, Frank awoke screaming about an earthquake. "And everybody," Horace said, laughing, "everybody thought he was some kinda lunatic!"

Given this behaviour, Margaret decided it was best to send Frank on ahead, while she and Heath waited for the luggage and Dog. Horace accompanied his father to ensure he wasn't lost, or asleep in the back of the cab, while the driver toured the city with the meter consuming their retirement funds.

"Where's Grandpa?"

I directed the boy to Goliath and, not long after, the limousine Arthur had sent drove up bearing Margaret, Heath, and Dog. By then, Arthur and Horace were riding Goliath again and again. Hamilton and I greeted Margaret and her new son.

Margaret seemed genuinely happy to be back at Klieg's. She introduced Heath, who studied me with serious eyes.

"Hello, Heath," I said.

"Hello," Heath said.

"What do you think of our Karnival?"

Heath turned. His eyes followed the path to the left arm of the midway, which was lined by the games of chance and skill. He gazed at the myriad prizes and patterns and colours and lights. "Well, I haven't really seen it yet. But I'm looking forward to it. Margaret's told me all about it."

"Which way is our tent, Madame?" Margaret asked. "I'd like to get these things put away and check on Frank."

Hamilton whistled. Within moments, several workmen appeared, picking up the luggage and heading toward the proper tent.

"Most of the boys are new since you were here last," I explained to Margaret as we trailed the workmen. "But all of them know who you are, and how Arthur expects you should be treated. The Snake Lady has left us again. The twins are still here, and the Sword Swallower, Fritz."

"Everything looks so different," Margaret said.

"New. The freak tent is freshly painted. And Arthur had some of the concessions remodelled. He's had everyone working around the clock to make it perfect for you."

"It's fabulous." Margaret stopped to look at me. "It is great to be back. Makes me wonder why I ever left."

"We all must go on," I said. "We each have a path." And as I spoke, once again Heath was studying me. "Perhaps young Heath would enjoy a visit with the dogs?" I asked.

"Would I!" Heath said, and Dog wagged his tail. "Can I?"

"Yes, you may," Margaret said. "Of course. Run along with your Uncle Ham." She kissed the top of his head and watched with great affection as Heath and Dog followed Hamilton to find the dog act in rehearsal.

"He is a lovely child," I told her.

Margaret turned to me with a smile. "I was so afraid something would happen, that the adoption wouldn't go through. But everything's fine. I feel so silly. I was even afraid I wouldn't be happy to be back."

That night, seated beside her bed, I was amazed that I had not known. When Margaret held me down on the ground so many nights before, I saw all that would befall her and all that ever had. I had seen her in this bed like this, but never saw what would put her there. Perhaps I could not foresee the event because her mind refused to accept it. As I sat beside her, holding her hand, I found myself connected, reliving the day from within her ...

Frustration and anger with Frank. Excitement to soon see her father. The crush at the airport, the interminable ride in the limousine, the flush of relief as she stepped onto the lot. The feeling that she had come home.

Pride and love for her new son, a sense of warmth as I left her and she entered the tent. Inside it was cool, with a faint mustiness. Walking around the tent, touching its sides, she felt the heat of the canvas against her fingers, her palms. She thought of her mother, and of Tim-Tina. She thought of Frank, the first time he had made love to her. It had been in a tent just like this one ...

She looked at Frank curled up on the cot. This is my life, she thought. It was odd to think it, frightening yet strangely comfortable. I have a husband and two fine sons. My father and aunt and uncle love me, and my mother ... my mother was a dream.

Moving away from the cot, taking a final look around the tent before stepping out into the sunshine. From anywhere on the lot it was possible to see Goliath, and she made her way, unerringly, along the midway to the giant roller coaster. People she knew greeted her as she went. She waved back at them, smiling, new faces turning to look at her, commit her to memory, until, at last, she reached Goliath.

Margaret put a hand to her forehead, shielding her eyes from the sunlight that glinted on the intricate structure. There were so many tracks and loops and double-loops, twists and turns and hills and valleys, that it was a moment before she spotted Horace and Arthur. Their car was climbing a hill. She would never ride this monstrosity herself – it was too big, too fast. It made her feel dizzy with lack of control.

The car crested the hill and plunged heavily downward. She felt her stomach knot as if she were there herself. She watched as it looped, gaining speed, slowing on a rise only to plummet once again, coming so quickly into a turn that she was certain the car would fly right off the track.

Then she noticed the sign. It loomed over the dips and twists of the roller coaster, lights ablaze in nine brilliant colours, reflected in the polished surfaces of the car.

The car slowed once more as it climbed the next hill, allowing its passengers a breather before the next bone-jarring plunge. Horace turned in the car to look out at the ground, saw Margaret, and waved. Blowing him a kiss, she watched her father glance at Horace, then in her direction. Arthur smiled and raised a hand in greeting as the car hurtled down.

The sign swayed to one side. A supporting arm gave way and gravity took hold. Like the blade of a guillotine set upon an inevitable course, the sign pitched forward into the car's path. With lights popping and metal groaning, it poised to strike.

Margaret prayed.

"Oh my God!" someone screamed behind her.

The car slammed with full force into the waiting sign, slicing Arthur neatly in half. Horace, swept from the car, bounced down through the rails to land with a dull heavy thud on the midway. The sign was wrenched aside, and crumpled to hang by one supporting arm, dangling over the track. The car lifted, hesitated before finding its course, and continued on.

Margaret felt paralyzed. The car was rattling through a loop, carrying the half body of her father. Her son was a heap of shattered limbs, immobile on the ground. The screams were deafening, and her throat was raw.

In her mind the final thought: No. I can't. I won't.

As workmen came running, Margaret fell silent.

The shock was too much for her, the doctor explained. She had retreated into a state of catatonia. There was no telling if she would ever come out of it, though she could go on to live for decades, silent and still within her bed.

"Perhaps the best thing," the doctor said, "would be to put her in an institution."

But we could not contemplate such a solution. We hired a team of nurses to look after her. They exercised Margaret's body periodically, inserted and removed the I.V. needles, changed the diapers and sanitary pads.

There was nothing that any of us could do for the shattered Horace. Hamilton left the lot in the ambulance that carried the boy away. As I stepped from the tent, leaving Margaret silent and still within, Frank, Heath, and Annette were waiting in the moonlight. We surveyed the lot. Frank could not possibly care for Margaret and Heath by himself, I was thinking. I knew Hamilton would feel as I did. It would not be right to continue the Karnival without them.

"We can't do all that travelling," Frank said.

"I know," I said.

"We've got to shut down," Frank said.

"No," Heath said.

We all turned to stare at him.

"No," Heath said again.

"But, Heath," Frank said, "your mother –"

"No. No!" Heath's eyes blazed. His fists clenched at his sides.

Frank's shoulders sagged. Until that day, nothing terrible had ever befallen him. He buried his face in his hands. "I don't know what to do!"

"We can buy the land," Heath said, looking at Annette and me. "We can reopen and stay right here."

I nodded, for this was how it was meant to be. I glanced at Annette who was watching Heath with wonder in her eyes.

Heath went to Annette and touched her gently. "Take care of my father," he said, and at that moment I could have sworn he was older than she.

Annette hurried to Frank's side. She pulled him into her arms, smoothing his hair as he wept into her shoulder. "It's going to be all right, Frank," she cooed as if to a child. "Everything's going to be all right ..."

*   *   *

Meanwhile, Ralph used virtually these very same words in an

effort to calm Nola. They were seated in a pediatrician's waiting room, the doctor's last appointment of the day. Chloe, then three, had yet to utter more than a few guttural sounds. Ralph insisted they bring her just to see what the doctor could tell them. Nola was certain she knew what the doctor would say, but she waited, silently shredding the cover of a magazine, as Chloe was examined behind one of the white doors, which led off the hallway beyond the receptionist's desk.

"It's going to be all right, Nola," Ralph said. He took her hand to still her fingers. "Whatever the doctor says, it's not going to make one lick of –"

"Please stop it," Nola said. "Just stop it." She tossed the magazine back onto the table and met Ralph's gaze with eyes that dared him to speak.

"Mr. and Mrs. Greeson, the doctor will see you now."

They followed the nurse into the doctor's private office. There was no sign of Chloe.

"Please have a seat," the doctor said as the nurse went out and closed the door.

"Where's Chloe?" Nola asked.

"She's in the playroom with a nurse's assistant," the doctor said. "I thought it would be best if we spoke a few moments alone."

"Why?" Nola eyed him, sinking into a chair. "Chloe knows she's different. What difference does it make if she hears you say it?"

The doctor cleared his throat. He began flipping through the open file folder on his desk. He showed them an x-ray that they did not understand, and explained that there was no hope of Chloe ever speaking. Her voice box had never properly formed. Her hearing appeared to be perfectly normal and, from what he could see, the girl was certainly not mentally handicapped. There was every reason to think that Chloe could easily learn to communicate through sign language, like millions of other mutes throughout the world.

"She'll never say a word?" Ralph asked.

"Never," the doctor said.

"What makes you so damn sure?" Nola said. "What makes all of you people so goddamned sure about everything all the time?"

"Honey, please," Ralph said.

The doctor, forcing a smile with failing patience, looked at Ralph when he spoke. "I assure you I am quite competent in my work," he said.

"Of course," Ralph said, automatically.

Nola frowned at him.

The doctor continued as if he were dealing with unintelligent children. Certain things were simply not possible, he told them. One of these impossibilities was Chloe ever speaking. The other, of course, had to do with the third arm. It would remain, as it was, forever. It was impossible for there to be any type of movement. There was nothing they could do about her voice, the doctor said, but certainly there was no reason for the girl to go through life further handicapped. It would be such a simple process to have the offending limb removed.

"Why?" Nola said. "All of you want to do the same thing and I just don't know how to see why."

"It serves no purpose," the doctor said. "It will remain a completely useless appendage."

"How do you know that?"

"Mrs. Greeson – why are you so opposed to this?"

"Because I don't believe you," Nola said.

"I beg your pardon?"

"I said I think you're full of shit. Just because you say it's useless doesn't mean it's useless. How do you know that?"

The doctor's ears reddened.

"What my wife means is," Ralph said, "we think things turn out just the way God has meant them to be. Since Chloe was born with it – well, then, to our way of thinking, there must be some reason for it."

"I don't think you understand," the doctor said.

Nola leaned forward, a hand perilously close to the letter opener on the desk. "I'll be damned," Nola said, "if I ever let you or anyone else mutilate my child."

"Correcting a mistake could hardly be confused with muti– "

"Who the hell are you to say what's a mistake?" Nola rose from her chair.

Ralph stopped her with a touch of her hand. "I'm sorry, doctor," Ralph said. "I think we better take Chloe and go."

In the transport truck, returning to their suburban rental with Chloe safely in the seat between them, Ralph did not know what to say to his wife. To this day, Nola had told him nothing about her past and, for all he knew, she had appeared fully formed from the vapours of his dreams the very day he had met her in the village diner. It was clear to him that the world was too hard for her. It was turning her softness brittle, her sweetness bitter.

"I want you to take us away," Nola said. She had been thinking about it for several months, sick of the taunts and the jokes, the stares and the judgments. They had rented five different houses in the previous three years, and everywhere they lived it was always the same. "I want you to find us a home far away from everyone. Acres. Acres and acres where Chloe can play without being seen."

"A farm?" Ralph asked.

For Nola, the word brought conflicting images to light. She did not want to think of her parents, and as Mollie sought entrance to her mind, Nola pushed her forcibly aside. "Acres and acres," Nola said. "Far away from everything, where there's no one to look at us. I mean it, Ralph."

"I know," Ralph said.

Chloe reached for Nola's hand, and Nola smiled down at her daughter. "We're going far away," she said, over and over to make it come true. "Far, far away ..."

V REVELATIONS

The decision was made that Klieg's would no longer be a truck show; thereafter, those who wished to experience our world were obliged to journey to us.

Arthur must have known that his time was coming to an end. Only weeks before his death, he purchased a major life insurance policy and hired a lawyer to draw up a will. His entire estate – and, most rightly, Klieg's – was to pass equally to Margaret and Hamilton. Were Margaret to predecease him, her share was to pass to her sons.

"Looks like this could all be yours one day," Annette said to Heath. She found herself quite taken with the boy, intrigued by his unexpected maturity.

"My mother's not dead," Heath told her.

"No, of course not, sweetie, I didn't mean that. What I meant was, you have somewhere to belong. Forever. You have a home that no one can take away from you."

"Don't you?" Heath asked.

Annette shook her head. "Until I met your aunt and uncle, all I ever had was a great big house. There's a big difference between a home and a house, you know."

The roller coaster accident was a lead story on the nightly news, and made front pages around the world. Eulogies ran in *Macleans*, *Rolling Stone*, and the amusement trade's *Billboard*, among other popular magazines. Supermarket tabloids revived the story of how Anna and Hank had died so many years before. The Maggots postponed further filming, and we closed for the season. We all needed time to mourn, to regroup and plan for the future. We did not know what challenges would await us when Horace awakened.

Horace had suffered extensive physical damage: every limb was broken, as well as several ribs and his back and neck; organs were crushed and ceased to function; yet, he survived. His brain appeared to be unharmed, but we would not know for certain until he returned to consciousness. To spare the boy agony, he was kept in drug-induced coma for months, while numerous operations were performed, and machines kept his body alive and working to restore itself. I spent most of my time beside his hospital bed, convinced that a part of him knew of my presence. When I grew tired, someone from the family would take my place, to speak to him in comforting tones, to read him Margaret's books, and sing his favourite lullabies. I could not bear the thought that he might awaken and not see a loving face.

After an initial visit, during which he lingered near the doorway as if desperate to flee, Heath was reluctant to return to the hospital. Frank, felled by grief and shock, could not be persuaded to leave Margaret's bedside. Splitting our energies between Horace and the new Klieg's, Annette, Hamilton, and I drove ourselves to near exhaustion.

It was easy to acquire the lot. The Maggots owned the property in their voluminous portfolio of real estate holdings. They quite happily allowed us to make the purchase for market value.

Once the papers were signed, we began to discuss plans for renovations to the Karnival, as befitted its new role as a stationary theme park. Annette invested her own funds to build the permanent housing quarters of eighteen bedrooms, two dining rooms, a community day room, and a gymnasium. Several of the employees took rooms, and Frank and Margaret resided in a private suite. Margaret was tended by a team of nurses as Dog remained a sentry beneath her bed. Most of the troupers chose to live in tents and trailers scattered throughout the backyard of the lot. Hamilton and I had our tent positioned near the office-trailer, and Heath and Annette occupied tents nearby. As The Fates would have it, Danny soon came to Klieg's.

Annette was overjoyed when her brother joined us, though the circumstances under which Danny arrived caused him a great deal of personal anguish. Ironically, while their mother had been pushing Annette to court the family lawyer, Malcolm Lewis, Danny was secretly in love with him.

Until long after he moved to Klieg's, Danny remained a virgin. But he had wanted Malcolm the moment he saw the handsome man in a dark blue suit stride through the mansion's entrance hall. Danny was sixteen, and Malcolm was a revelation, a font of unfulfilled fantasies and unpredictable erections. Danny was ashamed and terrified to learn so suddenly and completely what he was. If his parents spoke of homosexuals, it was always with disdain. No prospective servant perceived as such was ever hired for the estate, and effeminate waiters and salesmen often were subjected to cruel and hateful comments. As soon as he was old enough to do so on his own, Danny travelled to Mexico, Spain, Tokyo, and Switzerland to forget Malcolm. It was doubtful he would have ever returned to Canada had his parents not died in an act of sabotage.

Growing up, Danny had spent countless hours listening to Annette talk about Klieg's and how one day she would live at the Karnival. Once her fantasy became a reality, and Danny found himself alone in the mansion, he began to plan. He was certain that if his sister's dreams could come true, so could his own. High on his father's cocaine, he spent hours envisioning moments when Malcolm would crush him with his body.

But when Danny put his plan into action, when he let Malcolm know of his love, his want, his need for him, Malcolm laughed. Humiliated, Danny ran from the house, returning hours later to find Malcolm gone. Truly alone then – in Danny's mind, servants did not count – Danny needed love and comfort. His parents, just as when they had been alive, were completely inaccessible. Only Annette could make him feel wanted.

Malcolm began sending underlings with the contracts and papers that required Danny's signature. He was always "at lunch" or "in a meeting" whenever Danny telephoned the legal firm. Danny paced the staircases, hallways, and rooms of the mansion, lost. Lonely in the house that drug money had built, he listened to love songs and snorted cocaine and wept for hours.

One afternoon, without notice, as workers poured the concrete for the housing quarters, Danny appeared at the Karnival. He shook the gates that kept the public locked from the lot, holding a suitcase and bellowing for his sister. Nothing, he had decided, could be worse than living in that empty mansion.

"What are you doing here?" Annette asked.

"I'm sick of being by myself," Danny said. He had left the estate with minimal staff and ample maintenance funds. "I thought I'd visit with you for awhile and see what it's like to be a carny."

Danny followed Annette to her tent. Inside, he looked around at the simple furniture. The oak bureau with the circular mirror hanging above it. The wrought iron bed overflowing with the elaborate rainbow of pillows and plush animals. The pine drop-leaf table and chairs. That afternoon, Danny purchased a small, though well-equipped, trailer and moved into a corner of the backyard.

Left to himself for much of each day, Danny wandered the lot. He watched as new rides and games rose into place on the midway. He toured the freak tent, lingering in what had been Balzod's cubicle, absorbing the history of magic.

Further inspired by Annette's initiative regarding the housing quarters, Danny presented plans for the Karnival Museum. Annette, Heath, Hamilton, and I huddled over the blueprints, which engulfed the desk in the office-trailer as Danny explained in detail. The museum would be a massive structure, its interior designed to give the look and feel of a tent, down to the wood chips, the smell of the canvas, the faint mustiness of the air. It would be divided into rooms, one tracing the history of Klieg's itself, another the history of magic – much more comprehensive than that in Balzod's cubicle – in others the evolutions in sideshows, rides, and games of chance and skill.

"It's incredible," Hamilton said. "What are the estimates?"

Danny handed him a file of papers. After a quick look at the bottom line, Hamilton emitted a low whistle.

"I'm fully prepared to pay the whole shot," Danny said. "No need for you to worry about that. We'll charge a separate fee for admission to the building and work out a split between us."

Construction of the Karnival Museum commenced the next

week, immediately following the completion of the housing quarters. Workers were determined to finish the project before opening day in June. Each night, we fell asleep to a symphony of power tools and steel, concrete mixers and voices rich with purpose. Each morning, we awoke to find the museum still growing, even as shifts changed, as meals were called, as fog burned away in the midday sun, as rain showered the lot.

On a night in late March, we gathered in a room of the recently completed housing quarters to watch the network broadcast of my *Scarlet Beach* episode. Horace was still in coma, with Polly and Peg keeping vigil for the night. Frank was at Margaret's bedside, but Heath, Annette, Danny, Hamilton, and I laughed at first, and then were enthralled, as the television mystery played out.

No one guessed that my character was the serial murderer. After the programme, I accepted congratulations on my performance.

Annette, her eyes bright with happiness, took Hamilton's hand. "I'm glad we're here together," she said. "Because I've got a surprise." She reached into her shoulder bag and produced a framed document. "This is for both of you."

Hamilton and I glanced at each other. We both extended a hand to hold a side of the frame.

Heath tugged at Annette's sleeve. "What is it?"

"You'll see in a minute," she said as the boy craned his neck to look.

Having read the document, I turned to Hamilton with tears in my eyes. His lips quivered as he kissed me.

"What is it?" Heath asked again. We allowed him to take the frame from us. His eyes travelled slowly, studying the document it contained as Danny peered over his shoulder. "Annette Rochelle Klieg," Heath read.

"You changed your name?" Danny stared at her. "Your name?"

Annette ignored him, smiling at us as I clasped Hamilton's hand. Her eyes showed tenderness. One hand reached toward mine, and then withdrew. "I told you I wished you were my parents," she said.

"And now Hamilton's name will live on," I said. I cannot describe the joy I felt, and yet, this was shadowed by the toll The Fates exacted for their gift. How I longed at that moment to take the girl into my arms, to hug and kiss her as a mother should! I stepped back, watching as she bent to embrace Hamilton and kiss his cheek.

Danny looked at me pointedly. "Well, Annette – congratulations, I guess," he said.

"Does this make us related now?" Heath asked.

Annette laughed with delight. "Sure, why not? Now we're cousins."

Heath turned to Danny, whose face had abandoned disbelief for confusion. "What about you?" Heath asked.

Danny started. "Don't drag me into this," he said, though not unkindly. "I'm just an investor. And I happen to like my name, thank you very much."

Hamilton took my hand. "It's a wonderful gift," he said to Annette.

"Boy," Heath said. "Just wait till Horace finds out about this!"

Several weeks later – four months and forty-six operations after the accident – the doctors determined it was time to bring Horace out of the coma. They suggested we delay as long as possible telling the boy about his mother and grandfather. Too much of a shock could slow his return to strength, the doctors said. Though it disturbed me, I agreed to take part in the subterfuge, provided Horace did not ask me outright why his parents failed to visit him. Perhaps it was cowardly, but I would be thankful that he never did.

When Horace awakened, we learned that he had suffered no brain damage. Any remaining physical damage could be mended through intensive rehabilitation. Annette arranged for a substantial donation to the hospital, ensuring Horace access to the latest and best equipment and therapies.

Several times each week, Heath would ask one of the workers to drive him to the hospital. There he would stay with Horace late into the night, hiding from the nurses after visiting hours ended.

One evening, Hamilton and I were debating how best to

explain to Horace all that had happened, when Heath informed us that this would not be necessary.

"Don't worry," Heath said. "He knows. About his grandpa – Margaret – how long he's been asleep – everything."

We were intrigued. Doctors had speculated that Horace might suffer from a type of amnesia, which would block the accident itself from his mind.

"What was his reaction?" Hamilton asked. "Was he very upset?"

Heath shrugged. "He said Margaret had just seen one too many bad things. He said some people are strong enough to handle stuff like that and some people aren't."

"I see," Hamilton said.

"Horace said he's lucky he ever had a grandpa and a mom in the first place. He says we should just count our blessings and be glad she's still alive."

"And you?" I asked. "What do you think?"

Heath considered for a long moment. "I think Margaret thought Horace was dead."

As opening day neared, Hamilton rarely slept, consumed with overseeing every detail of the new Klieg's. But I could see that his heart was really not in it. He was completely stunned by his brother's death, not to mention Horace's fate and Margaret's retreat into catatonia. It was only Annette's boundless enthusiasm that kept him from sinking into a severe depression. Both she and Heath were beside him throughout much of each day. They learned every aspect of the business, from how to hammer a sidewall peg properly, to the installation of a new horse on a merry-go-round.

In late May, The Maggots released the first single from their new album. It quickly soared to the top of the charts. Shot at Klieg's the previous December, the accompanying video heightened interest in our world. Klieg's reopened, to much fanfare and an impressive gate, the first Saturday in June. Construction of the Karnival Museum was complete, but only five of its twelve rooms were accessible for viewing. Danny lingered outside the building, flushed with pride, as the entrance queue snaked into the midway.

That night, the gates and awnings locked, all but the midway's streetlights dim, we were exhilarated. We were proud to have kept Arthur's dream alive, but my heart ached for Hamilton. His eyes no longer sparkled when he looked out over the Karnival.

The summer went rapidly, and the gate further swelled. Queues formed hours before we opened each morning, and security swept the lot to clear stragglers each night.

I continued to make appearances on local television programmes – generally talk shows but, on several delightful occasions, game shows as well. My customers at Klieg's soon found it necessary to book appointments weeks in advance.

Annette requested I train her in the art of reading Tarot. She was a quick study, and her confidence with the cards grew much more swiftly than my own had under Madame Olga's tutelage. That autumn, she began to give readings from her own lantern-lit, curtained cubicle in the sideshow.

Horace was blessed with incredible determination, the best therapists, and the latest equipment. Nearly ten months after the accident, he had healed sufficiently and was released from the hospital. He took a room in the housing quarters, working with a tutor to complete his education, and continuing his physical rehabilitation in the gymnasium. Only now and then would he visit his parents, talking to his mother as she lay silent and still in her bed. Soon he no longer attempted to connect with Frank, who was all but consumed by grief and shock.

Over time – and with Horace returned to us more or less intact – the sparkle slowly returned to Hamilton's eyes. He focused on reviewing the numerous applications for employment. Our troupe was expanded to feature: two magicians, Lady Mysteria, who specialized in levitations and transformations, and The Brain, whose mind-reading act quickly became legendary; the "Alligator Triplets," afflicted by a condition that gave their skin a scale-like appearance, which they supplemented with green and brown body makeup and yellow contact lenses; a professional stunt diver, who risked her life in a ring constructed behind the giant freak tent; the ever-popular Carposi brothers, the largest of whom received standing-ovations when he juggled the three elder; and a man who professed to be centuries old, who guessed ages and weights for a dollar. Hamilton toured the lot and watched the performers with notepad in hand, and either Heath or Annette always at his side.

Annette bloomed at Klieg's, gaining self-assurance in her role as our daughter. She and Danny, like giddy children set free in a toy store, proceeded to invest millions of dollars in improvements to the Karnival. She encouraged Hamilton to evaluate and give his opinions on every plan and blueprint. In three short years, the freak tent was replaced with one twice its size, and the midway grew to include two double Ferris wheels, three haunted houses, five roller coasters in addition to Goliath, seven differently themed merry-go-rounds, and eighty-two other rides of all kinds. Games of chance and skill numbered in the hundreds, and food concessions of every description scented the lot with rich aromas. Without question, Annette and Danny's finest achievement was Kids Karnival, in size and scope a one-quarter-scale replica of the Klieg's Midway. Here, regardless of skill or chance, every game the children played won them a prize.

With Frank's permission, we arranged to continue the printing and distribution of Margaret's books. They would remain well-loved for years to come. Clifford Press books were stocked in all the Karnival gift shops, and customers frequently purchased the complete boxed set.

Nearly always at his wife's side, Frank soon lost all concern for life outside the housing quarters. He never got used to the constant changes that greeted him on those rare days he ventured onto the lot. Often he stood at one of the windows, ignoring the swarm of activity outside, feeding breadcrumbs to the chirping birds on the windowsill. From the dining rooms, Heath brought him bread for the birds and, most nights, Heath and Frank played cards at a table in a corner of the suite, either Fish, Old Maid, or Crazy Eights, which was Heath's favourite. As Frank held his cards, his eyes repeatedly strayed to Margaret's bed, and Heath would wait patiently for his father to remember the game.

Heath spent his days attending a local school. As had been the case in the lovely suburb of Niagara Falls, his fellow students held little interest for him. They all knew who he was, and sought his friendship in the hopes of obtaining free Karnival passes. But he declined invitations to join them for lunch, or for after school cig-arettes, or trips to the mall. His teachers, impressed with his matu-rity, diligence, and aptitude for learning, were disappointed that he failed to enroll for extra-curricular activities. Perhaps we should have encouraged Heath in such pursuits, but the boy's heart belonged to Klieg's. Whenever he could, he would be on the lot, assisting and learning from Hamilton.

When Frank on occasion left the suite, Heath would sit beside Margaret. Dog would sit at his feet as Heath held Margaret's hand and read aloud her books. There were fifty-seven books in all. He had finished nineteen of them by the time he turned twelve. That was the year we purchased the huge hot air balloons. The balloons floated on either side of the Karnival entrance – one's gondola blue, the other one's yellow – and offered aerial tours of the lot.

Heath read Margaret's books in the order in which she had written them. Eventually, he came to the one he had read to her so many nights before: A Dog's Tale. This he read slowly, his voice breaking. Heath was fifteen that night. As he shut the book, he felt a shift in his soul.

It was late when Heath left the housing quarters. The Karnival was closed, and night creatures patrolled the darkened midway, casting restless shadows in the moonlight. Faintly, drifting from the backyard, Heath could hear music and voices, a radio broadcast. He turned, striding away from the sounds.

He did not know what he was feeling. The book had taken him back to those first days with the Cliffords. With those memories also came an inexplicable anger.

In his years with the Children's Aid Society, Heath had often wondered why he had been abandoned, but he reconciled himself to never knowing. He came to believe he would remain at the home until he was of age, going out into the world a man with no ties. "People only want babies," the children said, but Margaret and

Frank were waiting for him when he was led into the office one day. He was certain that they would turn to the worker and shake their heads. But they smiled and told him how handsome he was, and how they hoped he soon would meet their son, Horace. Margaret, Frank, and Heath spent that first day together, then another, and a third. On the fourth visit Heath was introduced to Horace, and the two boys liked each other immediately. Heath could hardly believe it was happening when the workers told him to pack his things. All the children stared as he walked to the door with his suitcase, but, as proud as he was to be wanted at last, he did not feel the sense of triumph the children expected. What he felt was a palpable need to know why.

He did not know why he had been abandoned. He had to know why he was wanted. For months he watched Margaret, uncertain how to ask her, hoping an answer would show on her face as she flipped pancakes, oiled her printing press, or kissed him goodnight. But no answer ever came. All he knew was that Margaret, thinking that Horace was dead, had chosen to sleep rather than go on with Heath as her only son.

The edging on the midway caught Heath's foot, and he stumbled. When he looked up, he was surprised to see that he was standing before Kids Karnival. The tall double gates were unlocked and ajar, a shaft of light slicing into the midway. The twelve-foot, carved wooden clowns, which served as gateposts, held their arms invitingly, forever ushering children within. But their faces were shadowed, their eyes empty holes, and Heath looked away.

Then he heard voices coming from inside Kids Karnival. He crept closer to the gates. He could hear whispers and giggles, kissing sounds and a zipper.

"My parents will kill me," a girl said, and she giggled.

"I thought you sneaked out." The boy's voice was familiar.

"Well, I did, but – Geez, they weren't kidding. I've never seen one so big."

The boy laughed. It was Horace. Heath listened, but all he could hear then was the rustling of clothing, slurping sounds, and Horace moaning. After several minutes of this, Horace grunted, repeatedly and loudly, and the girl coughed, deep in her throat.

"Oh my God," the girl said, coughing.

Horace laughed.

What are they doing? Heath wondered, thinking that he knew. He heard the girl giggle again, saying, "As good as that slutty tramp Lily-Jean?"

The gates swung open, and Heath scurried behind a gatepost. His fingers clutched the clown's billowed pants. Silhouetted, Horace and the girl stepped onto the midway. The girl waited, arms crossed over her breasts, as Horace closed and locked the gates.

"I better get back," the girl said. She spread her arms to kiss him, a hand reaching down between Horace's legs. "Tomorrow?" she asked.

"I don't know," Horace said. "You better go."

With a parting kiss, the girl turned and, wood chips flying from beneath her feet, sprinted down the midway toward the backyard.

Heath leaned out to see who she was, lost his grip on the gatepost, and stumbled to reveal himself in the moonlight.

Horace glared at him, then flashed a sly grin. "Spying?" After nearly two years of intensive rehabilitation, Horace had continued to work his body in the housing quarters gymnasium. At seventeen, he was six-foot-two, handsome and nearly as sculpted as Strongman Hank at his peak. Periodically, he visited his mother, telling her the events of his life as he had when he was a child. On rare occasions, he would remain to join Heath and Frank for one of their then nightly card games. This night, he had not visited his family, but had several liaisons on the dark Karnival grounds. Manhood had endowed him with an enormous penis, which was the subject of much gossip – and a source of great delight – on the lot. Horace enjoyed his pick of lovers, though few ever suspected the sheer volume of his encounters. "What are you doing out here, Heath?"

"Nothing," Heath said. "What are you doing out here?"

"Nothing." Horace dug a package of cigarettes from his pocket.

"You were with that girl," Heath said.

Horace looked at him over the flame of a match. "So what? It's nothing you need to worry about."

"Who is she?"

"A gentleman should never kiss and tell. Remember that, Heath." Horace took a drag on the cigarette.

"You're with a lot of people," Heath said.

"Don't worry about it," Horace said.

"There's things you can catch," Heath said. "Girls can get pregnant, you know."

"Not doing that, they can't." Horace released a puff of smoke. "Really, Heath, don't worry about this stuff. Some day someone's going to come along and you're going to figure all this out."

Heath followed as Horace began to stroll toward the backyard. Heath's mind was full of questions, but he did not know how to phrase them, and he doubted that Horace would answer.

"So what were you doing out here, really?" Horace said.

"Walking. I was reading to Margaret."

"Thinking?"

"Yeah."

"Hoping?"

Heath was silent.

"She's never going to wake up, you know. She's going to lie there sleeping until she dies, and Dad's going to sit beside her feeding those birds –"

"Stop it," Heath said.

"Well, it's true and you may as well know it. Look, Heath. I love them – just as much as you do, if not more – but you've got to face it."

"You don't know," Heath said.

Horace sighed. "I just don't want you spending your life thinking something's going to happen when it isn't. If you spend all your time on the Karnival and Mom and Dad, then you're never going to have any fun."

"Fun like you do?"

Horace turned to him. "No ... Not like me."

"Why not?"

"Because you're different."

"What's that supposed to mean?"

"Not everybody wants the same thing," Horace said. "Some people are meant to fall in love and some people aren't. Some people could never fall in love even if they wanted to, and some people fall so much in love they lose themselves."

"Like Frank," Heath said.

Horace took a final drag and dropped his cigarette onto the midway, grinding it into the dirt under the wood chips with his foot. "Look, Heath. If you want to watch workers build rides all day and sit there playing cards with Dad night after night and reading to Mom, then fine. But sooner or later you're going to realize you're not doing any living."

Despite – or perhaps, because of – his brother's words that night, Heath began to take even more of an interest in the Karnival. As Hamilton's hearing and agility had declined with age, Heath started training with the dogs. He assisted in the office, taking over the counting of the gate, and then the monthly bookkeeping. He assumed more of Hamilton's duties as time went on; thus, when Shay arrived at Klieg's the following year, Heath was the one to interview her.

Taking a vacation from their small forgotten village in Alberta, Louise Markham and Aggie North also came to the Karnival that year, though they would not stay on. They had no idea that the kind young man who helped Aggie free her heel from a grating was the same boy who had been found with Mollie Wayne so long before. The women watched him stride away. Smiling at each other, they noted that there were not many such kind men in the world, the reason each gave for not having married. Pointedly avoiding Kids Karnival, as well as the various midway grab joints, Louise and Aggie enjoyed an informative stroll through the Karnival Museum. Leaving the freak tent – which they would not have entered at all had Tim-Tina still been inside – they shook their heads sadly, and Louise remarked on the cruelties of nature.

"There weren't that many real freaks," Aggie pointed out. "Perhaps God is getting better at this."

Shay had never forgotten Heath. He had been her only childhood friend. It was she he was hurrying to meet that day when he freed Aggie's heel. The moment Heath had rescued her kitten from the tree, Shay had begun to fall in love with him. She was crushed when she saw the "For Sale" sign hammered into the Clifford's front lawn, but she refused to believe that Heath could ever forget her. Over the intervening years, Shay had collected articles and photographs of Klieg's, much as Annette had done, vowing that one day she would find Heath.

With this in mind, she accelerated her schooling, and applied to an art college in Vancouver that she was certain would accept her. She had no intention of attending, but she knew that her parents would never allow her to leave home to live at Klieg's, and she could not bear to wait another year. Only weeks after the letter of acceptance arrived, with her mother and father's unwitting blessings and her brother's undying envy, she was on a bus headed west to Klieg's.

When Heath entered the office-trailer where she waited, suitcase set carefully on the floor beside her, Shay was struck by his businesslike manner. He's only sixteen! she thought. She had expected his father, but Heath was shaking her hand. He sat behind the desk, to all appearances a man in his early twenties, confident and self-contained. He was so handsome she wanted to throw herself into his arms.

"It's a pleasure to meet you, Miss Garrett," he said.

"It was," she corrected him. "The most important day of my life. Well – until today, that is."

He was confused. "I beg your pardon?"

Shay could not contain herself, and burst into helpless laughter. Of course he did not recognize her! With determination and exercise, she had grown into the extra weight. She had become a shapely young woman. "It's me," she said. "Gargantuan Garrett."

"Not gargantuan anymore, you're – wow!"

She was relieved at the look of pleasure on his face. "You, too," she said.

"I can't believe it! So you want to work here? You can't be the fat lady, that's for sure!"

Heath brought her to meet me. As I looked into her eyes, I saw the joy they would bring to each other. "My daughter, Annette, will be quite pleased," I told her.

"Why's that?" Heath asked.

"Annette saw this young woman in the Tarot. A raven-haired maiden in search of her destiny."

"Close enough," Shay said with a laugh. "What I'm really in search of right now is a job." She had brought her portfolio of artwork, and asked if we would hire her to repaint the giant freak tent's banners.

"Of course!" Heath said. "Uncle Ham's been wanting to do that for months, and you just kept saying –"

"It wasn't time," I said, and Shay returned my smile. "But now we have the right talent to accomplish the job."

Shay chose to live in a trailer in the backyard of the lot. She immediately set to work designing new banners for the freak tent. Her drawings, which she brought for our review, were stunning in their concept and execution. But it was obvious, due to the complexity of the designs, that the task was too much for one person. As the Amazing Armless Artist had retired shortly after Arthur's death, we hired a team of six professional painters that Shay oversaw in the completion of the work.

Though he never neglected his duties, Heath spent hours in the yard, watching Shay supervise the painting of the freak tent. He brought cool drinks for the painters and fresh fruit for Shay, which he shared with her in the shade of the canvas as they laughed at each other's stories and spoke in whispers.

"You've got it bad for her, don't you?" Horace asked Heath one day. At Heath's urging, Horace had become Karnival Strongman several months before Shay arrived. Already hugely popular, Horace performed near the stunt diver's platform behind the giant freak tent, wearing a loincloth that hid little of his incredible physique; thus, he was often witness to the growing romance.

"What do you mean?" Heath said.

"Shay," Horace said. "You're falling in love with her."

Heath looked from Horace to the canvas where Shay was working, and then back to Horace again. He looked at the ground.

"You're unbelievable!" Horace said. "How could someone be so in love and not even know it?"

Heath thought about Horace's words, wondering if what he felt for Shay was love. At night, alone in his tent, Heath fantasized about her, as frightened as he was warm with happiness.

The painting of the giant freak tent stretched on for months. The results were magnificent, and the painters themselves became an attraction. Crowds gathered in the yard and on the midway, buzzing with admiration. As foreman, Shay was as quick to praise as she was to point out a flaw in workmanship. Often she would take up a brush to complete what she felt had not been done to perfection.

One afternoon, Shay climbed a scaffold to touch up the eyes on Lady Mysteria's twelve-foot likeness. A tremor shook the region. Rides groaned, prizes collided, and tents swayed. Customers held each other, babbling and shouting, and those on the midway and in the yards planted their feet wide. The scaffold shifted to one side, and Shay tumbled to the earth, striking her head hard on the ground. Though a few people entered into hysterics, no one else was physically injured. The rides, concessions, and tents suffered no structural damage. On-site medical personnel took Shay to the housing quarters, where she lay unconscious for hours. Heath was terrified, weeping beside her bed, until she opened her eyes just after sunset.

"What's wrong with you?" she asked. Her head pounded.

"I didn't think you were going to wake up," Heath said. He took her hand, and he told her all that was in his heart, how he could not bear it if he were to lose her. "I love you," he said. "I've loved you forever."

Shay returned his kisses. Thereafter, the two were virtually inseparable.

Shay was soon supervising the completion of the banners. Much as Arthur had been with Anna, Heath kept Shay nearly always within his sight, and he had to restrain himself the first time he saw her climbing a scaffold. They sneaked away after dinner at night to kiss and make love under the stars.

Heath no longer slept beneath his bed. Hamilton was the first to notice. He stopped by Heath's tent with papers that required Heath's attention, got no answer to his call and, entering, caught sight of Heath asleep on the bed. For a moment he could not see why it struck him as odd. Then he recalled that Heath always slept on the floor of the tent, the bed above him, blankets hanging down to shield him from view.

Hamilton told Annette and me of this, and I knew it was a sign. "It is almost time," I said.

Annette leaned forward across my table. "What is it you see?"

"I am sorry," I told her. "If you have not seen, it is not for you to know."

Annette reached for a cigarette and lifted a lighter with shaking hands. "The cards speak of a mother, a sister. Heath's?"

"Annette. When you are older, you will learn that to wait is sometimes the very best action. There are things we must never question, motives we must never ask to know. What you feel coming is a change, a renewal, the number thirteen card of Tarot. A tearing down of old decaying walls and the rebuilding of new. That is what you are feeling, what you must not fear. Our world is a turning of cycle within cycle, wheel within wheel. Each event is significant, each person, each word, each action – all are but spokes of the wheel, each necessary, each bringing us toward completion only to start anew. Each is a miracle, a blessing. When we are faced with a choice, we must choose with great care. But we need not fear what The Fates have put into motion."

"But I want to see. I want to know!"

"As do I, child. As do I. But I have come to realize, as you one day must, that we are not meant to see all things. We can see landmarks, what we recognize as intersections along our path, and these we must embrace with all our being. We must trust ourselves to be ready, to see clearly which action is required and be prepared to take that action. That is the most for which you can ask, the most you can do. I lost my eye because I could not accept my

inability to see more. Had I gotten what I wanted – had I seen ..."
I shrugged and forced a smile. "A mother. A sister. Do not try to
know why they are coming and what they will bring. See them –
recognize them – and when their events overtake you, be ready. Be
prepared to act in the way most appropriate. Trust in yourself to
survive. You are meant to survive."

Annette ground out the cigarette. "I'm frightened."

"You are not. You would like to be, but you are not."

"Madame –"

"Enough." I held up my hand and Annette fell silent. "You will
not be frightened. Now. Go on, you have customers waiting."

I reached for Hamilton and together we watched as she left us.
I felt a great sympathy, for I knew she was lonely and it was not
easy for her to believe in her self outside her cubicle. To her mind,
she was frightened, but what she was feeling would more accurately be described as a lack of self-confidence. Due to her *knowing*, she was aware that The Fates were restless to see the results
of their handiwork; however, as she was unable to perceive what
would thus occur, she assumed that she would fail in whatever the
situation demanded. Just as she was lonely because she refused to
trust the motives of others, she lacked confidence because she
refused to trust in her self.

I never wanted to make life more difficult for Annette. I wanted her to grow strong, to find the belief in her own power within
her self. I knew that for her to survive she would have to confront
The Fates on her own.

As we were building a new home for Klieg's, Nola and Ralph
were enjoying a serene life with their daughter, Chloe.

Ralph had retired from hauling cartage. He sold the transport
truck, and purchased forty acres of farm, half of which was planted with pines destined to be Christmas trees. The farm was nestled
within the boundaries of woods, enclosed on three sides by vast
Crown lands. A stream from which they fished crayfish and trout
cut through the west acreage, deepening and running shallow as it
meandered through its course. One tiny road wound down and

around hills and eventually joined the remote highway that led under a covered bridge and into town. The farmhouse was tall and had once been white, its paint having yellowed over the years. There was a loft bedroom for Nola and Ralph, and an oddly placed room off the kitchen, which Chloe chose as her own.

Ralph acquired an array of books, covering everything from building and maintaining fences to smoking meat and canning vegetables. The first year, they fed chickens and pigs and milked a cow, but Chloe refused to take the eggs, and she could not bear to see the animals slaughtered. Ralph sold all the livestock the following summer and, thereafter, whatever animal products the family needed were purchased. Once a week, Ralph made a shopping trip into town. He brought the bulbs they planted, the seedlings and twine and stakes and loam, and the three of them set up preserves, and tended the flower and vegetable gardens.

Among the books that Ralph acquired was a volume on sign language. After dinner, in the kitchen at night, Chloe learned to speak with her hands. Nola and Ralph flipped through the pages of the book, deciphering their daughter's sentences.

The Greesons were happy in the home they built. For more than six years they enjoyed the peace of the wilderness, with no cruel laughter, no taunts, no judgments.

But then, about the time that Shay was shaken from the scaffold at Klieg's, Nola and Ralph were tormented when Chloe disappeared. Chloe often wandered the fields and woods, for she was fond of the various scents of root-growing things. One day she did not return before sunset, as was her custom.

Nola was frightened. "She's been gone too long, Ralph."

"She'll be fine, Nola." Ralph looked at his watch. It had been little more than three hours, not a long time for Chloe to be off in the fields and woods.

"But I'm worried about her," Nola said. She paced and wrung her hands. "What if she wanders into town? She can't speak, she can't scream if someone tries to hurt her."

"She's not in town, Nola," Ralph said. "It would take her days to walk there."

"Please, Ralph. Please let's go look for her."

"Nola." He pulled her to him, kissing her brow. But she was rigid with fear, and at last he began to share her concern. "All right. We'll go. But when we find her at the stream, remember I told you so."

But Chloe was not at the stream. She was not in the barn or the fields. Nola wanted to search the Crown lands, but Ralph would not let her. "You'll get lost in the dark," he said. "She'll come home while you're wandering and she'll start worrying about you. Let's go back to the house."

Chloe was not at the house, would not be in fact for three full days. Terrified of what people might say if they ever saw her daughter, Nola refused to allow Ralph to call in help. He went out each day in search of Chloe as Nola, frustrated that there was nothing she could do, paced the house, resisting sleep.

Just as they were certain they had no choice but to contact authorities, Chloe came home.

"Chloe!" Ralph said. He ran to kiss her and hold her close.

Nola was tight with anger, which had quickly replaced a brief flush of relief. She clenched her hands at her sides. "Where have you been all this time?" she demanded.

Chloe signed, Walking.

"Don't give me that," Nola said. "It's been three whole days! Walking where?"

Fields, Chloe signed. Woods.

"Did you see anyone?"

Chloe ignored her, hugging Ralph.

Nola took a step forward. "Did you see anyone?! Did anyone – ?"

"Stop it, Nola," Ralph said. "It doesn't matter. She's home and she's safe – that's what's important."

"Don't you ever take off like that again," Nola said. "Do you hear me, Chloe? I couldn't stand it if something happened to you."

Sorry, Chloe signed.

Nola's anger dissolved. The girl was well. Nothing harmful had befallen her and she remained, as always, poised with self-assurance unexpected in a nine-year-old.

"Are you hungry?" Nola asked.

Chloe shook her head. She reached into her pocket, drew out and pressed a colourful crumpled paper into Ralph's hands.

"What's this?" Ralph asked. Carefully he smoothed out the paper. It revealed itself as a glossy brochure. The front cover read "Klieg's" in gold script over a photograph of one of the huge hot air balloons. The back cover featured images of the giant freak tent and the Karnival Museum, the monkey family of skilled musicians, and the dog totem pole, Hamilton and Heath standing on either side, hands upraised. Folded out, the inside of the brochure displayed a full aerial view of the lot.

"Wow," Ralph said.

"What is that?" Nola asked. She took the brochure, turning it over in her hands. "Where did you get this?"

Chloe shrugged and pointed at the brochure. We go, she signed.

Nola, trembling, handed the brochure back to Chloe. "It's an awful long way," she said.

Chloe shook her head and waved the brochure in Nola's face.

"But, baby love, it's on the west coast and –"

Chloe began to stomp around the kitchen, waving the brochure and shaking her head.

"I've read about this place," Ralph said, watching her. "It's supposed to be something."

"I don't want to go," Nola said.

"Why not?"

Nola just looked at him and then she turned away.

Chloe ceased her stomping and stood to one side of the kitchen, gazing at her parents.

"Why not?" Ralph asked again. "We haven't been anywhere in years. We could hop in the pickup and be there in a day or so."

"Hear that, Chloe?" Nola said tonelessly. "Daddy wants to take you to a carnival."

Ralph studied Nola. "Why don't you want to go?"

"It's just – such a long way to go to see something like that."

"Something like what? It's a big amusement park designed like a carnival. It'll be fun," he said. "Trust me."

"Don't you think this is just a little bit creepy?" Nola asked. "She disappears for three solid days and then comes home with that!"

"It's a brochure for a famous place. There must be millions of these all over the world."

"What's it doing out here?"

"Who knows? Maybe someone threw it out of their car. You know what people are like – she probably picked it up in the middle of the woods."

"Then why does it look brand new?!"

"Brand new? It's –"

"So it's a little bit crumpled up," Nola said.

Ralph took a deep breath. "I don't know," he said. "What difference does it make?"

"Because it's creepy, that's what difference it makes! Her coming home with that thing in the middle of nowhere and now she wants to go? And you want to take her?"

"Well, why not? Why shouldn't we take her? My God, Nola, the girl can't just stay locked up here forever. Sooner or later, she's going to have to go out into the world and –"

"Over my dead body!" Nola shouted.

"What is wrong with you?"

"I don't want to go!"

"This isn't about you, Nola."

His tone was one she had never heard before. She stared at him, unable to speak.

"This is about our daughter. And the only thing she's ever asked for in her life."

Nola turned away from her husband. "I'm scared, Ralph. The way people will look at her. The way people always look at her. Please, Ralph, please – I don't want to go. We'll stay here like we always have, we'll be happy. Haven't we always been happy here?"

"Nola, I –"

"Please, Ralph, she'll be hurt, she'll be –"

"No one's going to hurt her," Ralph said. "She'll be fine. We'll all be fine."

"No." She was seized with an intense foreboding. "No."

"Honey – she's going to have to go out in the world some time. There's no way getting around that. Now we agreed when she was born that she'd been born to a purpose. And we didn't listen to the doctors, we listened to our hearts. We never said it'd be easy, but we promised each other ... Now she wants to go to this place. And we've got to take her, Nola. You know – we've got to take her."

"But what if –"

"What if we don't?" Ralph said. "You know like I do she'll just start walking and get there without us. Look at her – she's determined to go! I don't know, maybe this is it, maybe this is why ..."

Nola shut her eyes, terrified. "I love you, Ralph," she said. "But I –"

"We'll go as soon as I finish the south fence," Ralph said. He returned to his chair, and Chloe climbed into his lap.

That night, Annette began to dream about Chloe. A few hours after midnight, Annette awoke from a nightmare, which vanished from her consciousness the moment she attempted to recall its details. All she could remember was a nameless little girl who possessed three arms.

Sitting up in bed, Annette listened to the darkness around her. Aside from the night creatures, the Karnival lot was quiet. In the cool blue shadows of her tent, Annette climbed out of bed and slipped into her jeans, pulling a tee shirt over her head.

Annette enjoyed walking in these hours of restlessness. She would circle the lot, touching the different concessions and rides, roaming the darkened freak tent, admiring the Karnival Museum, and gazing at the housing quarters. Often she would climb into the gondola of one of the huge hot air balloons and lie there, looking out at the stars. At times she would see an airplane, lights flashing as it flew soundlessly through the sky. She would think of explosions and plane crashes, and a long dead set of parents failed by inept bodyguards.

Leaving her tent, Annette crossed the backyard and entered the midway. She was on her way to the balloons at the front gates when she came upon the conjoined twins passing a joint between them. Spotting her, they smiled and waved, calling her over. She hesitated briefly before she approached, accepted the joint, and took a long drag. "Thank you," she said. "This tastes wonderful."

"Our pleasure," Peg said. "Finish it, and we'll light another." And she did so, passing it to her sister, Polly.

"Have a seat," Polly said.

Annette lowered herself onto a bundle of straw, sitting cross-legged across from the twins.

"I wasn't aware that you smoked," Peg said.

"I haven't for years," Annette admitted. "But I've been ... edgy lately."

"So we've noticed," Polly said. "You've always kept so much to yourself it's no wonder you get stir crazy."

Annette looked away. "I've been less than polite with you, I know."

"What's done is done," Peg said.

"I never meant anything by it," Annette said. She was suddenly and intensely high.

"In what way?" Polly asked.

"I mean – it wasn't your – I – Peg –"

"Because we're freaks," Peg said, smiling. "You haven't avoided us because we're freaks."

"Yes," Annette said. "I just avoid everyone. Except my family, of course."

"It must be terribly lonely for you," Peg said. "I must admit I have no concept of the feeling. I've always got Polly with me and I always will have. I can't imagine how it must be to exist alone."

Annette felt an empty hollow form in the pit of her stomach. "There are worse things," she said.

"You're that afraid to be hurt?" Polly whispered.

Annette could not speak. Abruptly she stood, but the quickness of her actions caused her head to swim. She shut her eyes. Polly and Peg caught her as she fell, setting her gently into the straw. After a moment she opened her eyes to look at them. They are so pretty, Annette thought, and kind ... She could hear her own voice, talking on and on as the twins listened silently, her voice breaking, the twins holding her and smoothing her hair.

Idly, as though her mind no longer controlled her mouth, she wondered what she was saying. After some time she at last was quiet. As the twins bent down to kiss her, she lifted her arms in welcome, and was swept into what felt to be an exquisite, slow motion dance ...

*   *   *

Polly and Peg had joined Klieg's in late summer of our nineteenth season, during our stand in New Orleans. They were lovely girls – both physically and spiritually – having been born to a woman of exceptional grace and character.

Robin Tanner was never referred to as pretty. Not as a child, pampered and loved by her mother and father in a cottage on the shores of Lake Pontchartrain. Not as a teenage girl, devoid of romance. Not as a young woman, watching her parents' lifeless bodies washed ashore following an unexpected squall. Her parents had endowed her with a strong sense of self-respect and industry. After their deaths, Robin sold the cottage on Lake Pontchartrain, and purchased a Bed and Breakfast in the French Quarter. There, on occasion, her exceptional grace and character attracted the attentions of male guests. One Mardi Gras, Robin enjoyed several nights of passion with a young Bible salesman from San Francisco. In due course, she gave birth to her daughters.

The twins were properly plump and healthy, though attached at the lower torso and buttocks. Only briefly did Robin consider having her daughters separated. Upon being told that there might be complications both during and resulting from any surgical procedure, Robin tore the consent form in two. She instructed the nurse to prepare her daughters for the short trip home.

Polly and Peg were easy-going babies, content to amuse each other as they lay in their crib. They explored with fascination the toys in the playpen in a corner of the kitchen. As they grew, Robin tutored them at home. She taught them geography and history, English and mathematics, using the books she had brought from the cottage's library shelves. When the twins exhibited an interest in music, Robin rented a piano for the parlour. While she played, the girls would dance late into morning, graceful as butterflies.

Over time, the twins began to assist in the preparation of meals and rooms. They moved quickly through the doorways and hallways with rags and brooms, buckets and scrub brushes. They chopped and stirred and sautéed and baked as if of a single mind. They were perfectly and naturally adapted to each other. Guests often had to take a second look to see that the girls were indeed attached, and not simply huddled to giggle and whisper, as some young people do.

"Why are we together like this?" the twins asked their mother one day.

Robin smiled and put a hand under each of their chins, turning up their faces to look into their eyes. "Because you're special," she said. "So special, that God never wants either of you to ever be without someone to love you."

When the twins were in their early teens, Robin suffered a stroke. Her insurance covered only part of her care. She had no choice but to return the piano, and take a second mortgage on the Bed and Breakfast. A little over a year later, she passed from a subsequent stroke. Polly and Peg – then but fourteen – were consigned to an orphanage. The Bed and Breakfast was sold to pay the hospital and funeral bills.

Life in the orphanage was not kind, and was even harsher to the conjoined twins. The children teased Polly and Peg incessantly throughout their stay, most particularly on the subject of private bodily functions. One night, much as Tim-Tina had done so many years before, the twins sneaked from the building, down back streets, and through lawns and gardens and fields, and onto the Karnival lot.

Hamilton found them the next morning, asleep on the floor of a cubicle in the freak tent. "Well, now," he said. "What are you two doing there?"

With measured tones, and no trace of self-pity, they told their story. "And so we came here," Polly said in summation.

Hamilton brought them to the cook tent for breakfast. They joined me at a table in the sun, and Hamilton briefly outlined their situation.

"What are you intending to do?" I asked him.

"Well ..." Hamilton said.

"But how can we hope to get away with such a thing? They're certain to be questioned at the border – and what about passports or birth certificates?"

"I have an idea," Hamilton said. "You three get acquainted and I'll be right back." Hamilton hurried from the cook tent and I turned my attention to the twins.

They regarded me with innocent candor. "Your husband's really nice," Polly said, and Peg said, "They won't even care that we're gone."

"Please understand," I said. "It is not that I don't want to help you."

"Mama said rules are made to be broken," Polly said, and Peg said, "We have nowhere else to go."

Hamilton returned within minutes, grinning broadly and carrying a large manila envelope. "We're all set," he said. He handed me the envelope and turned to the twins. "Your names – if they ask you – are Chris and Toby Millar."

Without looking, I knew what the envelope must contain: birth certificates that once belonged to the "Siamese" twin boys crushed to death by Tiny.

"But their ages," I said. "And their sex! No one will ever believe that these girls are men in their thirties."

"With the right makeup and clothes they will. Besides – we're talking about border guards confronted by a caravan of freaks. They'll be gawking, not thinking."

Of course, Hamilton was absolutely right. The twins were allowed entrance into Canada and they easily adapted to life at Klieg's. Content unto themselves, they did not court friendships as they assisted in the cook tent. Soon they began to pester Hamilton until he permitted them to join the sideshows. On the main stage in the freak tent, the monkey family played accompaniment as the twins danced. Patrons – who at first whispered and gazed with pity – found themselves awed by the grace and elegance of the twins. Without exception, each performance earned a standing ovation.

Initially, I felt that I needed to mother them, but I quickly learned that such was not the case. They were well-educated girls, mature beyond their years. Robin had imbued them with a great sense of respect for life and self. Though they loved and missed their mother, they would always have each other, and the serene knowledge that they would never be alone. As the seasons passed, the girls grew into fine women, popular with patrons and troupers alike. They were frequently approached romantically – more often by the curious than the sincere – yet they spurned all advances, content unto themselves. I had always hoped that one day Polly and Peg would find love, though neither had ever given an indication of any such desire.

But on this night, so many years after they had come to Klieg's, as they held Annette and listened to her tortured words – words of which she was not consciously aware – their hearts opened to her.

*   *   *

No longer alone, Annette looked at the twins. The sun had risen. Something wonderful and indefinable united them. Polly and Peg smiled at her and she smiled back.

After a breakfast of wine and grapes and peaches, their conversation interspersed with laughter, Annette returned to her tent. She was startled to see Danny lounging on her bed, flipping through the pages of a magazine.

"Well, good morning! Quite an evening, I'd say."

Annette laughed. "Would you?"

"I can see it. You're positively glowing! Stand in front of the mirror and get a load of that aura. It's breathtaking!" He moved to her side and pulled her toward the mirror over the bureau.

"Danny!"

He let her go, smiling at her. "Aren't you going to tell me what happened?"

"I don't know." She was certain he would make a joke about the relationship. She moved past him to brush her hair in the mirror.

"See what I mean?"

She jumped as his reflection appeared beside her own. "I wasn't even looking at it," she said. She turned, setting down her hairbrush.

He caught her around the waist. "Tell me."

"You'll laugh."

"No, I won't," he said. "I promise."

"I know you, Danny, you'll laugh."

"Cross my heart." He rocked her back and forth. "I promise. And I promise I won't tell a soul."

"The twins."

For a moment it did not register. And then his eyes showed recognition. "Polly and Peg?"

"Polly and Peg," she said. "I knew you'd laugh."

"I'm not laughing," he said. "I think it's great."

Danny himself had fallen in love, and he took this opportunity to tell her. He and the Sword-and-Fire Swallower, Fritz, had been lovers for more than a year, meeting clandestinely in the night, few words ever spoken between them.

"Oh my God," Annette said.

"What?"

"I was just thinking. You and Fritz, me and the twins. What're the odds?"

"Maybe Mom and Dad did so many drugs it screwed up all their chromosomes." Danny chuckled bitterly at his own attempt to joke.

"That's hideous," Annette said.

"What? Why?"

"I'm not buying into the idea there's something wrong with me. And if you want to be happy, you won't either."

"Easier said than done," Danny sighed.

Truth told, Danny had not wanted to fall in love with Fritz. He had not wanted to fall in love with anyone after Malcolm, least of all another man. They had met in the dark. Without a word, Fritz drew Danny into his tent and Danny abandoned himself; no part of him spared Fritz's need. Afterward, Fritz hurried him from the tent, and Danny was certain he had done something wrong. The next day in the yard, Fritz pointedly turned his back when Danny approached. For days, Danny tortured himself, thinking of Malcolm, damning himself for ever imagining that Fritz could love him. Danny watched Fritz from a distance, and hated himself for wanting him.

But then Fritz stopped him again near his tent. He pulled Danny into his arms, tugging at his clothes before they were inside. When Fritz took him that night, Danny felt that his fears had been groundless. He believed he belonged irrevocably to the man above him.

For over a year Danny spent his nights on the lot, hovering near Fritz's tent, waiting for the look that would draw him within. Feeling an unusual confidence after his conversation with Annette, he mentioned to Fritz her relationship with the twins, jokingly estimating the odds.

Fritz's face reddened. "You told her?"

"Why not?"

"I told you to keep your fucking mouth shut."

"What difference does it make? She's my sister. So she knows we're in love, big deal."

"Love!" Fritz laughed. "You don't get it, do you? You're a hole, kid, only a little better than my hand!"

Early the next morning, Shay found Danny in the shadow of the giant freak tent, one of his wrists slashed, the ground stained with blood. Annette was convinced we would lose him. Shay stayed with her, keeping vigil at his bedside in the housing quarters.

"I can't even die right," Danny said once he awakened and saw his sister beside him. "Why didn't you let me go?"

Shay slipped from the room as Annette reached out to hold her brother.

"Don't," Annette said. "Please don't."

"Don't you see, Annette? This world isn't meant for me. This fucked up world and I'm the one who doesn't belong, who shouldn't exist! Can't you see that? Even Fritz believes that!"

"I'm sure that isn't true."

"Of course it's true. He was horrified, Annette. Horrified. No one's supposed to know." He shook his head, hearing Malcolm's laughter – Fritz's laughter – ringing in his ears. "I don't even belong here. You should have heard the things I said about Madame and Ham when you moved them into the house. Pygmies – I called them pygmies."

"But you didn't know them then! You don't still feel that way."

"I don't know what I feel except awful. I thought – you know, I thought if Fritz and I could be in love – then it would be all right. It wouldn't be some sick, twisted –"

"It isn't!"

"Oh, but it is ... it is."

Annette stormed across the yard to confront Fritz, but the man was nowhere on the lot, having packed his things and left in the night.

Unable to direct her anger at Fritz, Annette made issue with my absence from the housing quarters during the time that Danny was in crisis. "You weren't there," she accused me.

"I prayed for your brother. And you did not need me."

"I did need you."

"I will not always be here for you, Annette. You must learn to stand on your own, to find the strength within your self. Others cannot provide that in any lasting manner. I cannot – neither can the twins."

Annette became quiet.

"I am most happy for you," I said. "It is good what you have found. But what you are truly seeking can only be found within your self."

"I know that," Annette said.

"Have you so soon forgotten what I told you?"

"I haven't forgotten," Annette said.

"Then prepare, child. Prepare ..."

Shortly after Danny recovered, Heath and Shay announced their engagement. Frank was devastated to learn the news, for he realized just how much time had passed. His sons – with little, if any, of his guidance – had become young men. Heath was no longer the disadvantaged boy that he and Margaret had taken into their home.

"So soon?" Frank asked.

Heath nodded.

"But you were hardly a child. I didn't ever get to –" Frank choked back a sob, his head falling beside Margaret's ever-still form. Sweeping over him was an overwhelming wave of failure and guilt.

"It's all right," Heath said, touching him. "It's all right."

"We had less than six months together and then your mother ... And I've been here. Here. I've failed you. I abandoned you, just like –" Frank wept, his hands ripping at the sheet, his head banging against the mattress and Margaret's hip. "I abandoned you!"

Heath knelt beside his father, holding him, aware that he too was weeping. Heath wept for the parents he had never known, the grandfather he had never met. He wept for Dog, whom he felt he had lost to Margaret, for Margaret and Frank and Horace and himself. He wept from exhaustion, from pain long suppressed.

Heath wept, most of all, for the childhood he had only briefly lived, the childhood he now wanted.

That night, Frank sat alone at a window of the suite, looking out at the darkened Karnival lot. It was nearly morning when he fell asleep with his head on the windowsill. He awoke to the frantic chirping of hungry birds, the afternoon sun warm on his face. As he opened his eyes, he saw, as if for the very first time, the swarming yard and midway of the Karnival stretching as far as his eyes could see. Realizing how much the world had passed him by as he stayed at Margaret's bedside, regretting all the years he had missed with his sons, Frank was determined not to continue in his failure.

"I've been wrong," Frank said to Margaret's still form. "I've been here and they've been alone. Margaret, they're not hardly boys anymore. They're all grown up and running things. It hasn't been fair to them, Margaret, I haven't been fair to them." He took her hand. "I've got to go outside now. Did you hear? Heath's getting married. He's marrying that pretty girl, Shay ... He's not our little boy anymore. I don't know that he ever was, really. Anyway, I wanted to tell you so you wouldn't be frightened alone here. Dog will be here. And I'll be home at night, just like coming home after a day at work." He kissed her lips, her cheeks, her eyes. "I love you, Margaret. And I'm going outside now."

At the doorway, Frank turned back to look at his wife. His hands were shaking as he reached for the doorknob and pulled open the door. The corridor was long and wide. Tile echoed his footsteps as he went slowly, a hand trailing on the wall beside him. Through the glass doors at the entrance, he looked out over the Karnival. There were so many people, rushing back and forth, calling to each other, going places, doing things ... Taking a deep breath, Frank pushed open the doors, wincing at the blast of hot air as he stepped into the sunlight.

His intention was to find the boys, or Hamilton. He was certain that they would have work for him. Frank hurried down the steps and across the yard, slipped through the fence and entered the midway. If he could remember correctly, the office-trailer was to the left. Frank headed in that direction, dodging the children, the couples, the teenagers. A boy with an elaborate purple hairstyle bumped into him, snarling.

"What ya doon, ya flake?" the boy hissed at him.

Frank pulled back, striking his heels on a baby stroller.

"Watch it, damn you!" the stroller's driver said.

"I'm – I'm sorry," Frank said. He watched as the boy, the baby stroller and mother, disappeared into the crowd. His heart pounded, and his hand clutched his chest. There were so many people! They were all around him, closing in, bodies touching him, mouths issuing deafening sounds, which hammered at his skull. He struggled to push his way through the crowd, his heart pounding, his head swimming. Tears clouded his vision ... Margaret, he thought, I must find Margaret. But the people ... There were so many people ...

Annette was with the twins when she felt the tug at her heart. She sat up and tamped out the joint. In her mind, she heard Heath's voice: "Take care of my father."

"What's wrong?" Polly asked.

"I don't know," Annette said. "Yes, I do." She buttoned her blouse.

"Is it your brother?" Polly asked.

Annette hunted a cigarette from the package on the bureau, lighting the wrong end before digging out another and getting it right. She took a deep drag on the cigarette, wishing she had not shared the joint.

"Annette?" Peg said.

"Frank," Annette said. In the polished silver of the lighter in her hand, she saw him. He was lost in the midst of the crowds. "I have to go."

When Annette found him, curled in a foetal position behind the dunking booth, Frank had soiled himself. Annette pulled him into her arms.

"I couldn't find him," Frank said. "I looked, I tried. But the people ... so many people ..."

Annette rocked him. "It's all right," she said. "It's all right ..."

"I want to go home," Frank said. "Margaret will be worried."

"All right."

"I want to go home. The boys ... They're late coming home, have you seen them? Dog won't tell me."

"Hush," Annette said. "They're fine."

"They've come home?" He lifted his head. "They've come home?"

Halloween, Annette thought. "Yes," she said. "The boys are in their rooms." She helped him to his feet and started walking him slowly, ignoring the stares of passing strangers.

"They had Dog with them, but he ran away. Heath doesn't

know the neighbourhood," Frank said.

"He's fine," Annette said. A great weariness had overtaken her. Her arm was around Frank's waist, and his weight was heavy upon her shoulder. She felt as if the entire Karnival were resting on her back. "We'll get you home," she said. "Margaret is waiting for you."

"I hope she isn't worried. But I had to go looking. People do awful things to children. Inhuman things."

"I know."

"That old man – Old Man Martin. They didn't go there, I hope."

"I don't think so," she said. Ahead of them, she could see the housing quarters and quickened her pace.

"Good. He did things to a little girl. I'm glad the boys didn't go there."

"I'm sure they didn't," she said. "Anyway, they're home now. Everyone is safe."

"Good." He seemed sure of himself as they stepped through the gate and entered the backyard. "I had to look, though. I had to look."

"It was very brave of you."

"Yes, it was," Frank said. "It was dark. It was very dark, I had to take a flashlight."

"You're very brave."

"We're going to the Karnival, did you know? Margaret's father owns it. I used to work there."

"Did you?"

"Yes. That's where I met her. She was so beautiful."

"I know," Annette said.

"But –" He stopped and Annette stumbled. "She's not well," Frank said. "She's bedridden. She – she was worried about the children."

"I'm sorry to hear that." She tugged gently at his arm and they mounted the housing quarters steps.

"Something's wrong," Frank said. He tried to pull away from her, his eyes sweeping over the building's façade. "This isn't my home."

"Margaret –"

"Where is she? What have you done with her?"

"It's all right, Frank. Really, it's all right. She's inside. In her room."

"This isn't my home!"

"It's a hospital," Annette said, hoping that this would reassure him. "You said yourself that Margaret isn't well. She's inside."

He studied her as if seeing her for the first time. He looked out over the lot, looked through the glass doors. "Inside," he repeated. "I remember now."

"I thought you would." She opened the door and walked through with him, hoping they would encounter a nurse. She did not know what to do with him.

"I know where she is," Frank said proudly. He moved away from her, striding down the corridor to the suite. He paused at the door, opened it a crack, and peered inside. "She's sleeping. I don't think you should come in. She isn't well."

Annette nodded. "Will you be all right? Can I get you anything?"

"Thank you, I'll be fine," Frank said. "Just – please tell the boys not to eat any candy until we've had a chance to check it."

"Of course," she said. "I'll tell them."

"Thank you," Frank said. He extended his arm and shook her hand. "You're very kind to look out for me. Do I know you?"

"I'm a friend of your boys," she said.

"Fine boys ... Fine fine boys. We're going to adopt Heath, you know."

"I know."

"You'll tell them about the candy, you won't forget?"

"I won't forget." Annette watched as Frank entered the suite and shut the door.

Never again would Frank leave the housing quarters. When Annette later recounted the incident, Hamilton, Heath, Horace, and I felt a great loss. Once more, someone dearly loved had been taken from us.

Heath and Shay picked a day in late May for their wedding. As she had decided to keep the marriage secret from her family, Shay asked Hamilton to give her away. Though they knew it would not be official, she and Heath requested that I perform the ceremony. They did not care to have a stranger bind their hearts. I readily agreed, for they were as devoted to each other as Hamilton and I, Anna and Arthur, Margaret and Frank. Heedless of tradition, Shay chose not to have a maid-of-honour, though Heath asked Horace to stand beside him as best man.

On the eve of the wedding, we threw a family party. Polly and Peg loved to cook, and insisted on preparing the meal. In the housing quarters kitchen, they chopped and stirred and sautéed and baked as if performing an exquisite ballet.

It was nearly midnight when we gathered in one of the housing quarters dining rooms. The last customer had left the lot. The gate had been counted and locked away. Hamilton and I held hands, seated side-by-side at one of the large round tables. My gaze swept over the faces of the children: Annette on my left, her brother beside her; Shay and Heath, so affectionate; Polly and Peg, chatting happily as they passed the serving dishes; and, on Hamilton's right, Horace. This is my family, I thought. I cannot describe properly the feelings that welled within me. Joy and sorrow and wonder quickened my heart, and the love I felt was palpable, flooding my limbs with warmth.

With full plates awaiting us, I stood and raised my water glass in toast. "If you will permit me a moment of sentiment, I would like to say that I cherish you all. Hamilton and I could not be more proud of everything you have accomplished."

"Hear, hear!" Hamilton said.

"We are delighted to have such fine nephews," I went on. "And to have found such a talented and caring daughter, who brings with her such a loyal brother."

"Make me sound like a dog," Danny said.

"Hush now," Annette said.

"If you two can't play nice," Horace said.

We all laughed.

I looked at Heath and Shay. "Though we will never forget those we have lost, we must ever turn our hearts to the future. Shay – on behalf of all of us here – I welcome you to our family."

"Thank you," Shay said.

We sipped, and Heath and Shay shared a kiss. The children applauded and cheered the young lovers. Hamilton hugged me as I resumed my seat.

"Your turn, Uncle Ham!" Heath said.

The table took up the call until Hamilton stood.

"My brother and I started this Karnival more than forty years ago," Hamilton said. "I don't think Arthur ever imagined that Klieg's would become what it is today. I know I didn't. We would have been happy just to do well enough to continue, simply because we love the work and the people. Over the years, Klieg's has been a haven to so many who were unwanted. And I am proud that, of all our accomplishments, we are still – first and foremost – a home to those who need us."

"Amen!" Polly said.

Danny looked at his plate.

The children applauded, and then grew quiet.

"Tomorrow," Hamilton said, "our Heath is going to marry his childhood sweetheart." He raised his glass to Shay. "May the gods bless you both. May they keep you happy and safe for years to come."

"Thank you," Shay said. She turned to bury her face in Heath's neck.

"Thank you, Uncle Ham," Heath said.

Glasses were raised, touched together, and sipped.

"Eat up now, before it gets cold," Peg said.

Conversation filled the room as dishes and silverware clinked and clanged. We ate roast duck and steamed salmon, various salads and vegetables and breads, almond cake and cherry pie and ice cream with hot caramel. Oohs and aahs and other compliments were bestowed upon the cooks.

After the meal, drinking coffee, Shay remarked on the Karnival and how different it seemed when one was a customer.

"What do you mean?" Annette asked.

"Well," Shay said. "You walk through the gates and it's all magical and colourful and absolutely wonderful. The rides are breathtaking and bigger than anything you ever imagined. And the sideshows are exotic and somehow not real. But as a member of the troupe ... Well, when I walk on the midway, what I see are the banners that need touch-ups, and the hedges that need to be trimmed. I see the wires holding the witches and goblins in the haunted houses, and the fog is just smoke from dry ice pumped through a machine. I know that Goliath is no longer in the top three largest roller coasters. And the fortune-teller is not some mystical creature, but my fiancé's great aunt, and my friend."

"So we've been missing something all this time," Danny said. "Do you realize? I've never been on a single midway ride!"

"Me neither," Annette said. "And I'll bet you anything Madame hasn't."

"Oh no you don't," I said.

"She's afraid!" Horace said, at which point, of course, there was no arguing with any of them.

I soon found myself with Hamilton and the children on the scrambler, as Horace manned the controls. I clung to Hamilton and we all laughed and screamed, whirling in faster and faster circles beneath the full moon. We moved on to one of the Ferris wheels, strategically placed around its carousel like points on the compass. Rising high into the sky, we watched the city spread before us like a colourful quilt fashioned by giants. We crested and descended, the lot sweeping closer and then falling away. I tried my hand at a game of skill, while Annette tossed me the softballs and stacked the milk bottles as she had for The Maggots. The family laughed and cheered when I was awarded a pink and green plush elephant. Shay and Heath threw darts at balloons, Danny and Horace swung mallets at Whack the Cobras, and Polly and Peg outscored all of us at Skee Ball. Finally, we strolled through the Karnival Museum, marvelling at Klieg's evolution, telling stories of those who had come and gone.

In those early morning hours with Hamilton and the children,

I at last experienced what Klieg's gave to the world: childlike joy and wonder, a legacy of which to be proud.

When we retired to our tents and trailers, Heath and Shay slept apart for the first time in months. He wanted to stay with her, but she reminded him of the superstition about the groom seeing the bride the day of the wedding.

"You don't believe in all that, do you?" he teased her.

"I don't know," Shay said. "But I'm not taking any chances."

Reluctant to sleep alone, Heath sneaked in and coaxed Dog away from Margaret and Frank's suite. Together they cuddled beneath his bed, the smell of the floor comforting. Heath rubbed his face in the canvas, tasted it on his lips, and slept.

Not far away, in a North Vancouver motel room, Nola was awake. As Chloe and Ralph slept peacefully, she sat at the window, looking out at the pickup truck in the parking lot below. It occurred to her that Ralph never offered to teach her how to drive, as he had taught her how to read and write. This is horrible, she thought, this entire trip, just horrible. People were always staring, whispering, changing tables in restaurants, leaving their meals unfinished. Two little girls had giggled, pointing, and Nola wanted to slice their throats and watch them die. She hated them, all of them, every single person who looked at Chloe. Nola wanted them dead, swallowed by the ground and the ocean, burning alive, drowning, bleeding and decaying before her, as she laughed and spat on them.

We'll see freaks, she kept thinking, and Chloe will be at home with them. Nola had studied the brochure. Her eyes burned with the images of dwarves, "Alligator" triplets, and "Siamese" twins ... I love you, Chloe, she thought, I love you ... But this night she hated that arm and wished they had allowed the doctors to remove it.

Overlooking the pickup truck, unable to sleep, she was taunted by her own words: born to a purpose; a reason for the arm; a special daughter, gifted by God ... A freak of nature, Nola thought, certain she had deluded herself, making excuses for something grotesque and unnatural ... She believed her parents' sickness had overtaken her, passing on from Mollie and Thad to herself, from herself to her daughter, her carnival Chloe, her shame, her –

She felt a touch on her shoulder and cried out. Turning, she peered through darkness at the figure of her daughter. Seized with guilt and revulsion, Nola recoiled. "Get away!" she hissed, and Chloe took a step back. "Get away from me!"

Shock immobilized Nola as, dark in shadow, the chest-arm raised, a finger pointing into Nola's face.

Nola reeled. "Get away! Get it away!"

The chest-arm did not waver. Chloe stepped forward, radiant white in the glow from the parking lot's streetlights. As Nola stared, Chloe's eyes blinked once, and then her mouth moved easily.

"Nola," Chloe said.

Nola's senses shattered.

Chloe and Ralph were sleeping peacefully when Nola returned to consciousness. The pickup truck was still in the parking lot, waiting to take them to the Karnival. Nola, shaking, spent the rest of the night convincing herself that Chloe had not spoken, that the arm had not moved. "It didn't happen," she whispered over and over, repeating to herself what all the doctors had said: "She'll never speak. And the appendage will remain completely useless."

But Nola knew that she had never believed them.

Dog woke Heath with a series of sloppy kisses. Heath reached over, burying his face in soft fur. For one brief moment, he was in the lovely suburb of Niagara Falls. Margaret was downstairs in the kitchen fixing breakfast, Frank was sorting through bills, and Horace was whistling happily as he dressed. And then Heath came fully awake. Frank was insane, and Margaret was catatonic. He was getting married and Dog was beside him for the first time in years.

Heath wanted to run. Pack a bag, take food for Dog and himself and go – just go. Find a place where he and Dog could lie in the grass, count the stars, wade in streams. A place where he was not expected to run a business or marry ... How he longed to be a child, with loving parents to hold him, a house that would stand always to keep him safe within its comforting walls, and nights that were clear and bright with stars, free of the high, thin, angry voice calling for Baby ... He was frightened, convinced his next steps would destroy even the dream of such a childhood. And then he was angry: at his parents for leaving him; at Margaret and Frank for disappearing into the recesses of their own minds; at himself for his fear, for wanting and needing someone to love him and make him feel safe; at Shay for appearing and opening his heart, tormenting him with nightmares of losing her forever ...

Dog whined softly and licked Heath's face.

"I love you, Dog," Heath said, and his anger and fear dissolved. He would not run, he told himself. He could not. He would marry Shay and continue with the Karnival and –

No, he thought, and it chilled him.

He showered and dressed then, keeping his mind on other things so as not to recall the word. He thought of Shay, of holding her, making love to her, joining in her sweet laughter. And then they walked, he and Dog, around the perimeter of the Karnival, into the woods that had yet to be cleared, leaves and branches crunching underfoot, the trees rustling above them. For hours they walked until he felt he would fall from exhaustion. They came upon a small stream and he sat on its bank. Dog played in the water, while Heath watched the tiny fish that flitted over the stones on the streambed. A place like this, Heath thought. It was then that he heard it, shrill and bone-jarring, his breath catching in his throat. The voice overpowered his consciousness and threw him into blackness.

After some time the woods returned, the rustling of the trees, the splash of the water as Dog chased dragonflies. Heath stood and called to Dog, anxious to touch the animal and feel his warmth. But not even Dog could dispel the thought of Her, and in a sudden blind panic, Heath began running. He stumbled over tree roots, bushes slapping at him, Dog at his heels. At the edge of the woods, he fell to the ground and lay panting. Dog nuzzled him, licking away the tears as he wept ...

When Heath had stopped weeping, he pushed himself to his feet. Leaving the woods, and prolonging return to the backyard and his tent, Heath slipped through a gap in the fence to enter the midway. Klieg's had been closed for the day – ostensibly for the sake of the wedding – and there were no crowds to distract or hurry him as he walked, Dog beside him, from concession to concession, ride to ride, as if seeking to commit each to memory. The games of chance and skill were silent, colourful prizes hidden behind collapsible metal awnings. The rides were still, their lights dark, their gates shut and locked, looking like skeletons of giant beasts no longer of this earth. When he reached Goliath, Heath stood for some time, marvelling at the intricacy of its design and feeling a palpable hate, as if it were a sentient being. When at last he left the midway and returned to his tent, he found his brother waiting for him.

"Forget what day it is?" Horace said. He was seated at the desk reading one of Margaret's books.

"I had some thinking to do," Heath said.

Horace set the book aside to study him. "You're not getting cold feet, are you? That's crazy."

"Why would that be crazy?" Heath said.

"Because you love each other! Not everybody gets to have that, you know. And you're different, remember?"

Heath sat down on his bed. "Everybody's different," Heath said.

Horace lit a cigarette, watching him. "What's up with you? This is more than cold feet, I think."

"Don't you ever wish we hadn't come here?" Heath met Horace's gaze, unable to believe he was actually saying it. "Don't you ever wish I never asked Margaret to bring us here? Really, Horace – don't you ever wish they never wanted me?"

"What the hell are you talking about?"

"None of this would of happened," Heath said. "Don't you ever wish that none of this ever happened?"

"Look, Heath –"

"Don't you ever wish you were a kid like everyone else? With a house and a yard and parents who taught you what things are about?"

"What's the point?" Horace said. "That's not what happened. And we're not kids – not anymore." Horace took a drag on the cigarette. "Look, Heath, if you're trying to get me to say I'm sorry you're my brother – well, forget it. That's not going to happen because that's not how I feel. Got it?"

Heath stood, face flushed as he loomed over Horace. "Aren't you ever scared? Aren't you ever afraid of what's going to happen the next time you turn a corner? What terrible thing's going to happen to the next person you care about?"

"No."

"Damn it, Horace! Why doesn't it ever bother you? Everything that's happened – your accident and your grandfather and Margaret's endless sleeping ... And now Frank is –"

"What's the point?" Horace said again. "We live through the things that don't kill us, and we just keep going on."

Heath thrust shaking hands into his pockets. "Doesn't it ever make you angry? Your grandfather's gone and your parents are gone and why doesn't it make you angry!"

"I don't want to be angry," Horace said. "I don't want to be resentful or sad or lonely or any of those things that make people unhappy."

"I don't get you," Heath said. "After everything and everybody ... And nothing happens to you."

Horace took a deep breath. He felt that he understood why Heath was so agitated this day. "I made a choice, Heath," Horace said. "For me, the past is the past. I don't want to wonder why things happened the way they did. I don't want to wish things had happened any other way. I just want to enjoy what I have while I have it, because who knows how long any of it will be here."

"Now who's crazy?" Heath said.

Horace ground his cigarette into an ashtray. "Do you remember that night at Kids Karnival? When you asked me what I was doing and I told you one day you'd understand?"

"What about it?"

"You know the feeling you get when you're with Shay?"

Heath nodded. Even then it warmed him.

"Well, I've never felt that, Heath. Not for the girl that night. Not for any of the people I've been with. I don't think I can feel that. And believe me – I've tried. So when you talk about letting things in the past get in the way of today ... When you're afraid to be happy just because you're waiting for the next bad thing ... Well, you can't. You just can't. Especially when it comes to love. That's just not the way that things are supposed to be."

That morning, as Hamilton oversaw the preparation of the yard, I sat at Margaret's bedside. While Frank slept curled peacefully, his back to us, I quieted my mind and waited, clinging to Margaret's hand ...

The *knowing* did not come.

I placed my palm over her heart, touched her cheeks with my fingertips, cupped her chin in my hands. I smoothed her hair, my fingers dancing over her eyelids. I gently kissed her lips. But all to no avail.

And then – and not for the first time – I begged her to return to us, telling her how badly we needed her, crying out to her with all my soul. And still, there was nothing. Conceding at last, I stepped away from her. Margaret was as empty as a seashell washed upon the sand ...

Hours later, Hamilton found me seated at my table in the freak tent. I was staring into my glass eye, striving in vain to see beyond Ralph, Nola, and Chloe's arrival.

Hamilton knelt beside me and placed his arm around my shoulder. "Something new?"

"Today," I said. "It is today."

I felt him stiffen. He was silent for a moment, uncertain whether he wanted to know. "And Heath?"

"I cannot see," I said. I moistened the eye with my lips and returned it to its socket. I reached for Hamilton's hand. My fingers closed tightly around his.

"What will we do?" Hamilton asked. "I was hoping we would

have more time ..."

"You're thinking he will leave us."

He nodded, swallowing, and I could see a mist cloud his eyes. "If he goes away with them ..."

I kissed his lips to suppress his words. "Darling, please ... Please don't torture yourself like this. Whatever may happen, Heath will not forget his love for his family, nor his love for Klieg's. We must believe that."

Hamilton nodded. He put his head in my lap. I stroked his hair, thinking of all the years we had spent together. I still felt the sheer magic of touching him. Silently, just as I had every day since he proposed, I thanked the gods for bringing him to me.

"I love you, Alice," Hamilton whispered. His hands clung to my legs. "With all my heart and soul, I love you. Through every crisis – every happy moment, every horror – I have loved you."

"I know," I said. I stroked his cheek. "And I love you more deeply than I ever thought possible."

Hamilton took me in his arms, drawing me close and kissing me. We slipped to the canvas and made love with a passion surpassing all others.

Annette was dressing for the ceremony when she caught sight of Danny in the mirror. She turned to face him. "Are you all right?" she asked.

"Oh sure," he said. He dropped onto her bed. "Perfectly fine." Unshaven, wearing torn overalls, he stared at the ceiling, his arms cocked behind his head.

"Aren't you going?" she asked.

He chuckled bitterly. "How could I ever be so rude? Really, Annette."

She studied him. "What's happened? Last night we all had so much fun and –"

"Speak for yourself."

At a loss, she looked away and buttoned her blouse. "If you're going to be like this, then maybe you shouldn't go."

"But I must. We must all be there." He was mocking what I

had told them earlier.

"Don't," she said.

"Hit a nerve?"

"Danny, I know you think it's all hogwash. I know you think they're just cards and Madame's just a good judge of character and –"

"How do you know all that?"

She wanted to slap him. "Why are you so upset?"

"Because it isn't fair! Here I'm expected to go and celebrate two people having what I've always wanted and I can't have – and I just don't feel like doing it. I don't want to pretend to be happy for them, when all I feel is resentment."

"I don't understand this. Why can't you be happy for them?"

"I'm just not – I'm too angry."

"That's childish," Annette said. She turned back to the mirror and began to brush her hair, looking at his reflection. And then something occurred to her. "You're really enjoying this, aren't you?"

"What?"

"This little role you're playing. The poor doomed faggot. And it's all built on the fact that our parents never would have accepted you. Well, dear brother, they're dead. Blown to pieces, in case you've forgotten! And all around you are people who love you and accept you for who you are and you're still acting like –" She focused her attention on her jewellery box, not wanting to look at him. "I'm sick of it, Danny. It's an old story, and only true if you let it be."

He laughed, sitting up on the bed. "And your story's better? The unloved waif becomes a gypsy girl?"

Annette bypassed the hoop earrings for which she had been reaching and picked up the diamond studs. "Ha-ha."

"Really, Annette. Don't tell me you're still enjoying all this. Sure it was fun for awhile, but come off it. This Karnival is just another way to make money. Daddy sold drugs – we sell thrills and illusions and freaks."

"Stop it! Just ... Stop it." She shut her eyes, leaning against the bureau. "Is that why you stay? For more money?" When Danny did not answer, Annette lifted her head, watching him in the mirror. "I love you, Danny. More than you'll ever believe, more than anything on this earth. I know your life hasn't been easy, but neither has mine. I'm happy here. I belong here. And I thought you did too. All the work we've done – the museum and the rides and the games and Kids Karnival ... Was it all a lie? Was it all just a way to turn a dollar into two?"

Danny dropped his gaze. He covered his eyes with his hands.

"I don't think you mean what you've said," Annette continued. "I don't think you really resent their happiness. I pray to God that you don't. This all seems to me like a childish play for attention ... But, just in case I'm wrong, I'll tell you this, and only once: I won't have you spoiling this event. I won't have it."

"Annette ..." He lowered his hands and sighed, but he did not meet her gaze. "All right," he said. "I'll shut up about it. I'll go to this wedding, I'll smile, and I just might squeeze out a tear or two. After that?" He shrugged.

"Whatever will make you happy," she said.

"Of course. My happiness." Danny left the bed, heading toward the flap of the tent. "We'll see," he said, and was gone.

It was about this time that Nola, Ralph, and Chloe left their North Vancouver motel en route to the Karnival. The sun was bright overhead, and the pickup truck was stifling. Even with the windows open, Nola felt as if she were in an oven, the sweat rolling from her body, her clothes sticking to her skin. She shifted a little further away from Chloe and angled her face toward the window. She closed her eyes as hot air moved over her.

Chloe was on her knees, hands gripping the door, eyes ever watchful as the truck chugged along the highway. Ralph chatted at her, but Chloe gave no indication that she heard him. Not that Ralph would mind her not listening. He was as excited as she. He had awakened that morning with an energy alien to him. He was anxious to get going, and it seemed to him that Nola was stalling as she dressed, messing with her hair, fussing over her clothes.

"Look, Chloe," Ralph said as they neared a Klieg's sign.

Chloe bounced on the seat and clapped her hands.

"Won't be long now," Ralph said.

Thank God, Nola thought, it's almost over. She had wanted to stay at the motel – (Let Ralph parade Chloe around letting people think she's part of the show, Nola thought) – but could not figure out a way to tell him. Eventually she had decided that she may as well go. After all, she had come this far ...

Nola was thinking about Mollie and Thad when Ralph steered left, taking the final turn onto the road that led to the Karnival. She was thinking about her first ride in the transport truck with Ralph when they entered the parking lot. She left her reverie as a security guard approached.

Ralph stepped out to greet him. "Problem?" Ralph asked.

"The Karnival's closed for the day," the guard said. "Got a wedding going on. We'll be open tonight."

"I see," Ralph said. He glanced at Nola who was trying to hide her elation.

Nola slid over the seat and smiled at the guard. "What time tonight?" she asked.

"Come back around six," the guard said, tipping his hat at her. "I'm surprised you people haven't heard about this."

"A wedding?" Ralph asked.

The guard nodded. "It's been in all the papers and television newscasts. People got an idea it's quite an event."

"Don't watch television," Ralph said. "Well, thanks. I guess we'll come back later tonight."

"I'm sorry you came all this way for nothing," the guard said. He shook Ralph's hand.

"It's okay," Ralph said. "My little girl –"

"Ralph," Nola said. She clutched his arm. "Where's Chloe?"

Oddly, none of us but Frank noticed that the birds neither sang nor flew that morning. Alone with Margaret in the housing quarters, Frank stood at the window looking out over the yard, the breadcrumbs untouched on the windowsill. He could see, in the yard, the rows of chairs facing the podium, the tiers of flowers ... The nurse had said that his son was getting married, but he knew she had been joking. In his mind, Horace was too young, and there was no time for Horace to marry anyone this day. Frank and Margaret were taking him to the Children's Aid Society to meet a little boy named Heath. Margaret wanted another child.

The shadows were shortening. Frank knew he had better get dressed and wake Margaret or they would be late. Seeing her sleeping so peacefully, he decided to let her be for another ten minutes. At the closet, slipping into a suit, he started thinking about the old Karnival and Arthur. Knotting his tie, he completely forgot why he was dressing, paused and looked back at the bed. He saw that Margaret was waiting for him. Whistling happily, Frank began to unknot his tie when there was a knock at the door.

"Frank?"

"Come in!"

It was Annette, stopping by to check on him. "How are you this morning?" she asked.

He did not recognize her. "Quite well, thank you. And yourself?"

"I'm fine, thanks. I thought maybe you'd changed your mind about coming to the wedding."

"Wedding?" Frank asked. He glanced at Margaret and came to Annette's side. His voice dropped to a whisper. "She doesn't know," Frank said. "I haven't asked her yet."

"I see," Annette said. She studied him, then, consulting her watch, she kissed him. "I've got to go," she said. "Let me know if Margaret says yes."

Once again alone with his wife, Frank finished undressing. He crossed to the window, looking out. The chairs were all full. And there was a big book open on the podium. Now? he thought. Today? Are we getting married today? He turned to ask Margaret, and then he saw the tubes running into her arms. A pounding began at his temples, growing ever more insistent.

Frank shut his eyes. "Margaret?"

There was no answer.

Eyes closed, Frank climbed into bed. His hands fumbled over the sheets to find Margaret, and he pulled her into his arms. "I love you," Frank said. "Please won't you marry me, Margaret?"

Annette hurried to her seat in the yard, the twins on her right, and Danny's empty chair on her left. She smiled at me as I walked to the podium, and I nodded as she took Polly's hand.

"Hi, Annette," Danny said, plopping into his chair. He kissed his sister's cheek and offered a joint.

"Damn it," she said. "Couldn't you have finished it?"

"Didn't want to be late." He winked at her. "I took the time to shave, at least."

Annette turned away. "You're hilarious," she said.

The animals were strangely restless. The monkeys chattered and argued, and the eldest monkey scolded the others until they had finally quieted. Then he raised his long arms and they lifted their instruments, snapping tiny sounds at each other. The dogs' minds were not focused. Heath gave the command three times before they came to attention. On Heath's signal, the dogs formed an archway before the podium. A variation on the totem pole, the archway was expressly conceived for this occasion, with a seventh dog bridging two columns of three. Heath and Horace took their places beside the archway, and the eldest monkey dropped his long arms to begin the symphony.

In Shay's trailer, Hamilton helped her adjust the flowers woven into her hair. "You look beautiful," he told her.

Shay squeezed his hand. "I can't believe this is actually going to happen. Do you have any idea how long I've dreamed about this day?"

Hamilton kissed her cheek. "Heath loves you a great deal," he said.

"Oh, Ham, you have no idea how much I love him! It's funny, isn't it? He was the only bright spot in my entire childhood – what am I saying? – my entire life! And it's all because of a scared little kitten."

At the main gates, Nola and Ralph spotted Chloe just as she reached the fence. Nola called out to her, but the girl dropped to her knees and emerged on the inside of the Karnival, running. Nola gripped the wires, shaking the fence. She shouted Chloe's name as the girl disappeared from sight.

"You've got to let us in there," Ralph said to the guard.

The guard hesitated.

"Damn it," Ralph said. "We can't fit under there. If she gets too far we'll never find her!"

"All right. Come on." The guard led them to a gate and unlocked it. "You better give me your name," he said. "Just in case."

"Here." Ralph ripped his wallet from his pocket. "I'll be back for it. Come on, Nola."

Nola clung to Ralph's arm as they raced through the Karnival. They called for Chloe, over and over, and Nola's throat became raw. They caught a glimpse of Chloe, standing near a cotton candy stand, just looking at them. They stopped, out of breath, only to watch as the girl turned and ran deeper into the lot.

Winded, they rounded a corner of the midway and came to a halt. Not far away, Chloe stood, chest-arm pointing. Nola gasped, fighting nausea. Ahead of them, the wedding party and guests were gathered, Shay walking down the aisle on Hamilton's arm.

"Oh God, Ralph," Nola said.

Ralph took a step forward.

As Shay and Hamilton continued down the aisle, Annette turned in her seat to watch. Her eyes were drawn to Chloe, and confusion swept over her. Then suddenly she recognized the girl from her recurring dreams. A cry caught in Annette's throat. Half-rising from her seat, she felt the twins stir.

Polly squeezed Annette's hand. "What's wrong?"

Annette could only stare. Chloe approached the archway, chest-arm pointing, mouth moving without sound. Shay, nearing Heath, turned wide eyes over her shoulder.

It was then that I found myself forced aside. It was as if someone or something had struck me hard on the back and sent me reeling. I endeavoured to orient myself and her name was hurtled into the yard.

"NOLA!"

It echoed through the Karnival, was caught and enveloped by the canvas of the tents, thrown back by the walls of the buildings and the gates of Kids Karnival, pinging off the metal of the trailers and awnings, the rides and games of chance and skill.

"NOLA!"

Recovering from the shock of the blow, I turned toward the origin of the voice. I was stunned. The body I knew as Madame Isis stood at the podium, far from me.

I had known that Nola was coming, but to be pushed aside and used in such manner was maddening. "Stop it!" But my words did not carry. "They deserve to be happy! Why is this happening?"

Abruptly I was engulfed by a wave of *knowing*, like none I had ever experienced. I watched as Nola was born and raised, terrified and abused on the Wayne Farm. I felt the pain inflicted upon Ralph, the deepening bond as he and Nola battled the doctors on behalf of their silent daughter, Chloe. I was witness to Heath's birth, saw him abandoned to a dog, found by Louise Markham, and then by Margaret to be taken to her heart. I heard the words of Old Man Martin, spoken in the dark of a faraway Halloween night. I accompanied The Fates to place a Klieg's brochure into Chloe's hands, as she slept within the peaceful boundaries of vast Crown lands. At once I endured and understood all that had happened to each of us to lead us to this moment. And I knew that, with what they had revealed, The Fates would forbid my return to life in the limiting form of Madame Isis.

I was no longer to exist as Madame Isis, who had once been Alice Clemmons. Though I possessed her every memory and emotion, these were as a facet of a diamond too immense for a mortal to comprehend, only one of many lives that had formed the consciousness I now understand and know as My Self. I could no longer intercede as I watched events unfold.

Nola felt a coldness clutch her heart. She recognized the voice, and her mind struggled to comprehend that her mother was present. But the body she saw calling her was not and could not be Mollie.

"Nola? Nola! Where the hell is you, girl? Nola!"

Unable to stop herself, Nola started forward.

For Heath, the Karnival vanished the moment he heard Mollie Wayne's voice. He was thrust into cool darkness, Dog curled beside him, sunlight stretching to reach them beneath the porch. She was walking above him, the wood creaking and groaning in protest of her pounding steps.

"Nooolaaa!"

He huddled closer to Dog, terrified that she would discover him. He heard her step down from the porch and cross the yard, giving up on Nola and calling for him. Dog nuzzled him, pushing him away, and he crawled from beneath the porch. Squinting in the sunlight, he was unable to find her with his eyes before she was shaking him, demanding to know where Nola was. Now, Heath thought, now is when Dog leaps on her back and –

"No!" Heath whirled. The Karnival flooded his consciousness.

The dogs abandoned the archway, barking and jumping about in the yard. The monkeys began to chatter and argue, instruments clanging together. Shay pulled at Heath's arm, calling him over the screaming for Nola and Baby. Chloe, chest-arm pointing, blinked once and smiled at Heath.

Heath stared at her.

"Nola," Chloe said. She turned to point at her mother, who was striding down the aisle.

"Nola! Where the hell is you, girl? Nola!"

Nola stopped a few feet away, just looking at them. "Come on, Chloe," she said.

But Chloe stepped back. "Nola," she said.

Nola went white.

"Baby? Where are you, Baby? Baby!"

Chloe's chest-arm pointed at Heath, a finger touching his abdomen. "Baby," she said.

"Nooolaaa! Baby? Baaabyyy!"

"No," Heath said. "No."

"Baby," Chloe said, that finger touching him. "Baby." She turned and pointed at her mother. "Nola."

Nola took a step toward Heath, her eyes wide. Her hand reached out, then stopped. "Baby?"

All at once Heath remembered Thad's burial, the dog, Mollie ... "Nola," Heath said. He lunged at her, seized her by the shoulders, and shook her. "You left me! You left me to animals!"

"Baby?"

"Yes – Baby, damn it!"

"No! You don't exist!" Nola's mind was reeling. She fought to pull away, but he held her fast. "Ralph!"

But Ralph was shocked into immobility. He stood staring at his daughter, his mind unable to comprehend what he was witnessing, his senses unable to see or hear anything else.

"Where the hell is you, girl? Nola!"

"Let me go, please, I don't know you, you don't exist! Ralph!"

"Baby? Baby!"

Heath gripped Nola by the throat. "She wanted you. You!"

"No!" Nola gasped for air. Her head swam.

"She called you and called you but you had gone. And she found me. Me! She wanted you but you had gone and Dog – Dog –" The memory crystallized, the dog leaping expertly onto Mollie's back, teeth ripping into her neck. Mollie fell, her limbs jerking oddly before she was still. The dog nuzzled her, calling Heath over, then tore off the arm and began to roll it toward him. "I ate her. I ate her!" He tightened his grip on Nola's throat. "Do you hear me?"

Horace rushed forward. He grabbed his brother's arms. "Heath, stop it! Let her go, you'll kill her!"

Heath released her and she crumpled, coughing and gasping for air. Heath pulled away from Horace. He raised his head and saw Chloe, her chest-arm no longer pointing. He turned at the touch of a hand and saw Shay, her eyes full with tears.

"Heath?"

"I ate her." Heath stumbled back. He tasted blood and flesh in his mouth. His stomach lurched.

"Heath, what is it? What happened?"

Heath looked at Nola, again at Shay. A shiver of self-revulsion swept through him. And then, Dog and the dog act at his heels, he escaped to the woods.

Shay collapsed. "Heath!"

"Let him go, child. Let him go."

Shay looked up. Mollie was gone. The Fates had allowed my brief return, and I extended a hand. "He will find you," I said, and then my body slipped lifeless to the earth.

Shay screamed. Annette pushed her aside, dropping to her knees, and the earthquake struck.

The first tremor shook the flowers from their tiers, brought down the freak tent, and upset the podium. The wedding party and guests were jolted, some thrown to the ground. Holding my body in her lap, Annette raised her eyes.

It seemed the Karnival itself was panicking. Chairs tipped over as people fled into and along the midway, past the hot air balloons, into the parking lot, running blindly. The monkeys flung their instruments and darted in circles, chattering and slapping at each other. The eldest monkey jumped up and down, and waved his long arms. The petting zoo animals hissed and honked and bleated and neighed as they took to the woods and the sky.

Roused from shock, Ralph hurried to Nola and lifted her. He called for Chloe, but Chloe blew him a kiss and then turned away.

Chloe's right hand reached out. She touched Annette's cheek. "Annette," Chloe said.

The second tremor was stronger. Power lines snapped. Fissures appeared. The Karnival lot heaved. The "Reptile Show" trailer toppled and shattered, spilling serpents and lizards and insects into the midway. A wall of the housing quarters cracked from foundation to roof.

"The balloon!" Hamilton shouted at Annette. "Hurry, get the others! The balloon!"

Annette scrambled to her feet, letting my body slide from her lap. Instinctively, she snatched up Chloe as she ran. "Get Shay!" she yelled at Danny. "Get Shay!" She did not turn to see that he was following her instructions. She staggered across the yard, clinging to Chloe. The monkeys, shrieking, chased behind them.

Horace was racing for the housing quarters when it collapsed. The Karnival Museum groaned. The Ferris wheel we had ridden the night before dislodged its carousel, which rolled across the yard and then crashed, smashing games of chance and skill.

All at once, as if made of the sticks from candy apples, Goliath went to pieces.

At the balloon, Annette set Chloe into the blue gondola and turned up the burner. The monkeys scampered to the mooring lines. On the midway, Polly and Peg tripped over each other as they ran. Horace reached Danny's side and they pulled Shay along between them, kicking snakes from their path. Shay struggled to free herself, screaming for Heath.

"Hurry!" Annette shouted. "Hurry!" She strained her eyes, looking for Hamilton. He appeared stumbling through a cloud of dust. She ran to him and picked him up. She carried him back to the balloon as the ground heaved again beneath her feet. She handed him to the twins, who were safe inside the gondola, helping Danny with Shay. Shay continued to struggle, calling for Heath. Another tremor knocked Annette to the ground, and she lay for a moment dazed. Then Horace reached out with one hand and lifted her, setting her into Polly and Peg's arms.

The balloon began to drift upward. The Karnival Museum gave a final groan and caved in. A flash fire flared, caught the wood chips, and swept along the midway. The fissures widened, sending forth clouds of steam and dust.

From everywhere – above and below and all around – was a horrible, maddening, deafening roar.

As he neared the entrance, Ralph saw the first balloon rising. Carrying Nola, he ran to the second balloon and set her into the yellow gondola. He cranked the burner. He was untying the last of the mooring lines when the next tremor hit. Shaken loose, a large gatepost leaned perilously, hesitated, and then fell. Nola cried out as bricks and mortar slammed Ralph to the ground. She strove to climb from the gondola. Ralph stretched his arms to tug at the mooring line, his legs twisted oddly, broken. Nola was about to jump, but the balloon, set free, caught an air current and shot to the sky.

"Ralph!" As Nola watched in horror, the ground opened and Ralph disappeared. With a final scream, Nola lost consciousness, and the balloon carried her northward.

Rides crumbled like dry skeletons. Concessions and tents were aflame as they sank into snaking fissures. The Kids Karnival gateposts tumbled into a rift. Their billowy carved legs stuck out of the ground, and then were swallowed.

In the blue gondola, Shay wept. Horace held her in his huge arms. Danny lit a joint, muttering, "What the fuck was that for?" over and over. Polly and Peg were silent, cradling Annette, faces tense. Chloe was asleep, curled against the side of the gondola. The monkeys, hanging from the mooring lines swaying in the wind, berated The Fates for the terror unleashed ...

Annette shut her eyes. She thought of Frank and Margaret crushed in their suite, of Heath and the dogs ... And her fingers closed to hold a warm round object, which Hamilton placed in the palm of her hand.

"Your legacy," Hamilton said.

It was my glass eye.

VI DELIVERANCE

Two days after the earthquake, having long since returned home from vacation at Klieg's, Louise Markham nursed a secret desire as she lovingly tended Aggie North. She dabbed at Aggie's face with a washcloth dipped in cool water. All the while, Louise was wishing for further damage to British Columbia and Washington State as numerous aftershocks plagued the region. From a distant cousin, Louise had inherited land on the far western ridge of the mountains. Should the lowlands continue to sink and flood, she knew she would have herself a substantial piece of oceanfront property. She envisioned a bright future for herself, but she feared that Aggie was soon to draw her final breath. Louise at last deigned to answer Aggie's question regarding that day at the Wayne farm.

It was after one a.m., well past both of their usual bedtimes, but Aggie was dying, slowly if not painfully. As she lay in her bed, her light gently fading, she whispered, one last time, "Cannibals, Louise?"

"There was a cannibal," Louise said soothingly.

Aggie smiled. "Yes?"

"Just one," Louise said. "The little boy. When I got there –"

"Yes?" Aggie said.

"He was eating Mollie's arm. The dog –"

"Oh!" Aggie said.

Louise patted Aggie's hand. "The poor thing didn't know what he was doing, of course. He was hungry. They hadn't fed him, you see."

"Oh, Louise," Aggie said. "Thank you, darling, thank you ..."

"You're welcome, dear," Louise said. She reached for the remote to increase the volume on the television. Sheila Beck, then a correspondent for a syndicated tabloid news programme, was reporting:

"Amidst a sea of countless bodies, countless lives lost or forever altered by the earthquake, there is hope – at least for some. There is evidence that some of the residents of Klieg's Karnival may have survived. The Karnival – for years British Columbia's most famous attraction – was the epicentre of the largest earthquake in provincial history. The Karnival itself was swallowed by the earth, though most of the surrounding area has remained intact. Earlier today, one of the two Klieg's hot air balloons was found tangled in a wooded area quite far northwest of the disaster. Inside the gondola of the balloon was a woman's shoe. Authorities are still searching the area for survivors, and we will keep you informed of further developments. From Vancouver in beautiful British Columbia, I'm Sheila Beck."

"Louise?" Aggie said.

"Yes, dear?"

"Isn't that the same reporter who was at the Wayne farm?"

"I believe so, dear," Louise said.

"Much better suited to radio, don't you think?"

When Louise turned to answer her, Aggie was dead.

Later that morning, as the sun was just beginning to rise, a decades-old Winnebago pulled to a stop on a remote highway. Annette was driving, still with a little difficulty steering. The other children slept on the vehicle's numerous fold-out beds and couches.

In the front passenger seat, Hamilton studied the handwritten directions on the back of a paper placemat. He folded the placemat and tossed it onto the dashboard. "I think this is it," Hamilton said.

The balloon had carried them safely beyond the mountains. The trip, as one might expect, was not particularly comfortable. They were all filthy from dust and ashes, and Danny's continued bad temper proved to be draining.

"So what the hell was all that about?" Danny demanded of Annette. Only hours after they were airborne, the sun was beginning to set, and Danny was giving way to anger. Chloe was sleeping, Shay weeping and not caring what occurred around her, but Polly and Peg and Horace listened, they, too, wanting to know.

"I don't think I have the full answer to that," Annette said. "Nola was —"

"I'm talking about that goddamned earthquake!" Danny shouted. "What the hell did we ever do to deserve that?"

Annette stared at him. There were several thoughts in her mind, but what she found herself saying was, "How can you take it personally?"

Danny's eyes narrowed. His lips twisted into a bitter smile. "Wasn't it?"

She wanted to scream. She wanted to slap him and throw him from the gondola. "I don't know," she said. "Just stop it."

"Cut it out," Polly said.

"All right, then," Danny said, "you tell me this: what are we going to do now? Are we headed anywhere in particular? Or we're just drifting with the wind?"

"I don't know," Annette said. "Where do you want to go?"

"Home! Where the hell do you think?"

"Keep it down," Peg said, "the kid's still asleep."

"The estate is gone," Annette said softly, and Danny stared at her. Reflected in my glass eye, she could see the jagged remains of the bluff upon which the mansion had stood. What survived of the gardens were the plots of herbs and a corner of the maze, its sharp turns leading to precipitous drops onto pounding surf below. The pony galloped along the beach, his hooves kicking up sand.

"How do you – ?" Danny stopped, looking at my glass eye. As Annette closed her hand, he met her gaze. "So what are we supposed to do?"

"I don't know about you," she said. "But I'm going to look after my family and this little girl."

There was not much to occupy them in the balloon. Danny, searching for a joint, was shocked to find his wallet in his back pocket. In the fading sunlight, with his back to Annette, he inventoried its contents. Shay sat huddled to one side of the gondola, her wedding gown in tatters around her. Several of the monkeys cuddled up against her as she wept. Horace, contemplating Shay, struggled not to imagine what had become of Heath. He soon retreated into a prolonged and deep dreamless sleep.

Polly and Peg, ever aware of Annette, busied themselves looking for signs of civilization amidst which to land. But all they saw were the grey and brown of mountain peaks jabbing at the sky, the green of trees and shrubs that whispered as they moved, the rippling purples, whites, pinks, and yellows of wildflower fields in the breeze, the sparkling blues of streams and rivers and lakes. As day became night and stars appeared, the colours all blended to a milky silver in the moonlight. Polly and Peg drifted into sleep.

The night was quiet, though bats and owls circled the balloon, keeping watch on those within. Danny soon fell asleep as well, but Annette and Hamilton remained awake. In her mind, Annette could not help but relive the horrors The Fates had unleashed. "I'm so frightened," she whispered to Hamilton. She looked to ensure that no one else had heard.

"There is no need," Hamilton said. He had known for some time that he would outlive me, and he had promised to be brave for the sake of the children. "Remember that Madame believes in you," he told her.

"But she's gone!" Annette hid her face in his chest.

Hamilton rocked her. "Madame is not gone. She is with us even now. Can you not feel her around you?" He cupped her hand over my glass eye. "Life does not end, love does not die." He took her face in his hands. "We must believe that, and we must be strong. Together. There are others who need our strength, others who do not, cannot yet understand what has happened and why."

"Shay," Annette whispered.

Hamilton nodded. "There is so much to do before she gives birth." At Annette's gasp, he smiled. "So you see? We have survived and life awaits. That is what is important, not what we have lost. There is no time to regret, to wish that this had not happened. There are lessons to be learned, to be taught and understood. Madame knows you are strong, that you are equal to the task before you."

"And I shouldn't fail her."

Hamilton shook his head. "It is your self whom you must not fail. It is your self to whom you must answer."

Startled into thought, Annette turned to look at Shay, who sat huddled in a corner of the gondola. Several of the monkeys still cuddled up against her, silently watching her with sympathetic eyes. Suddenly determined, Annette released Hamilton's hand and stepped over Polly and Peg and Horace to reach Shay's side.

Shay looked up, and the monkeys cuddled more tightly against her.

"Are you feeling any better?" Annette asked.

"I feel so lost without him." Shay averted her eyes, stroking the head of the smallest monkey. "I just can't seem to believe I'll ever see him again." She shut her eyes as Annette sat beside her. "You have no idea," Shay continued after awhile. "No idea ... I was so happy that finally, after all these years I had found my dream, found Heath ... And then – out of nowhere ... Nowhere!" Her voice took on a tone of defiance. "Who was that woman? Who was she!"

"His mother."

"His mother ... And she?" Shay thrust her chin in Chloe's direction.

"His sister."

Shay's eyes were burning coals focused on Chloe. "Damn you! Damn you!" She gripped the gondola, and began to pull herself to her feet.

The monkeys, dislodged from Shay's side, chattered in displeasure, and the smallest tugged at the sleeve of her dress.

"Shay, please." Annette placed a hand on Shay's arm.

Shay sat down, and Chloe rolled over in sleep.

"She only did what she had to do," Annette said. "It is necessary for Heath to –"

"Necessary?! Was it necessary to take away the man I love? To so horrify him that he would –" Shay buried her face in her hands. The monkeys threw their arms around her, turning questioning eyes to Annette. "I don't want to hate her," Shay said. "I swear I don't, but –"

"I understand," Annette said softly. "But she's only a child."

Shay lifted her head to study Chloe. How innocent she looked in sleep ... For a moment, Shay was unable to believe that Chloe possessed a third arm, which had pointed from her chest and brought such terror. But she knew it had happened, as unbelievable as it seemed, for uppermost in her mind was the look of self-revulsion on Heath's face when he turned and fled toward the woods. "I'll never see him again," Shay said. "I know it. I just know it."

"You mustn't think that way," Annette said. She clutched Shay's hand. "You mustn't give in, mustn't give up hope. Heath will find us and –"

"How?" Shay demanded. "How do you expect him to find us now? How do you know he isn't already dead? You saw what happened, Annette! You saw the ground open and –"

"Hush now." She pulled Shay into her arms, praying for the fire and fight to leave Shay's body. Desperate to find the right words to say, Annette closed her eyes, trying to quiet her mind. "There is so much we don't understand," Annette whispered. "And yet we must trust that all has happened for a reason, that each event is fulfilling its purpose." The words felt right and sure. "Each of us is so much more than we know ... And we have to believe that there is a part of us for which these tragedies are necessary."

"All I ever wanted was to love him, for him to love me." Shay pulled away to meet Annette's gaze. "Was that really so much to ask? Can you really expect me to believe that there is a part of me that wants to lose him, that wants him to –" She shook her head. "No. I can't believe that."

"What do you believe?"

"Now?" Shay laughed bitterly. "Nothing. I believe in nothing."

"Not even your love?" Annette's fingers tightened around my glass eye. Her voice grew strong with conviction. "You will see him again. He will come home to you. But before that day arrives there are lessons you must learn. And beyond all else is this: love must endure, love must triumph – or this life means nothing."

"I'll always love him. How could you think I would –"

"I do not speak of Heath."

Shay looked at Chloe as Annette went on.

"What has happened – everything that has happened – has happened for a reason. You must come to understand that this child has brought Heath something he has longed for, perhaps without even knowing it: a chance to reconcile with his past. And if you love him, you will not begrudge him this chance, nor condemn his sister for giving him such a truly wonderful gift."

Shay covered her eyes. "I don't know if I can do this ..."

"And yet you must."

Shay shook her head. "If she hadn't come – if she hadn't brought that woman –"

"Then your dream would have died." Annette grasped Shay's shoulders and turned the young woman to face her. "You must understand there was no other way. You have brought Heath the first real happiness he has ever known. But that happiness can quickly fade, become obliterated by the past which has so haunted him. For Heath to be the man that you want him to be – that he wants and needs himself to be – his questions must be answered. He must confront his mother and reconcile his past. Otherwise, he could never truly be the man you say you love, the man you dreamed about for so long. The day would come when he would be only a shell ... For your dream to become a reality, there is – and can only be – one course of action." Annette's tone softened. "A gift," she repeated. She touched Shay's cheek with her fingertips. "You know this. You know in your heart and in your soul that what I tell you now is the truth."

"I don't know ..."

"You do know. You must put aside your self-pity and trust in the love you share. You must see how fortunate Heath is that this has come about. Don't condemn her. Don't allow yourself to resent her for what she has done. You must come to know that she had no other choice. And if you cannot – if you will not – then your love will become a lie."

"Annette –"

"There is no other way. And you know it."

Shay nodded slowly. "In my heart ..." She sighed heavily, brushing the hair from her face. "I do love him. With all my heart and soul. And I want to believe what you're saying, I want to believe that this is right, that everything will ... But it's so difficult to believe ..."

"Look around you. Together, we can be strong. Together, we can all put aside our grief and go on."

Shay gasped, then turned away, ashamed. "How you must hate me."

"I don't understand."

"Madame," Shay said, clenching and unclenching her hands. "I didn't even think how you must be feeling, how Ham and Horace ... Margaret and Frank must be ..." Her gaze fell on Chloe. "She lost her mother ..." Shay turned to Annette. "How could I be so selfish!"

"That isn't important now," Annette said. "We're all bound to behave oddly after such a shock."

"But I didn't even think about –"

"It's done," Annette said. "Just try to get some rest. Who knows what morning will bring."

"Stay with me," Shay said. "Please ..."

"All right." Annette settled beside her, and the smallest monkey climbed into Annette's lap.

Shay closed her eyes, leaning her head on Annette's shoulder. "Do you really believe what you said?" Shay asked.

"Get some rest," Annette said. She stroked the monkey's head, listening as Shay's breathing slowed to the even tempo of sleeping.

Hamilton kept watch as Annette, at last, slept. Chloe soon awakened and sat by his side, smiling at him and calling his attention to certain constellations.

Come sunrise, they began to look for a suitable place to land, as the tanks were nearly exhausted of fuel.

"There," Polly said. She pointed off to one side. "That's a little town, isn't it? And that looks like a scrap yard, see?"

"We could get an old bus or something," Peg said. "If we make it to that field, it doesn't look like too far a walk."

Danny grunted. "Couldn't we set down where there's a decent car dealership?"

"At this stage, we've got no choice," Hamilton said. He lowered the flame on the burner.

The balloon descended, moving suddenly northward, then westward, then south, and then gently eastward once more, as it drifted down through the different currents of air. Reaching the field, the gondola bounced several times across the grass, and then came to rest. The balloon began to deflate and sag.

The root-growing things waved in greeting, insects and tiny animals scurrying about the blue gondola, sniffing, investigating.

"Thank God there's a stream," Polly said, and Peg said, "Amen to that."

The monkeys scrambled down and jumped from the mooring lines, shrieking as they danced about in the grass. Everyone but Horace and Shay climbed from the gondola and gratefully stepped onto solid ground.

"Are you two coming?" Danny asked Horace.

Horace was speaking in quiet tones to Shay. "You don't want to stay here, do you? There's a stream where we can get cleaned up."

Shay looked at her tattered dress, pulling faded flowers from her tangled hair. "Do we even know where we are?"

"I think so," Horace said. "We're in friendly territory, anyway, I'm pretty sure of that. Come on now, let's go."

Horace helped Shay from the gondola, and together they joined the others at the stream. Chloe was careful to remove a locket on a chain from around her neck, setting the jewellery onto the grass beside Danny's wallet. They bathed with their clothes on, washing away the dust and ashes.

As the family lay in the sun to dry, Chloe wandered along the bank of the stream. She returned some time later with a large pile of blackberries and wild strawberries held on a platter of tree bark.

"Danny and I'll walk into town," Annette said as they savoured the berries. "We'll buy a bus or something at the scrap yard and bring lunch."

"Do I get a say in this?" Danny said.

Annette smiled at him. "You're the only one with access to money at the moment. So, whether you like it or not, this family needs you."

Annette and Danny made mental notes to purchase – in addition to lunch and a vehicle – cigarettes, fresh fruit, soap, toothbrushes, toothpaste, and toilet tissue. Chloe opened her locket and withdrew a small folded piece of paper. She unfolded it, smoothing its edges, and handed it to Annette.

"What's that?" Hamilton asked.

"Some sort of handwritten citation," Annette said. " 'In acknowledgement of her love for Nature, Chloe Greeson is hereby granted the title of Honourary Forester.' "

"Honourary what?" Danny said.

"Forester," Annette said. "Signed Joseph Danton, Forester."

"Isn't that something," Polly said.

"Is that your name, honey?" Annette asked. "Chloe?"

Chloe nodded. She pointed to the back of the paper. There, written neatly in ink, was a telephone number. Chloe pointed to the number, then to the signature on the front of the paper.

"Joseph's phone number?" Annette asked, and Chloe nodded.

"Maybe he can tell us where Chloe lives," Peg said.

"I can't believe I'm doing this," Danny said as he and Annette trudged through the field to the road.

"Life's an adventure," Annette said, and Danny burst into laughter. "Just help me get Chloe home," Annette said. "Then I'll call Malcolm Lewis and you can do whatever you want."

Malcolm, my ass, Danny thought. First thing I'll do is find us a new lawyer ...

Only two cars passed them on the road, and these were headed in the opposite direction. About halfway to town, they spotted the "For Sale" sign on the decades-old Winnebago, which was parked in front of a rambling ranch house.

They were inspecting the vehicle when an old woman appeared beside them. "She may be getting on, but she runs like a top," the old woman said.

Danny started. "Where'd you come from?"

"Hello," Annette said.

The old woman smiled. "Willing to let her go for next to nothing," she said. "I'm not about to drive this contraption, and Henry sure won't be driving anything anymore. You got a big family?"

"Yes," Annette said. "We're taking a road trip."

"Great for a family," the old woman said, showing them into the vehicle. "Sleeps eight, you know, once you fold out the couches and drop down the loft above the front seats. Ten, if you count the seats. There's a bathroom, such as it is, and a little built-in kitchen with stove and fridge and a sink. Just remember to keep the water tanks full, and empty the septic. Got a full set of pots and pans, a little coffee pot, plus dishes and silverware and glasses and what-not. Henry was mighty proud, you know, drove us everywhere in this contraption, all over the country and back again. Never stayed in a bed other than my own after Henry bought this."

"It'd do, I suppose," Danny said.

The old woman smiled at him. "There's always the scrap yard, of course," she said. "Just another mile or so up the road."

"This is lovely," Annette said. "It's just perfect."

"Next to nothing," the old woman said, "provided you pay cash. You stop at the bank and ask Patricia to put the money in my account. Mrs. Henry Ellis is the account," she said once she and Danny agreed on a price. "My name's Elizabeth. You ask Patricia to call me when you're done."

"I assume there's a grocery," Annette said. "And a diner, maybe?"

"Stop at The Scaredy Cat."

"The what?" Danny said.

"It's a restaurant," Mrs. Ellis said. She gave Annette the keys to Henry's pickup truck. "Lucille will fix you up with a right smart lunch. The bank is across the street – remember, you have Patricia call me when you're done, now – and the grocery is next door to the bank. Meantime, I'll prepare the papers for this contraption and warm her up. The old gal hasn't been running in a while."

Annette drove Henry's pickup truck to town. As Danny entered the bank to speak with Patricia, she strolled to The Scaredy Cat and ordered boxed lunches from Lucille. "May I use your phone?" Annette asked.

"Long distance, I figure?" Lucille said.

"I'm afraid so," Annette said. "But my brother's at the bank now, and I'll certainly pay you whatever you like."

"Just a minute," Lucille said. She lifted the telephone receiver and dialed. "Hetty? It's Lucille Thomas at The Scaredy Cat. Got a gal here needs to make a long distance call. You keep the clock running and give me the cost when she's done, will you?" Lucille smiled reassuringly at Annette as Hetty's voice crackled on the other end of the line. "Yes, I know that's not how things are done," Lucille said after a moment, "but Mrs. Ellis sent her ... Yes, yes that's right. They're buying Henry's old Winnebago ... Thank you, Hetty." Lucille handed Annette the receiver. "Just give her the number, dear, and she'll connect you."

"Thank you," Annette said. She read the number into the telephone, wondering how Lucille had known. She imagined that soon everyone in town would learn that she was purchasing Henry's old Winnebago and placing a long distance call from The Scaredy Cat.

"Go ahead, please," Hetty said.

The number connected to a mobile telephone. "Danton, here," a masculine voice said.

"Joseph Danton?" Annette said. "Forester Joseph Danton?"

"Call me Joe. What can I do for you?"

"I'm Annette Klieg. You don't know me. I was given your number by a little girl named Chloe Greeson."

"Chloe?" Annette could hear the concern in his voice. "Is she okay?"

"She's fine, Mr. Danton, really. We would like to bring her home."

"I don't understand," Joe said. "What's happened? Chloe was on vacation with her parents."

"They came to our Karnival. Maybe you've heard of us? Klieg's Karnival."

"Uh huh," Joe said. "That's where they were going."

"Well, they arrived," Annette said. "But then there was an earthquake and – well, we floated off in one of the hot air balloons, and Chloe was right beside me and I just snatched her up without even thinking about it."

"I heard about the earthquake," Joe said. "What about her parents?"

"I'm not sure," Annette said. "But Chloe gave us your phone number, and I felt we should bring her home where they could find her. If they – well, you know."

"I'll tell you how to get there," Joe said. "Do you have a pencil and paper?"

Annette took down the directions, writing on the back of a paper placemat. "Thank you, Joe," she said. "I imagine it'll take us almost two days."

Danny entered the restaurant as Hetty was telling Lucille the price of the call. "Everything's squared away," Danny said to Annette. "She knew I was there to buy the old thing before I even said a single word, can you believe it? No skeletons rattling around in any of these closets, I'll bet you ... Anyway, I withdrew a chunk of cash so we wouldn't be strapped. What's that?"

"Directions to where we're going." Annette folded the paper placemat.

"In the middle of nowhere, right?"

"How did you know?" Annette said. "You must be psychic."

Danny paid the bill for the lunches and telephone call. With the directions in her pocket, Annette thanked Lucille profusely, tipped her generously, and hurried with Danny to the grocery across the street. Annette filled a shopping basket with various pastas and sauces, bacon, eggs, and potatoes, cheese, bread, and jam, juices and soft drinks and fresh ground coffee. Not forgetting bags of peanuts for the monkeys – nor the cigarettes, fresh fruit, soap, toothbrushes, toothpaste, and toilet tissue – they thanked the cashier for his assurances that Henry's Winnebago really was top-notch. Back at the Ellis ranch house, the Winnebago's engine purred as they set their purchases inside, stocking the refrigerator and cupboard shelves.

"The septic is fine and she's got full tanks – both water and gas," Mrs. Ellis said. She accepted the keys to Henry's pickup truck. "And she won't give you any trouble, I promise you that. She may be getting on, but Henry kept her running brand spanking new." Mrs. Ellis gave Danny the paperwork and closed the door behind her as she stepped from the Winnebago. "Enjoy your road trip," Mrs. Ellis called out as Annette – with some difficulty – steered the vehicle onto the road. "You stop back by if she ever gives you the least bit of trouble."

Meanwhile, in the field, Horace and Hamilton finished deflating the balloon. They folded it and stuffed it into the gondola.

"I'm so sorry about Madame," Horace said. "I don't think it's really sunk in yet, but ... I think we're all going to miss her."

"And Margaret," Hamilton said. "And Frank."

Horace stared at the ground. "They were gone a long time ago," he said. "Years ago."

"They still loved you," Hamilton said. "Both of you."

Horace thought a long moment. "I know," he said at last. "But not enough ... Not enough to choose us." Horace turned away and crossed the field to check on Shay, who was seated with the monkeys as they groomed her hair.

At Peg's request, Chloe began teaching sign language to the twins.

"Can you spell Klieg's?" Peg asked.

Chloe quickly did so.

"Wow," Polly said. "That looks so pretty! Show us again – slowly, please."

Annette parked the Winnebago on the side of the road. She and Danny raced across the field. "You won't believe our luck," Annette said, handing out the lunches. "Let's eat and then we'll show you." Annette returned the handwritten citation to Chloe. "I called your friend Joe. He gave me directions to take you home."

After lunch, they used the mooring lines to tie the gondola to the top of the Winnebago and headed eastward, following Joe's directions. As no one else knew how to drive, Annette and Danny decided to take turns at the wheel. Hamilton served as navigator in the front passenger seat.

Annette drove the remainder of that day. Polly and Peg prepared dinner in the little built-in kitchen, and the family ate in a roadside park as orange and pink and red streaked the sky. After dinner, Danny took the wheel as the children and monkeys settled onto the numerous fold-out beds and couches.

"You may as well sleep, too," Danny said to Hamilton. Night had fallen and stars had begun to appear. "We're on this road for another six to seven hours, at least."

"It's difficult to sleep," Hamilton said. His gaze remained on the paper placemat.

Danny glanced at him, then looked away, uncertain if he should speak. "How are you holding up?" he asked.

Hamilton turned to the side window, watching as the moon followed them through the night. "I miss her greatly," Hamilton said. "But I have you children. I'm thankful that I won't be alone."

"It's terrible to be alone," Danny said.

"Not always," Hamilton said. "But we all need to feel that we are loved and accepted. Madame was always saddened that you would not think of yourself as part of our family."

"But I – what?"

"She thought of you as such," Hamilton said truthfully. "Just as I do. Like Polly and Peg and Shay and Annette, you are as much a part of our family as Horace and Heath ... Madame and I could never have children of our own. You are our children. And, without you, I would have little reason not to join my beautiful Alice."

"I don't know what to say."

"You don't need to say anything." Hamilton leaned back in the seat. His eyes eased closed. "Wake me if you get lonely," Hamilton said.

Danny was lost in thought when Annette awakened at daybreak and came to his side.

"Sleepy?" she asked.

"Not really. Hungry."

"I'll fix you something. Much further to go?"

"Another day, I guess."

Danny's estimate proved accurate. The next morning, only hours after Aggie North passed away, the sun was rising as Annette stopped the Winnebago at the gate of the Greeson farm.

"Home."

Annette and Hamilton turned, startled to see Chloe standing beside them.

"Can you open the gate?" Annette asked.

Chloe nodded and skipped from the Winnebago. She spun the dial on the gate lock, popped the lock, and swung the gate wide. Annette drove through, then waited for Chloe to secure the gate and return to the vehicle before continuing on.

Tree branches screeched along the Winnebago's roof and sides as the vehicle wound slowly up and around hills. The noise roused the children and monkeys from sleep. Suddenly the wooded area gave way to a wide field, golden in the sunrise, overlooked from a hill by the tall house that had once been white. Beyond the house were the twenty acres of pines destined to be Christmas trees.

"Wake up!" Annette called. "Everyone, look!"

"Nice place," Hamilton said to Chloe.

At the crest of the hill, Annette parked the Winnebago. They stepped out to survey the yard, the tall house, the barn, and the assorted outbuildings. The yard filled with the buzz of insects, the singing of birds, and the ceaseless excitement of the monkeys.

"Looks deserted," Danny said. He hollered a greeting, which echoed across the yard.

At the side of the tall house, Joe – whom no one had called Joey since he was fifteen – heard Danny's hollered greeting, and set down the watering can. As a Forester, he was responsible for most of the vast Crown lands that enclosed Ralph and Nola's Christmas tree farm. Though he was in no way responsible for what happened on their farm, he had taken it upon himself to tend the flower garden. He knew of Chloe's fondness for the various scents of root-growing things.

For years, Chloe had delighted in wandering the fields and woods, and Joe had encountered her on numerous occasions. Often she would walk beside him as he toured the Crown lands. He would tell her the names of the plants she fancied, kneeling beside her on the forest floor. When Chloe went missing, Joe was the one to find her the night she returned home. He had come across her sleeping against the trunk of a tree, the Klieg's brochure tight in her hand. They had learned, over time, how to communicate with each other, and that night, escorting her back to her house, Joe asked her about the brochure. She would not tell him where she had obtained it, but she insisted her parents were going to take her to the Karnival. Watching until Chloe stepped safely through the kitchen door, Joe thought about the fire that night so long before, and the beautiful Tim-Tina, who had not let him carry the burden of guilt alone.

Joe and Mark had remained special friends for years after the fire. Then one day Mark announced that he was getting married. Joe pleaded with him to reconsider, but Mark was adamant. He did not want to endure living as a homosexual.

Joe had loved Mark ever since he could remember, and not once had imagined a future without him. Joe vowed that he would never again fall in love. Shortly after Mark's marriage, Joe learned of a career in Forestry and was intrigued by a life that would place him far from others. He completed the necessary schooling, leaving family and home and all he had ever known for a secluded existence on the vast Crown lands.

As Joe emerged from the side of the tall house, eyes shifted their gaze from Danny to him. Danny turned and immediately felt a lump in his throat.

Chloe ran to Joe and jumped into the air.

Joe caught her easily. "Safe and sound!" He threw back his head in laughter.

"That must be Joseph," Peg said.

Danny could not look away as Joe set Chloe down and continued forward.

Joe's eyes swept over them in rapid appraisal. "Hello," he said. "I'm Joe Danton." He extended a hand to Annette.

"We spoke on the phone," Annette said. "I'm Annette Klieg." She introduced the others, though she felt it unnecessary to introduce each of the monkeys by name.

"Pleased to meet you," Joe said, shaking hands in turn. "Still no word of Chloe's parents?"

Shay gasped at the thought of Nola. Horace put his arm

around her and walked her slowly toward the tall house.

"Forgive us," Annette said. "We're still somewhat disoriented."

"I understand." Joe knelt beside Chloe, his eyes showing tenderness. "I'm sorry about your mom and dad," he told her.

Chloe kissed his cheek and hugged his neck. Releasing him, Chloe began to sign as Joe watched carefully.

"Long as you're sure," he said.

Chloe nodded.

Joe smiled, turning to look at Annette. "Apparently, you're all going to live here for awhile."

"Thank you," Annette said.

"Thank Chloe," Joe said. "Well, I guess I'll let you get settled." He gave Chloe a parting hug and began to walk away down the hill.

"Come back for dinner tonight," Peg called.

Joe looked back, grinned, and waved.

"What a sweet man," Polly said.

"And handsome, eh, Danny?" Peg said.

Danny frowned as Chloe clapped her hands. "Don't tease me, little girl," Danny said.

Chloe smiled.

In the tall house, Polly and Peg moved quickly through the kitchen, preparing crackers and cheese and eggs and canned soup. Annette carried a tray of food into the living room, where Shay lay on the couch tossing restlessly beneath a quilt. Horace was seated beside the window, staring out across the acres of pines destined to be Christmas trees.

"The twins cooked," Annette said. She set down the tray. "Is she sleeping?"

"I hope so," Horace said. He lifted a slice of cheese and chewed it thoughtfully. "She says you told her he'd find us here. It seems to have calmed her down a bit."

"I'm glad of that," Annette said. She tried to picture Heath in her mind. "I just pray I'm right."

After breakfast, as Hamilton and Annette cleaned the dishes and wiped the table, Polly and Peg made a list of necessary supplies.

Danny wandered out to the porch and sat on the steps. He looked out across the farm and the vast Crown lands, wondering if he could be so lucky as to stumble onto a patch of marijuana. He was lighting a cigarette when Joe drove his green truck into the yard.

"Hi, Danny," Joe said.

Danny smiled, pleased the man had remembered his name. "Hi, Joe."

Joe sat beside him on the porch steps. "I got to thinking maybe you need to go into town. You'll never fit that Winnebago through the covered bridge."

"There's a covered bridge?" Danny said. "I thought they'd all been torn down and burned as firewood."

"I know," Joe said. "Surprised me, too, first time I saw it. But time pretty much stops in places like this."

"Oh, it must be hopping on a Saturday night."

"There's a movie house," Joe said. "But most of the movies they show are older than we are. I'll take you one night, if you like."

Danny's heart fluttered. "Really?"

"Sure. As long as you're not picky about what we see."

"Not at all," Danny said.

"Maybe a drink after?"

"Whatever you want," Danny said. "I mean – sure, a drink."

Armed with Polly and Peg's shopping list, Danny and Joe climbed into the green truck and drove into town. "So how did you end up at the Karnival?" Joe asked to make conversation.

"My sister," Danny said. "She wanted to live there all her life, and, after our parents were killed, she got herself adopted by Madame and Hamilton."

"Madame Isis?" Joe said. "But where's she?"

"She ... died," Danny said. "Right before the earthquake hit."

"That's a shame," Joe said.

"Yeah," Danny said. He was surprised to feel a personal sense of loss.

"I envy you, though," Joe said.

"Me? Why?"

"The Karnival! What an incredible place to live," Joe said. "It was magical ... There were times I thought about running away from everything and signing on."

"You've been there?"

Joe glanced at him. "Of course, they were still touring then, I ... I was there the night Anna Klieg died."

"One tragedy after another with these people," Danny said carefully.

"Whatever happened to the hermaphrodite?" Joe asked. "Tim-Tina."

"Cancer," Danny said, remembering from the Karnival Museum.

Joe was silent as he manoeuvred the green truck through the covered bridge.

"I never knew her – him – whichever," Danny said. "You?"

Joe nodded. "She was a beautiful person. But she had something in her eyes, very much like you."

"Me?"

"A deep sadness," Joe said. "I don't think she knew how to love herself."

Danny turned away.

"So, with you people staying on ... going to rebuild?"

Danny looked at him. "What makes you say that?"

"There a reason why not?"

"No, of course not, but – I guess it's a little early to start thinking about that."

"I'd like to help," Joe said. "If and when you do, of course, and if you'd let me. I owe a debt." He had been considering this since Annette telephoned, his chance to atone, in part, for his actions that night so long before. "What do you say?"

Danny's eyes widened. "Why would you?"

"I told you. I owe a debt." Their eyes met and held. Joe smiled. He reached for Danny's hand. "I'm just saying – if you people need me, then I want to help. And I think it'd be a shame if you didn't rebuild some day."

Danny felt a warmth course through him, and he agreed, not knowing what he was saying.

"Here's our little burg," Joe said. He withdrew his hand to steer the green truck to a stop.

At the hardware store, Danny purchased cots and blankets and pillows and lanterns, as well as several tents. He and Joe loaded these into the green truck and continued on to the grocery. There, Danny bought everything on the list that Polly and Peg had made, and the boxes with these items were set beside the other things in the back of the truck. At the clothing store, Danny selected jeans and tee shirts and socks and sweaters in several different sizes, estimating as best he could who would fit what. Fashionable or not, everyone would have something clean to wear, until they could make their own trips into town.

Back at the farm, Danny and Joe brought the clothing and food items into the kitchen. They piled the tents of numerous shapes and sizes in the field near the base of the hill. The first tent was nearly complete when Annette, Polly and Peg, Horace, and Hamilton raced down the hill.

Annette was the first to reach them. "What's this?" she asked.

Danny dropped an arm over her shoulder. "Well, we all can't live in the house and the Winnebago."

"I guess not," Annette said.

"I arranged credit in town," Danny said, feeling energized. "We'll all need more clothes and a hundred other things, I'm certain. There's even a music store where we can buy instruments for the monkeys."

They worked at erecting the other tents, spreading them out in a semi-circle behind what Ralph had dug as a fire pit. The cots and blankets and pillows and lanterns were placed inside the tents. Hamilton and Horace collected firewood for the pit.

Meanwhile, up the hill, Shay investigated the tall house. She climbed the ladder to view the loft, saw Nola's things on the dressing table, and knew that this must have been their room. Rushing down the ladder, she stepped onto the kitchen floor and turned to see Chloe in the doorway of her bedroom. Shay took a step back.

Chloe's eyes showed innocent confusion. She beckoned Shay forward. After a moment, Shay followed her into the oddly placed bedroom, crossing to where Chloe stood at the window. Looking out, they could see down the hill, where the others were working at erecting the tents. Chloe tugged at Shay's arm, pointing with her left hand down the hill, at Shay, at the Winnebago, at Shay, shaking her head.

"I don't understand," Shay said.

Chloe thought a moment. She pointed at Shay's womb, made a rocking motion as if holding a baby in her arms, pointed down the hill once again, and shook her head.

"How did you know?" Shay asked.

Chloe shrugged.

"Well," Shay said, "just be glad something like this isn't all that new to me."

Chloe smiled. Again she pointed at Shay, and then spread her arms wide to indicate the room.

"You're kidding," Shay said. "Where are you going to sleep?"

Chloe pointed at the ceiling above her, indicating the loft.

"Okay," Shay said. "I suppose you're right. It would be better for the baby."

Chloe nodded vigorously and, bidding Shay to follow, she skipped to the bookcase built into the wall. There stood all fifty-seven of Margaret's books. Chloe pointed at Shay's womb, pointed at the books, and Shay began to weep, slipping to sit on the bed. Gently, Chloe stroked Shay's hair until Shay was calm.

"Now, listen," Shay said. "You do understand what I'm saying to you, right?"

Chloe nodded.

"Okay, then," Shay said, wiping her eyes. "First of all, I want to say thank you. For your room ... the books ... You can't possibly imagine how much this means to me. Now, I want you to know that I'm going to try. Really, I am ... But if Heath doesn't find us like Annette and Madame said he would, I ... Well, then, I don't know what we're going to do."

That night, Polly and Peg cooked a scrumptious feast, which none of them fully appreciated. They sat together near the fire pit, the sun setting as they ate in silence. After dinner, as the lanterns cast shadows and stars began to appear, Joe expressed his condolences for what they had lost – for Chloe's parents, for Margaret and Frank and Heath. "And for your wife," he said to Hamilton. "I remember her from my favourite cop show."

"*Scarlet Beach*!" Hamilton said. He laughed when Joe nodded. "She loved filming that. It was just before we found our Annette."

"What's *Scarlet Beach*?" Shay asked.

Annette explained about the episode of the series, in which I had played a serial killer. "She was so good in it!" Annette said. "She would have made a terrific actress."

"She was offered other parts, you know," Hamilton told them. "But she turned them down because she knew she would miss the Karnival."

They talked late into morning, until the sun began to rise, about Arthur and Anna, Hank and Tim-Tina, Margaret and Frank and Heath – about all who had come and gone and been loved – fond memories of days past beginning the healing of their hearts....

Far away, unaware that his family had travelled to safety, Heath roamed the woods of British Columbia. He came upon a stream and slipped to its bank, scooping water in the palm of his hand to drink. Dog and the dogs hurried to join him. He lay back to rest as they lapped at the stream.

It all seemed so unbelievable to him. Fleeing the scene of the wedding, he had barely reached the woods when the earthquake struck. He was knocked to the ground, hitting his head. His vision cleared as the first balloon, the one with the blue gondola that carried his family, floated eastward, passing over him. Below, still in the yard, Ralph untied the last of the mooring lines, setting free the second balloon, which sailed upward, carrying Nola away to the north.

And then the ground opened and swallowed Klieg's Karnival.

When all was quiet once again, Heath and the dogs stood amidst a thick cloud of dust and soot, overlooking the rift in the earth. There was not a vestige of the Karnival to be seen. At once, he envied Frank and Margaret, spared the pain of going on ...

Turning away, he and the dogs headed northward into the

woods. Some time later he recognized one of the balloons tangled in the limbs of a dying oak tree. Praying that its gondola was blue, he ran for the balloon, rocks and roots catching his feet as he went. But the gondola was yellow. He stared at the yellow gondola, Dog and the dogs sniffing about the tree and the snarled mooring lines. With a yelp, Dog lifted his head, calling for Heath to follow, and they walked northward, cutting west, then east, then, once again, northward through the woods.

Exhausted, Heath fell to the ground and slept. He awoke to continue walking. As the days passed, time lost its meaning, and he could not help but think of Nola. "No!" she had screamed at him. "You don't exist!" When first voiced, those words had wounded him deeply. As time went ceaselessly on, he dared not imagine the cruelty she had endured to strive so earnestly to negate his existence.

"Nola!"

The dogs lifted their heads, turning to look at him, ears twisting back and forth, searching.

Heath shouted her name again, waiting, listening, but there was no answering call. Again he leaned over the stream to drink and was confronted by his reflection in the water. His skin and clothing were covered with a thick layer of dust and soot. His hair was filthy and matted. His eyes were puffy and red, tears having left jagged streaks down his face.

With a cry, Heath ripped the clothing from his body and plunged into the stream. The water was icy, catching his breath in his throat, his muscles seizing. He swam to the bottom, his hands searching the streambed. His fingers tightened around a large rock. He held on, keeping himself submerged as his lungs gave up their last breath, stars whirled before him, his head pounded, and his chest began to ache. At last he let go. Springing for the surface and gasping for air, he surged into the sunlight.

He scrubbed at his skin with his hands, washing away the dust and soot. Again he dove, rolling onto his back to look up at the sky through the swirling water.

Moving past him, touching and seeming to flow right through

him, he heard a silvery voice.

"She is lost," the voice whispered. "Find her. Find her ..."

Nola was hungry. She pawed along in the dirt looking for the remains of the rabbit. Some time before, she had killed it with a rock and raised the still-warm body to her mouth. She had been about to rip her teeth into its neck when the fur tickled her face and her stomach turned over. She had tossed the carcass to the ground, vowing that she would never sink to such debasement. At this moment, she could find nothing further to eat, and even the carcass had somehow disappeared. She had finished all the berries on the bushes near her den, and she was afraid to go deeper into the woods. She just knew something would pounce on her the way she had pounced on the rabbit.

Frustrated, Nola made her way back to the den and crawled inside. The cool of the earth was her only comfort, and she curled up on the pile of leaves she had made against one wall. Lying on her side, she looked out through the bushes that shielded the entrance to her den so she would see, should anything enter her clearing.

It was horrible to live in such manner, like a feral thing in the woods. But her heart no longer cared. It seemed fitting that she be forever damned to live like this, her punishment for having abandoned her son, for having lost faith in her daughter. Forever damned without hope of salvation, without the chance to beg forgiveness, to right the wrongs she had committed against her own children. She was convinced that her son hated her, Chloe was gone, and Ralph had been swallowed by the ground. From the moment she had awakened aloft and alone, she knew that she was to go on without Ralph. Nola wept. And she continued to weep, even after the balloon had become tangled in the limbs of the dying oak tree. Through sunrises and sunsets she wept, until at last, she stopped. She had climbed from the gondola then, hungry, not caring where her feet should take her, stumbling upon the den and climbing inside to fall into sleep.

"Nola!"

Once again, she had slept. She awoke with a start, hearing her name. Whether it had come from the woods or her own mind, she did not know. She looked out from her den and saw the dogs sniffing about the clearing. She held her breath. One dog came perilously close, but then a voice rang out and the dog lifted its head and scampered away.

Nola released her breath. Her head swam. She had seen him and she was certain he would kill her. Terrified that they would return, she scurried from the den and fled in the opposite direction.

Nola ran until her sides ached and she was winded. She slipped to the ground, blades of grass tickling her skin. As her panting slowed, the pain in her sides easing, Nola sat up to look around. She saw the water and this confused her. She was positive she had been running in a different direction. Panic gripped Nola's heart, and she covered her eyes with her hands, lost.

"Nola!"

"I'm here!" The involuntary words, once shouted, seemed to hang suspended in the air around her. "I'm here," she whispered, and a sudden chill swept through her body. Glancing back over her shoulder, she saw the safety of the woods and pushed herself to her feet. As she staggered forward, Heath stepped from the trees, his eyes fixed upon her, the dogs circled in a pack behind him.

He would kill her. She knew it. In her mind she saw him advancing toward her, hands upraised, grasping her throat. Nola whirled and bolted away from him, heading toward the stream, turning and running along its bank, fighting against the pain that tugged at her sides. He was not far behind her, calling out, his breath hot against the back of her neck, closer and closer and –

Suddenly Dog appeared before her, teeth bared. She screamed and veered from the animal's path, falling heavily to the ground, dazed. She felt the touch on her shoulder and swung her fists, but he pulled her into his arms, holding her fast.

"Stop it," Heath said. "You're safe now. I won't hurt you again."

His gentle voice drained the fight from her body. Nola lay passively in her son's embrace. "Baby?"

"Yes."

She burst into tears, and struggled to speak through her weeping, desperate that he understand, that he know and, if he could, if there were a way, that he forgive her ...

*   *   *

My time here is soon ended, this cycle nearly complete. And still with so much I wish to tell you! I pray that my words will reach you, for you to understand that in each life there are lessons to be learned ...

I know that I am expected elsewhere. Others are waiting to escort me away. But earthly time is of little consequence to me now, and I am not without self-determination. Truth told, I have the distinct feeling I shall never return to mortal form, though this may be only the last vestige of human vanity.

And so I have lingered with Hamilton and the children. I am proud to see what they have accomplished in building a new home. How quickly they have taken Chloe to their hearts! How fully she has accepted them into her life! Together, they have found the strength to continue on, to begin anew.

As these words are written, summer has blossomed. Each day, the sun shines brightly on the Greeson farm. Rain clouds sweep in when needed, water the earth, and then move on. At night, stars blanket the sky, as if all the lights of all the places that Klieg's ever visited had been plucked from the buildings and sidewalks and vehicles, and set into the canopy high above. The pines destined to be Christmas trees are lofty and their boughs full. Their abundant needles scent the air as day follows night, and night follows day.

The tall house is once again white, and surrounded by flourishing flowerbeds. Hostas, ivies, mints, and baby's breath are rampant beneath the oaks and maples. Daisies, morning glories, snapdragons, lavender, marigolds, stock, and roses press heavy blooms against the house's windows, and spill into places the shade does not reach.

At Chloe's insistence, and with the proper permits obtained, workers were hired to convert the barn. Its main floor now boasts one large room, with an open-concept kitchen and a door to a lovely bathroom overlooking the pines. A dining area seats comfortably all the family. Polly and Peg prepare the meals in the well-appointed open-concept kitchen. Adjacent to the kitchen is a lounging area, with satellite television, VCR, and stereo equipment. Shelves of books and video tapes line the walls. Big picture windows offer a view of the yard, the tall house that is once again white, and the new cabins. Much of the room is given over to a pool table, an air hockey game, and several different types of pinball machines – none of which had ever been installed at Klieg's. The barn echoes with music and laughter, and the clacks and clunks and clinks and bells of the games.

Perhaps only Annette and Hamilton are aware of my presence as I move among the family, warmed by lively conversation and loving interaction. Laughter is the most beautiful sound! A joyous song that sweeps across the planet and rises to the heavens, more far-reaching than you may realize.

The loft of the barn has become a full second floor, divided into suites for Polly and Peg, Annette, and Horace. Though Annette keeps a private suite, her love for the twins – and theirs for her – continues to deepen.

The barn's interior walls are painted a rainbow of colours. The exterior is a soft yellow, the doors and windows and porch and railings accenting the clapboards with blue. The front porch extends the full width of the barn, with a swing on one side of the double front door and rocking chairs on the other. Potted flowers bloom in the porch's cool shade. Herb and vegetable plots attend the remaining three sides of the barn, which – despite its renovations – will always be referred to as such.

Again at Chloe's urging, the outbuildings, once intended for animals, were razed and their foundations used for new dwellings. With Joe's assistance, Danny designed for himself a small private cabin. The cabin's exterior is painted the same soft yellow as the barn, but there are no attendant structured flowerbeds, nor herb or vegetable plots. A profusion of wildflowers surrounds Danny's cabin, for he has discovered that he does not care to garden.

On a small rise, a two-bedroom cabin awaits its inhabitants. Shay has sewn bright curtains for the windows, and matching pillows for the sofa, which sits beneath the windows along one wall. In anticipation of motherhood, she has decorated the bright second bedroom as a blue and yellow nursery, with crib and changing table, built-in shelves for books and toys, and a rocking chair perfectly positioned at the window. She has placed pots of pink geraniums on either side of the cabin's small porch, and flower boxes along the outer sills. Chloe brings cuttings from the tall house's gardens for Shay to plant in freshly-dug beds.

Margaret's books have been moved to the built-in shelves in the cabin's bright second bedroom nursery. But Shay continues to sleep in the tall house, declaring the cabin her honeymoon cottage. Each night, Shay tucks Chloe into bed in the loft bedroom of the tall house, reads to her from one of Margaret's books, and then retires to the oddly placed bedroom off the kitchen. In the morning, she returns the book to her cabin, and sets it in proper order beside the other books.

Nestled beside the pines, a third cabin was built to scale for Hamilton. Its counters and shelves are at accessible heights, its furniture and windows low to the floor. Here, when I am able and Hamilton is alone, I bring him pleasant reveries, and visit him in dreams to hold him close.

Hamilton now enjoys endless hours spent with the children. They dine together at the table in the barn. They relax in the lounging area, and challenge each other at the games. Aided by Malcolm Lewis – who also agreed to look after the legalities of the Karnival's destruction, and her estate's slippage into the sea – Annette has obtained video tapes of all my talk show and game show appearances, as well as my *Scarlet Beach* episode. Together late at night, she and Hamilton frequently watch one or more of the tapes, holding hands and reminiscing.

Horace takes Hamilton fishing at the creek that cuts through the west acreage, though they usually return their catch to the water. Frank and Margaret are rarely mentioned in Horace and

Hamilton's long conversations. Though I whisper their names into his ear, Horace wishes only to look toward the future. Still, Horace has taken steps to ensure that Clifford Press books remain in print.

When Chloe is not wandering the vast Crown lands – or assisting in the gardens or the fields or the barn's kitchen – she often prepares in Hamilton's tiny cabin elaborate teas for herself and Hamilton. At times she invites the monkey family to join them.

The monkeys live in the Winnebago, rehearsing their symphonies and playing cards at the small table off the little built-in kitchen. Throughout the day, and late into the night, the music drifts across the yard, into the tall house, the barn and the new cabins, down the hill and across the fields, at last to be swallowed by the dense forest of the vast Crown lands.

With the barn's renovations and the cabins complete, furniture purchased and artfully arranged, linens and dishes and silverware shelved to be used and washed and shelved once more, the tents in the field were dismantled. Ingeniously, they were fashioned together to form one large pavilion, which stands near the fire pit in the field. Two picnic tables have been placed end-to-end inside the pavilion. Horace and Hamilton have constructed an impressive barbecue, with grill, side burner, and oven. On occasions when they use the barbecue, Horace cooks, and Polly and Peg enjoy the respite from the barn's kitchen.

The twins revel in their domestic duties, having rarely undertaken such work since leaving their mother's Bed and Breakfast. They spend hours in the barn's kitchen creating new recipes, canning jams and jellies, baking pies and cakes and bread. They make certain to provide a well-balanced diet, and just the proper amount of sweets to reward the consumption of vegetables. With the stereo playing accompaniment, they dust and sweep and scrub and polish the barn and its furnishings, moving up and down the staircase and across the floors as if performing an exquisite ballet. Chloe teaches them sign language, and they teach her lively dances such as the Polka, the Jitterbug, and the Mashed Potato. The three are often in the yard, whirling in the sunlight.

How joyful they are at those moments! And how truly blessed!

If you remember only a single lesson, let it be this: no child should ever be caused to question his or her rightness of being.

How different Tim-Tina's life could have been! Had her parents known of the tens of thousands of similar children born each year – had she been born to a woman of Robin's or Nola's character – perhaps she could have formed a strong sense of identity. Perhaps she never would have seen herself as a thing. I ache for those who are and have been mistreated as Tim-Tina was. For those who are mutilated by horribly misguided doctors. For any child whose body or spirit is crushed to fit a mould of human design. I long for the day when such ignorance and arrogance will end.

I pray you will listen well and remember: it is not for you to judge those the gods have placed rightly upon this earth. Guard your every action. To treat any one life as anything other than sacred is to denigrate all life. You must be exceedingly wise and act with the greatest of caution. Each and every one of us has a unique purpose. None of us can possess the full knowledge of this rich tapestry's interweaving. But, should you look, I believe you will find the truth in each event, the rightness of each step along the paths The Fates have scattered before us. For each and every one of us is both a student and a teacher.

I applaud Nola for her strength in the face of "medical expertise." Chloe is an exceptional child, intelligent and sure of herself, with an innate acceptance of life's rhythms. It is wonderful to see such a pure and bright light! Though she dearly misses her parents, she enjoys the family's attention and, with incredible stores of energy, she is in the fields, in the pines, in the gardens, in the barn, and in the tall house, seemingly all at once. She tidies Hamilton's cabin, enlisting the youngest of the monkeys to help. She has shown Horace how Ralph had pruned the pines to encourage their symmetrical growth. She accompanies Horace for the work, the two returning with armfuls of boughs, which will scent the buildings with their abundant needles. I marvel as she assists Annette in the herb and vegetable plots, Shay in her gardens, and Polly and Peg in the barn's kitchen. She delights in her walks through the vast Crown lands, and sustains a deepening friendship with Joe.

Joe has become an important part of their lives. He brought the brushes and rollers and barrels of whitewash, and helped the family repaint the tall house. He facilitated the building permits and oversaw the workers. He escorted Hamilton to the doctor to be fitted for a hearing aid, and frequently drives family members to town or the city on shopping trips. He shares meals and stories and lively conversation.

After years of near-seclusion on the vast Crown lands, Joe has found that he has missed and appreciates the company of others, and he and Danny especially have grown close over time. Together they designed and helped to build the cabins. They often attend the local movie house and, on occasion, dine in a nearby restaurant, or sip drinks in the town bar. They play pinball and pool in the barn, and talk for hours beside the fire pit, its rocks ghostly white in moonlight. The family has encouraged their love, for Danny and Joe are as perfectly suited as Arthur and Anna, Margaret and Frank. At last, on a recent night at the movies, Joe reached for Danny's hand in the dark, and held tight until the credits rolled and the lights came up. Later, as they lay together in Danny's cabin, they talked and made love until dawn. When the sun began to rise, they held each other, promising their hearts before drifting into sleep. Danny has learned that a true bond of love develops only with time, and only after shared experiences that are lived outside of passion.

Annette is overjoyed for her brother, and the family has welcomed Joe without reservation. Only Shay is unhappy, unwilling to accept what must be.

As Danny had once been jealous of her happiness with Heath, Shay is now resentful that Danny has found love as she cradles a broken heart. Though she wants to believe Annette's reassurances – and her own words to Chloe the day they arrived – her actions have made this impossible. On a trip to the city with Annette, Danny, and Joe, while selecting the perfect items for the bright second bedroom nursery, she insisted they find an investigator to search for Heath. Awaiting the man's reports, she busies herself with her house and her gardens. One moment she believes Heath is climbing the rise to her cabin, or has just been found by the investigator. The next moment she is certain he has been dead for months, or The Fates will strike him down to punish her for questioning their design. It saddens me that she will not allow herself to believe.

As for my dearest Annette, she has come to see that her instincts will not fail her. Having performed the act that will speed reunion, a growing belief in the strength of her spirit warms her each day as she rises, each night as she lies down to sleep, whether alone or with the twins. She feels a sense of calm and self-acceptance that had once seemed unattainable, which can never be purchased with any amount of funds.

Each evening, after seeing Hamilton safely to his cabin, Annette returns to her suite in the barn. At the table, the room illuminated only by the light of a single candle, she holds my glass eye in one hand, a pencil in the other. With a quiet mind, her consciousness set aside, she permits me to write these words with her hand.

But this shall end. They are waiting to escort me away, Arthur and Anna, Tim-Tina and Hank.

They are drawing near.

Of late, Shay suffers further unrest. As survivors must, the family has begun to plan for the future, and talk has turned to rebuilding Klieg's. Shay is horrified that they would consider this when they have had no word of Heath. Despite their insistence that no one has forgotten Heath – and Annette's reassurances that he is on his way to her – Shay adamantly refuses to take part. I have whispered encouraging words, and I have visited her dreams, but to no avail.

This morning, Shay came upon Hamilton and the others huddled over a sketch of the original Karnival layout. She stormed from the barn and stayed locked in her cabin throughout the rest of the day. The dinner basket Polly and Peg left on her porch remains untouched. Only tonight did Shay leave her cabin, stepping over the basket to cross the yard beneath the full moon, enter the tall house, and tuck Chloe into bed.

How much easier it would be for Shay, if only she would allow herself to believe! If only she would think of Frank and Margaret. Then she would remember that what we endure is designed to strengthen us. That we choose whether lesser tests prepare us for future trials, or consume our spirit. But Shay has not seen the wisdom of this lesson. She risks stepping onto a path that will lead to a decision not unlike Margaret's. I beseech you: regardless of your circumstances, despite the seeming-harshness of your lessons, you must never abandon hope. Each moment is a lesson, a step along your path that fulfills a purpose. Never forget that your path is but a journey to a new beginning. Embrace each and every moment the gods have granted, for a lifetime is a fleeting experience. Allow your trials to fortify you. Learn what you are meant to learn, and then continue on. When days are darkest – when you feel that you cannot continue on – what you need in order to endure will be found in the strength and love that you provide for others.

Although they are moving ahead with plans to rebuild the Karnival, the family is not insensitive to Shay's feelings. Their belief is strong and, as survivors must, they cannot but turn their hearts to the future. The Karnival is in their blood, and a profound sense of purpose compels them to take action.

Oh! So soon they have arrived, the harbingers of reunion! Already I can hear the dogs ... Their barking grows louder as they hurry through the Crown lands and toward the fields. I can feel Arthur and Anna, Tim-Tina and Hank ... They are moving closer, intent like a powerful tide sweeping in to carry me away ...

And still I am not prepared to leave you!

I pray that you will search your heart, that you will remember and heed my words. You must be ever vigilant. Ensure that all are treated with the utmost care and respect, that they may be whole and embrace the world because they have learned to embrace themselves. Only in such richness of spirit can there be any hope for lasting peace and happiness, for a life's ultimate realization ...

At the fire pit, Danny and Joe jump to their feet. Clinging to Shay's hand, Chloe pulls her from the tall house, through the garden, and into the yard.

The dogs burst from the trees and race through the fields. Danny is running toward the barn, surrounded by the yelping dogs, announcing their arrival.

Arthur, please! Wait! Anna!

Chloe slips free of Shay and skips down the hill. Nola and Heath step from the woods. Heath's face is haggard. He is tired, yet his legs take him surely and ever faster up the hill. Shay stands in the yard, frozen as he nears. Her arms ache to hold him, as I ache to hold my Hamilton one last time.

Annette grows restless. I can feel her wanting to rise to her feet and –

Tim-Tina, not yet! Please!

Danny and the dogs reach the top of the hill as Hamilton, Horace, Polly and Peg rush into the yard. The Winnebago's door bangs open and the monkeys scamper out, jabbering and jumping and waving their long arms.

Nola is on her knees, weeping. Chloe is joyous in her embrace.

Guide them well, Annette!

Shay is safe in Heath's arms. And the tide has reached me.

My love for you all is boundless ...

I pray that you will remember ...

The author wishes to thank:

Madalene, for her enduring belief.

For thoughts on plot and characters: Zareh Oshagan; Lorene Stanwick; Leonore Johnston; Sandra Morris.

For financial assistance: Bradley; J.S.; the Ontario Arts Council Writer's Reserve.

Consultants: Lynne Martin, R.N.; Reg Brick, Forester, B.C.

My deepest gratitude to Bruce Walsh, who took on the challenge of finding a publisher. And to Cathy Baran, who presented the original manuscript to Sam.

An extra-special "Muchas gracias!" to Elliot Stanwick.

My best wishes and kindest regards to Ms. Teri Garr, my initial inspiration.